A **Hotel** In **Venice**

By

Margot Justes

A Hotel in Venice

Copyright © 2015 by Margot Justes

Chapter 1

The stars seemed to follow the black gondola as it flowed along the Grand Canal, and in the distance, a dark and narrow passage beckoned for a romantic interlude.

Iridescent shards glistened in the moonlight. The golden glow and the ripples in the water reminded Minola Grey of Shelley's poem *Love's Philosophy.* "And the moonbeams kissed the sea." As the gondola glided along the canal, the old *palazzos,* one building after another, appeared to sway with the hushed tones of the lapping water.

Peter Riley had wanted some peace and quiet and asked the gondolier to choose a less travelled way along a narrow and more intimate path.

"Welcome to Venice, Miss Grey." Peter's finger traced the line of her cheekbone and then her neck. "I'm very much in love with you," he whispered in her ear and felt her lean into him. This was the way it should be, just the two of them together. Alone. Nothing stood in their way. They were in Venice for a wedding. Theirs. Minola loved glass and art. Because of the Biennale Art Festival and Murano, another island world-renowned for blown glass that was only fifteen minutes away by water taxi, they had chosen Venice as the perfect destination.

Minola Grey turned toward him and brushed her lips against his, the touch whisper soft. "I'm very much in love with you, too. Anywhere with you is romantic, but Venice is magnificent. Incomparable," she purred like a contented kitten, nestling deeper into his arms and gazing across the canal.

He was completely absorbed in the peaceful moment, until Minola tilted her head away from him and murmured in his ear, "Peter. Isn't that strange?" She pointed above her head at the pier and stared at what seemed like a mound of multi-colored mosaics. From her vantage point, the glass appeared to be a colorful blanket. "It's like a sculpture, sort of."

"Miss Grey, may I remind you we're in a gondola in Venice. The moon is shining." He ran his fingers over her cheek once again, his touch firm and persuasive. "I'm caressing your face. We're together. You, Love of my Life, should be looking at me, not glass. I know, after our visit to Murano, you have glass on your mind, but really, where is your sense of romance?"

"Peter, I'm sorry. I am romantic. You tell me I'm romantic when we make…"

"Love? Yes, you are. Passionate and romantic, you turn my world upside down, and not just when we make love. However, now would be a good time to slip into that romantic mood again." His lips curved up in a smile. He couldn't help himself. Everything she did made him smile, with the exception of getting into trouble and endangering her life. She had an uncanny talent for finding bodies, and the end result terrified him.

They had met in Paris. He was with Interpol, and his money laundering case almost cost Minola her life. In Bath, her life was threatened, and worse, he couldn't control her impulse to help. Peter loved his work—he excelled at it—but now he focused on keeping the woman sitting beside him safe from harm. That was not as easy as it appeared. She was a remarkable artist who knew how to get into trouble and could never deny anyone's cry for help.

"But, Peter, it's unusual. I know we're on the Grand Canal. Well, we turned and are now on this lonely, dark, narrow, and romantic canal—okay, sort of an alley, except that this is Venice and it is a canal. Just take a peek…" Minola Grey would not let go and pointed again to the glass enclosure when she heard Peter groan. "I'm sorry. But…but…" She stuttered.

"Minola, what am I going to do with you? We have moonlight, a dark intimate canal in front of us, a lantern, and a gondolier who is not going to sing to us. A perfect setting."

"Perfect setting? For what?" she asked, still captivated by the colorful display on the pier, and she moved closer to the edge of the gondola so she could see better.

"You're going to reduce my vocabulary to *Arrgh*." Peter's voice sounded resigned. He motioned to the gondolier. "Roberto, please bring us closer to that pile of glass, whatever it is." Peter watched as the gondolier expertly used his foot and a wall to push off so he could maneuver his gondola as close to the pier as possible, allowing Peter to step out. "Stay put," he ordered as she tried to follow him. "I mean it." He gazed back at her and frowned. "Stay."

Minola bristled at the order. "I'm not a doggie." She glanced at his resolute expression and grudgingly replied, "Fine. I won't budge." Minola settled back in the gondola and saw Peter bend down.

Tiny pieces of glass were molded together to form what appeared to be a blanket for whatever was underneath. The center was well-crafted, and the colors brilliant. The edges, not finished well, were sharp and haphazard. Suddenly, he felt those goose bumps on the back of his neck that told him more than just glass rested on the secluded dock.

"I have a bad feeling about this," he murmured.

"Peter, did you say something?" Minola raised her voice to be heard. She rarely shouted and found the sound unpleasant. Her preference lay in peaceful contemplation and quiet conversation. Loud noises did not appeal to her gentle soul, and she avoided situations that involved screaming and throngs of people. Even her art exhibits were tempered, and Peter made sure she was protected at all times. He understood her and would do anything to keep her from harm. Anything. She appreciated that, but often did not agree with his assessments and his need to shield her.

"Stay put. I'm going to be a little longer."

"Nooo… not without me. I'm not staying in the gondola alone."

"You're not alone. I'm right here, and so is Roberto." Peter stooped down and viewed the bizarre sight. The flashlight on his cell helped him to see the blood around the base of the glass. He pointed the light toward the edge of the pier and saw the blood trail lead to water.

Peter tried to lift the hefty glass, and using both hands, he could hardly budge it. Straining hard, he lifted the mound a tiny notch, enough to tell him all was not well. The familiar stench that reached his nostrils caused him to instinctively control his breathing. He'd recognize the odor of a decomposing body anywhere. The sweet acrid smell, the reek that defies description but lingers long after, told him a body was hidden underneath the glass sarcophagus. He turned, quickly stepped down, and boarded the gondola before calling the police.

Peter's bleak expression told her all she needed to know. "Peter, that's a body covered by glass, isn't it? A dead body?"

"Are there any others?" he quipped, running his hand down her arm for support. "The police are on the way."

"What would it be doing there? This is Venice. A piece that large had to come from a big furnace. Are there large furnaces in Venice? I thought they all moved to Murano centuries ago."

"I don't know. You're the glass expert. That is why we spent so much time in Murano, isn't it?" His voice was short. He was in unfamiliar territory, and at the moment, he had no contacts in Venice. None that would allow him access to this investigation.

"No, we came here on vacation, to be together, visit a friend, a few galleries, and see Murano," she spoke softly, afraid she ruined their time together. "We came here to be married."

"So far, we haven't spent much time together. You've been busy." A muscle flickered in his jaw, and he felt himself tense. "And now we won't have much peace."

"I know. I'm sorry. I wanted to visit the Castigli family. They are friends, their furnace produces exquisite glass, and Jennifer needed to talk." She saw his reaction and bit her lip until she tasted blood, a habit indicating her nerves. Licking her lips and swallowing, she looked up and found Peter's gaze focused on her mouth.

"Yes, I know. I was there…with you. How quickly you forget." His reply was curt. Nothing good was going to come out of this.

"I didn't forget. Peter, I'm sorry." She bent her head down to hide the sorrow. She'd hurt him, something she never wanted to do. "I always know when you're with me." She took his hand in hers and touched his palm, hoping to erase the pain she caused. "Peter, I always know."

"You might want to let me know once in a while." Peter looked out to the Grand Canal and the narrow canal where they now found themselves docked, gazing at the beauty surrounding them. The various lanterns and lit homes that lined the Grand Canal reflected a burnished glow in the water as a vaporetto, the typical utilitarian mode of travel used by locals and savvy tourists alike, sped by. Even the standard public transportation was romantic.

He raised her hand to his lips, the embrace as soft as a gentle breeze. Above all else, he loved the woman sitting next to him. His life changed for the better when they met in Paris after she became involved in a murder investigation. His murder investigation. She bloody well wrapped herself around his very soul and very nearly died in the process. It must not happen here. She would not become involved. Despite his firm resolve, he knew she would help, and he, in turn, would follow her anywhere to keep her safe.

"Always. I promise. Peter, you do know that I'm in love with you. That I'm yours and always will be." She brushed her lips against his cheek. The touch was at once gentle and erotic. The spark against her fingertips as she touched him reminded her of their first meeting, and her volatile and intimate reaction to him. She would later learn he had an English and an American education. He could read people well, and that made him excel at his job.

"That's better." Once she allowed him into her life, he never doubted her love and commitment to him. His always savage response to her when they were together was tempered by her gentleness. He wanted her at all times, something he never imagined possible. The more he knew her, the more he loved and the more he wanted. *How is that feasible?*

"Peter, you don't think this is connected to the missing master glass blower or the problems at the Castigli Furnace, do you?" The words slipped before she had a chance to stop them. During their earlier visit to the Castigli furnace, her friend Jennifer had been distracted. One of her employees had not shown up for work for over a week, and Jennifer knew he wouldn't leave without saying a word. They were working on a project together, and Minola's inquisitive nature just couldn't let go of the mystery. "We're not in Murano, and I'm imagining things. There are many furnaces in Murano." A shadow of alarm touched her face.

"No, this is Venice. This is where I wanted a romantic gondola ride with the love of my life. This is where I wanted to…Damn it; you just had to find a body," he groused.

"This is where you wanted what?" Minola asked.

"I'm not going there now. We're waiting for the police, and we have to tell them we found a body. We're out of our element here, Miss Grey."

"Why? You're Interpol-that means International Police. Venice is international."

"Not funny, Miss Grey." He shook his head and replied smoothly, "I have no contacts here at this time."

"Shouldn't you have international contacts?" Her voice was fragile, uncertain. She didn't want to inflict additional strain on their relationship and hoped they had come to terms with his obsessive need to always protect her.

"I do, just not in Venice, not at the moment." He sensed her disquiet as they sat in silence and waited for the carabinieri to arrive. Peter was quite familiar with their history. They were the national military police of Italy, formally known as *Arma dei Carabinieri*— loosely translated as Arm of the Police or Militia. Policing both military personnel and civilians, their past was long and involved. "Minola, this will not be easy. The carabinieri are not just a police force. Do you know they were originally the police force of the Kingdom of Sardinia? They are not to be trifled with."

"That means they realize what needs to be done and will work with Interpol—that's you."

"Hardly." Peter comprehended their mission, and that they took it seriously. They had a unit that could defend Italy, plus another unit that focused and dealt with organized crime, terrorist, and subversive activities. They did their job well, understood the criminal mind on all levels, and did not trust easily.

He watched the gloomy gondolier sit down and rub his hands together. He seemed nervous as he shoved his hand through his hair, a sure sign of agitation. Peter didn't blame him. Roberto, like many other Venetians, was trying to eek-out a living as a gondolier in a difficult economy, and now he was stuck waiting for the police. Peter turned toward Minola and saw her looking at him.

"Peter, were you able to see anything?"

"Minola, it's dark. I couldn't lift the glass, far too heavy, and besides, if I were the local police, I'd be angry if someone interfered with the crime scene. I'm a cop and should be well versed in police procedures, no point in ruffling feathers. Especially carabinieri feathers. We'll just have to wait. All I can tell you—we have a body."

"Dead?" She whimpered, still hoping it was not so.

"You didn't just ask me that?" He smiled in spite of the difficult circumstances.

"Well, yes, I did. Wasn't thinking," she replied sheepishly.

"I see." His lips curved up a little. "Until we know more about the body, we'll refrain from discussing the issues at the Castigli furnace."

"Why?"

"When you spoke with Jennifer Castigli, did she mention police involvement?"

"No, she just indicated Julio was missing, and they had issues with the glass blending formula or something like that. They were going to handle it internally. I didn't ask any questions. She wanted to talk, and then she didn't. She was concerned, and I didn't want to push her. Didn't see the point at the time."

"Maybe we should pay another visit," Peter suggested

"I think so, too, and we have an excuse. Should anyone ask, they are friends who are making the vases for the wedding. She had her glass pieces exhibited at the Standish Galley in Chicago. That is how we met. She's a talented glass blower, and I've always had a thing for glass. We kept in touch."

"A thing for glass, Miss Grey?"

"Yes, I love it. Sort of like a thing for you. I love you. Deeply." Her lips touched his neck, and she felt a brief shiver ripple through her body. It would always be like this with him. He was her *everything*.

"Thank you for that caress. You always know what to do." He gripped her hand in his and smiled. "Now you're bringing romance into the picture, while we're waiting for the police and a body is keeping us company. There is something to be said for your timing, my love. Jennifer. Tell me more about Jennifer. I need to keep my mind off your body and the things I'd like to do with you, and to you," he whispered in her ear then took a deep breath.

"Stop right there or I'm going to be in trouble." A tingling settled in the pit of her stomach. Every time he looked at her, her pulse quickened. He'd unlocked her heart and soul. "Jennifer. Right," she sighed and continued. "Well, she went to Murano about three years ago, just for the summer. She returned to Chicago, did some amazing blown glass. The colors were just unbelievable. They seemed to glow and float, one color next to the other. I've never seen anything like it. It reminded me a bit of the Tiffany colors, but the glass was more translucent instead of Tiffany's opalescent and iridescent styles. I have a piece. Becky is storing it for me."

"Storing it for you?"

"Yes, when I left Chicago, I literally left with just the clothes on my back and the necessary art supplies. Well, I did take the few vintage clothing pieces I owned. I scoured countless consignment stores for them, spent a lot of time finding my treasures, and I wasn't about to leave them. Anyway, Becky stored the few pieces of art I owned, and the rest went to charity. When I make a break, I make a clean break." Her decision to leave home had been quick and matter of fact. What she'd thought was a relationship did not exist, and she learned the hard way to distrust men in general. *Peter had his work cut out for him, but he stuck around.* For that, she was profoundly grateful.

"I see." He chuckled softly. She wanted a full partnership in their relationship, and his gripping fear for her security led them along a stormy path that only recently had calmed. He hoped. Peter knew well that the criminal elements at the international level had a long reach. Being with Minola Grey in the public eye did not give him any peace of mind. He could be hurt through her.

Minola was not immune to violence. Attempts on her life had been made before, leaving Peter unable to focus on his job. Their issues revolved around his lack of communication, as she put it, and her determination to lead a normal life amidst threats and danger. He understood the criminal elements and the danger they posed, while she lived an innocent life and had believed in the goodness of others, until she met him.

"How did Jennifer wind up living in Murano?" he asked.

"She fell in love with Antonio Castigli and decided to move permanently to Murano. He was a master glass blower and may still be blowing glass. The family goes back centuries. Jennifer once told me he was a master at design and blowing. That is an impressive combination. We haven't really kept in touch until recently. They were married a couple of years ago and seemed very much on love."

"If, and it's a big if, that body is the missing glass blower, we have a problem."

"Just one?"

"For the moment," he replied with quiet confidence. He knew the carabinieri would not play nice. Their turf, and they protected it well.

"How will we know who it is?" she asked quietly.

"I assume, more like hope against hope, the local police might extend a courteous hand to Interpol. If not, someone in the London office might have a connection. Things are a bit difficult between Interpol and the local police here. We'll worry about that later. Now I think you need to call Jennifer and have a chat."

"Why would we believe it's Julio? It could be anyone." Minola was afraid for her friends.

"Yes, it could. But somehow, I doubt it. We have a coffin made of glass, a missing master glass blower, and a recent visit to Murano. Not to mention, you made the news, and so did I as your lover." He looked down at their intertwined hands. His grip tightened, and he continued. "Isn't that how the papers described me?"

"Peter, does it bother you?" she asked in a broken whisper.

"To be your lover? No. That is what I am and always will be." His fingers touched her collarbone, lingering there intimately. "But the publicity and your safety, yes, you know I'm bothered a great deal by any risk to you."

"I didn't say anything to the press. It was supposed to be a quiet vacation. I don't know how they found out about us."

"Well, for one, you are here during the Biennale Art Festival." He knew she wanted to see the world-renowned festival that dated back to 1895, held every other year. The modern art exhibition turned many unsuspected nooks and crannies into temporary galleries. "You're a known artist, fresh from a murder investigation in Bath and a successful showing in London. We have been together since Paris. Need I say more? And I have been with you every step of the way as your lover. They are right."

"Peter, I'm so sorry." She swallowed hard and bit back the tears that threatened to fall. He cherished his privacy as much as she did, yet her profession somehow threw her into the public eye, along with Peter.

"Nothing to be sorry about. This is our life, and I wouldn't change a thing. We're together. That is all that matters." His voice was calm, and his gaze steady on her face. Above all, he wanted to reassure her that, no matter what, they belonged together.

"Thank you for understanding," she whispered. "When I call Jennifer, what do I tell her? That you found a body and it could be

Julio? Why upset her before we have concrete information? Maybe we can identify the shards of glass as belonging to a specific furnace. Wouldn't that be a start?" Minola asked.

"I'm going back to take a few pictures." Peter stepped out of the gondola, reached into his pocket, took out his cell, and then walked over to the glass display and snapped about a dozen shots. He put his cell away, stepped back into the gondola, and saw Roberto was quietly and unobtrusively watching him. Taking out his identification, he showed it to the gondolier. Roberto nodded and lowered his head in acknowledgement.

Waiting in silence, they saw the police boat smoothly maneuver around the traffic on the Grand Canal and turn the corner alongside their gondola. The flashing lights added another sparkle to the lively water traffic. He remembered Minola comparing the Grand Canal to other grand avenues in Paris, New York, and Chicago, except this one was wet. Peter stared in the face of the agility of the boaters to maneuver around tight corners and other boats, a well-choreographed dance on water.

Peter helped Minola step out of the gondola. He thanked the gondolier and asked him to take them back to the hotel after the police were done, with a promise of additional compensation. Peter watched as the police questioned the gondolier. They were short and precise. An effort was made to establish their time of arrival at the intersection and why they stopped. Roberto answered succinctly and did not offer anything else. The police then turned their attention to Captain Peter Riley, Interpol, and Minola Grey, American artist. Roberto maneuvered his gondola against a wall and waited.

"What made you go there? Isn't that a little *insolito—eh—*unusual for a *turista*?" the first officer asked.

Taking out his identification, Peter introduced Minola and himself. "Miss Grey noticed the glass and was curious. We stopped so that we could see it better." Peter did not elaborate further. He didn't have a warm and fuzzy feeling about this interrogation.

"Interpol?" the officer snorted. "And what did you find?"

"I tried to lift the glass, and I was able to identify the smell easily enough." Peter was surprised at the ease with which the officer spoke English.

"I see. Who noticed the glass?"

Peter wanted to be snippy. He already told him it was Minola. What, did they think that in the span of a few minutes his story would change?

Minola quickly replied, "I did. The moonlight reflected the colors brilliantly. So much color—unusual, vibrant…strange," More than a little nervous, she continued. "So vivid and beautiful."

"What else can you tell me? Did you know what it was?"

"Well, no. I saw it from a distance, and in the moonlight, it appeared to be a huge piece of art…because of all the many different colors, I thought maybe a mosaic," Minola advised quietly.

"How did you know what it was?" the officer persisted.

"I didn't. From afar, it might have been a sculpture. I wanted to see it a little closer."

"I ask again, why, Miss Grey?"

"Because I'm an artist and was curious," she replied simply.

"What do you know of Venetian Glass that you would be so curious?"

What she wanted to do was tell him that she didn't need to know anything about Venetian glass, or any other glass, to be curious and acknowledge its beauty, but instead she replied in an even voice, "I didn't know it was Venetian. It seemed intriguing and quite beautiful."

"You had to satisfy your curiosity," he insisted.

"No, I did not. Captain Riley went to do that. The pieces seemed to be shard leftovers from a furnace." Minola bit her lip when she realized she'd said too much.

"How would you know that?"

"I'm an artist. I paint," she repeated. "And I also love glass. I visited Murano today and know that the shards are often reused, kept in a bucket and eventually wind up in smaller jewelry pieces or glass bricks. They are sharp, therefore kept in containment for safety reasons.

Outsiders have no access. Out of courtesy, I was given a private tour. I just wondered what it was and why it was left on the pier. I was curious. That is all." She took a deep breath and literally could have kicked herself for allowing him to get the upper hand. She knew better.

"As an artist and a tourist, you visited a furnace in Murano?" he emphasized.

"Yes, like all the other tourists and artists who visit Murano, I did the touristy thing and saw a couple of furnaces. That is why I wondered how such a huge sculpture was just sitting on a secluded pier. We turned from the Grand Canal into this small canal, and I…It does look like a sculpture." She glanced at the pile and shuddered. "The fact that it resembled a sarcophagus seemed bizarre. Rather striking if you don't think about what it covers…don't you agree?" She tended to babble when nervous, and this was no exception. She reached toward Peter and knew he'd be there to support her, and he didn't disappoint. He wound his fingers around hers.

"That seems to be *sensate*… reasonable explanation," the first officer nodded and turned toward Peter. "Captain, where are you staying? I would recommend you do not leave town."

Peter smiled at the pronouncement, giving them the name of the hotel and their length of stay.

"Are you here on holiday?" the second officer asked, addressing Peter.

"Yes, we are. As stated before, Miss Grey is an artist, and we came to enjoy the Biennale." Peter wasn't about to share the more intimate reason for their visit. It would most probably have to come out, but as far as he was concerned, at this time, there was no incentive to divulge anything remotely personal. They already had more than enough information.

"We will wait for the…*medico legale* to arrive, but you may go. We know how to reach you," came the warning. At least Peter took it as a warning. *Do not leave town.*

"Is there a possibility that we can find out the identity of the victim? As a police officer, you understand…" Peter let the request trail, and watched as the scene was photographed from every angle.

"Yes, of course, unfinished business. Common courtesy would signify that we notify you of the victim's identity." The officer's reply was terse and non-committal.

"Thank you." Peter felt effectively dismissed and wasn't sure if he would ever find out who the victim was, certainly not from the police. They didn't even promise anything that vaguely resembled a courtesy call. Peter asked Roberto to take them back to their original destination. No point in pursuing a romantic rendezvous with the image of a body still fresh in their minds. Peter watched Minola's silent retreat. The horrific mound of glass so starkly visible in the moonlit sky was hauntingly beautiful.

The big question was why dump the body and cover it with what was essentially a work of art? The piece was stunning. The various earthy colors were uneven and most likely discarded pieces. Such a large piece took time to create. Was it a work of art that was meant to be used elsewhere, or was it specifically designed to become a casket? If so, the murder had to be premeditated. Why use the remnants of glass? Or was the piece already made and only used as a coffin at the last minute? Was it commissioned? If so, would it be missed?

"Minola, the composition of the shards, the colors used, it must have been somehow relevant to the crime. If it is indeed Julio, then how he was killed and covered must be significant. Something so elaborate can't have been just a body dump."

"I thought the same thing, but only Jennifer can tell us. Good thing you took all those pictures. Hopefully, she'll know if it came from her furnace," Minola replied.

"I think the death is somehow related to the furnace, and the missing person." His instincts never failed him; he'd been in the business too long to take things at face value.

Peter wondered what they had gotten themselves into. He was a seasoned cop, and he didn't believe in coincidences. If the glass was from the Castigli furnace, Minola was once again in the middle of a murder.

He'd met Antonio Castigli briefly on their earlier visit to the furnace. Minola introduced them, and they also met a family friend and member of a competing furnace, Pia Deniccali. The striking, self-assured woman, who Peter felt sure would demand to be the center of attention in any gathering, left him untouched by her cold and calculating beauty. He was all too familiar with the type.

Peter remembered that, after the introductions were made, he found Pia Deniccali staring at him as if she were appraising his worth, or maybe something else. He couldn't understand her fascination with him and felt uncomfortable with the scrutiny, but he thought maybe she wanted his help. Odd that Minola did not matter to Pia. She glared at him. He'd heard the expression *man-eater* before, and she fit the description quite well.

So far he'd met some interesting people, and a fascinating mystery beckoned. In this case, Peter had no contacts, unless he ingratiated himself with the local police, and the carabinieri did not seem too receptive. In fact, they seemed downright hostile.

Chapter 2

On their return trip back to the hotel, Peter watched as the gondolier smoothly turned toward the Grand Canal. The bright moonlight in the distance reflected in the water, and the single lantern in the gondola cast a dim shadow on their seat. The water lapped along the edges of the gondola. Somehow, the soothing sound calmed his spirit despite the gruesome discovery.

More than just the Biennale Art festival brought them to Venice. Peter wanted to celebrate their engagement and, ultimately, their wedding. He'd invited family and friends to celebrate their marriage: A small gathering that included his parents and sister with her family, Minola's best friends Sally and Robert Jones, along with David Abington and Ashby Sutton, gallery owners and excellent friends from Bath.

He'd also invited Rebecca Standish and Kirk Adams, along with Tracy Billings and Gordon Kerric from Minola's hometown in Chicago. He had to admit that Sally Jones, Minola's best friend, took charge of the planning, but he, like Minola, wanted to share their happiness with the people who were important to them. Minola had no relatives other than close friends, whom she considered family.

Venice, the magnificent art festival, her love of glass—it seemed the perfect romantic venue. The perfect choice. On a gondola under a full moon, she had to find a body. She left a bloody trail of bodies. Everywhere they'd been together, a body waited for Minola to discover.

Peter felt her lean into him, as if she sensed his distress. He put his hand around her waist and pulled her closer to him. Her body warmed his. The magnificent *palazzos* they passed on the way spoke of the wealth and power that once was Venice—the Venice of old with great political power, intrigue, and commerce. The colorful buildings seemed to float along the water. The paddle rhythmically moved the gondola along. The soulful music carried over the water. A brightly lit restaurant facing the Grand Canal with colorful lamps vividly guided their way home. Laughter and conversations echoed around them.

For Minola, somewhere along the way, the romantic setting and the ride back lost its luster. Even the romance of the Grand Canal was gone. She needed Peter. She needed to be alone with him, to apologize for asking him to look. "I should not have insisted." Her voice was shaky and uneven. How could she find a body in the middle of a romantic gondola ride with the man she loved above all? *Do I possess some kind of dead body magnet?*

"I'm glad you did. Otherwise, it would have bothered you. I know you. We'll handle it, together." He kissed her hair, simply because he had to touch her. He needed to connect with her on all levels.

"Peter, we'll be fine. We're together. That is all that matters." The charm and romance of Venice no longer captivated, but the mystery of Venice now prevailed and persisted more than ever. The small canals that seemed to blend into one another, dark and damp narrow alleys, the uneven cobblestones, the shadows reflected on walls from the dimly lit lamps, the echoes of happy and laughing voices in the distance—all that made Venice captivating, somehow elusive, as if one were chasing phantoms from the past, always out of reach. Hauntingly beautiful. The *Carnevale*, the various eerie masks she'd seen on display, along with the magnificently aged costumes readily available in shops gave Venice a seductive, ghostly allure. A Venice entrenched in centuries of mystery, magic and superstition. A Venice cast in perpetual shadows.

She shivered and snuggled closer to Peter. This was the Venice of Casanova, the romantic, debonair, and mysterious lover of women.

This was the Venice of ancient scholars, artists, and political schemes that far outweighed today's scandals.

Venice enthralled Minola, steeped in history with age old palaces, magnificent art everywhere she turned, gilded churches, and narrow, dark streets where the only source of flickering light was another street somewhere in the near distance, a veritable delight everywhere one turned.

A faint reflection from the water eerily lit another pathway, and some of the meandering narrow alleys were not lit at all. She should be here with Peter, and only Peter, not have a dead body along for the ride.

"I don't know what made me look. What is the matter with me?" she whispered again, her voice trembled.

Peter knew she was on the verge of tears. "Nothing is the matter with you, my love. We'll sort this through. Let's go back to our room and order coffee." Peter played the coffee angle. She was addicted to the brew, and it relaxed her. She seemed to mellow out with a few cups of coffee.

"How are we going to handle it?"

"Together. The cop voice is telling me you have to get in touch with Jennifer, e-mail her the pictures I took, and ask her if she can identify the colors of the glass. If I remember what I read correctly, some are specific to the furnaces; the formulas are kept secret. Maybe Jennifer could identify the blanket of glass as part of the Castigli furnace. Especially since it's large enough to show off the patterns and colors. See, I paid attention," he smiled.

"Yes, I can see that you paid attention. But we don't even know how the person was killed."

"The blood around the edge of the glass was not fresh, at least from what I could see with the flashlight. Based on the smell, the body had been there a while. I wonder how and where the death occurred."

"Why do you think it happened elsewhere?"

"Because the body was lying on what I can only assume was a large piece of wood, most likely carried onto the pier. Not enough blood. And we have the small trail of blood leading to the pier from the water, and not from the building. That tells me there was blood on whatever brought him to his last resting place. I assume the body is that of a male. I also saw some kind of heavy plastic sticking out, but couldn't see enough to confirm it."

"Could two people have carried the body and the glass from a boat to the dock?"

"No, too heavy by far, but a body covered in a bag could have been dumped and set on the wooden plank, and the glass carried the same way and placed to cover the body."

"How did the blood get all over the area if covered in plastic?"

"Good point, Miss Grey. Many jagged edges could explain the rips."

"Why there? Is the location significant?"

"You're asking the wrong man. I'm not familiar enough with Venice to guess why here, but an unobtrusive and hidden place would be a good choice to hide a body. Remember, the gondolier turned into the small canal for a little romance and intimacy? It couldn't be seen from the Grand Canal. The perfect place, if someone didn't want an eminent discovery."

"Well, for one, if this body came from Murano, why not dump it somewhere in Murano? Safer and faster. Why Venice?"

"Another good question. Maybe as a warning to someone? Maybe the area was significant to the murderer or the victim, or even both. Or simply a convenient place to dump the body and continue on. A private and secluded residence seemingly abandoned would be perfect. The possibilities are endless." Out of habit, or his well-developed sixth sense, Peter checked to see if they were being followed. Maybe he missed something, but he didn't see a flicker of suspicion, just the usual Grand Canal traffic, yet he felt uneasy. "I believe we'll be spending a bit of time in Murano. Ah, we're almost here." Peter turned and tipped Roberto, gave him his business card, thanked him, and helped Minola step out of the Gondola. A short walk brought them to Piazza San Marco.

"Peter, could we walk a little? I don't want to go to the hotel yet."

"Of course." He led her toward the music and the famous Caffe Florian, where people danced right in the middle of the square as they listened to the band play. Sitting down at a table came with a hefty service charge for the privilege of listening to the musicians and being served by waiters wearing formal attire; however, there was no fee for standing and listening or even dancing to the international tunes they played. Minola expected only Italian pieces, but that was not the case. The cafe played the music at an international level to attract one and all. A famous tourist trap to be sure, but magnificent at the same time, and it was her favorite respite before going to the hotel.

The dimly lit square had a haunted feel to it. The gleam of moonshine gave the place a rather starry and romantic atmosphere, the perfect setting for their current mood. The Doge's Palace stood in the shadows, and the stream of lights on one side of the piazza cast a grey haze over a couple lost in a waltz.

Peter gathered her in his arms and held her snuggly. He kissed her hair and whispered, "I love you. It will be fine." Together, they swayed to the music and, for the moment, were lost in each other.

"I know, but someone died. Presumably, he had a family, someone who loved him, and someone who hated him. Hated enough to kill. From the appearance, you suspect murder?"

"Yes, most probably," was all he said. He was used to this side of life. He was a cop; she was not. She was an artist with a remarkable talent. Along the way, she'd been exposed to crime and murder because of her association with him. He wasn't about to let her go, but he was going to let go of Interpol. She just didn't know it yet, something he'd have to mention and soon. It went back to their communication issues and his deep and desperate need to keep her from harm. Not telling her would result in trust issues and another misunderstanding. Maybe after the wedding, he would surprise her.

Peter had seen her talent change, growing darker, grittier. He knew he couldn't continue to expose her to his current life with the brutality of drug addiction, murder, and greed and all the incredible ways a human being maimed and butchered another. He saw first-hand what it did to her.

She'd denied it in the past, claiming she fell in love with the total man and that included his life as a cop. He couldn't, wouldn't allow it to continue. He had responsibilities at home, in England, and he needed to assume them. That was his plan after they married. He would set up a studio for her in his home in Slough. She would paint, and he would run the estate. Hopefully, someday, they would have a family and live like normal people. Whatever that meant…Minola was an artist, sensitive, caring and vulnerable. Normal probably would never apply to them.

In the meantime, she found a body, and here they were, immersed in another murder. He knew Minola well. Intimately. She would want to solve the puzzle, especially if her friend Jennifer was somehow connected.

Peter pulled her toward the cafe. They sat down and ordered coffee. He watched as Minola leaned back in the chair, closed her eyes, and listened to the music, but the tension did not leave her body. Her hands clenched. She opened her eyes and gazed at him. Even in the shadows, he saw her abiding love and regret reflected in her magnetic eyes. They drew him in every time. Once she admitted she loved him, she didn't hide from him and held nothing back. An incomparable lover, she gave him everything and demanded the same from him.

She took a sip of her coffee, licked her lips, and said, "Thank you, Peter. This is perfect." She sighed contentedly.

"You're welcome. Feeling better?"

She nodded at him, and a small smile quivered on her lips. "See the piazza from here, the flickering lights and shadows. The canal and the magnificent view. Everywhere you turn, simply stunning. Listen to the sound of the swishing water as the boats glide on the canal. The lighting is ideal. So lovely here under the moon with the reflecting glow on top of the Ducal Palace. This is perfection. Did I mention that I love you with all my heart and soul?" She took another swallow of the espresso. She didn't gulp it down like the Italians. Instead, she sipped it lovingly.

"Not recently. No. But I appreciate hearing it, even though I cannot do anything about it at the moment." His voice broke with huskiness.

She moved her chair closer to him so their thighs touched and whispered in his ear, "What did you have in mind?"

"What I always have in mind when it comes to you. I want to love you. Ready to go in?" He paid the bill, helped her up, and then nuzzled her hair as he gathered her in his arms.

"Yes, I am. You picked the perfect location for the hotel. I love it." She reached up and lightly brushed her lips against his cheek, snuggling closer and needing the proximity and warmth of his body.

The hotel faced the Grand Canal and was secluded from the tourist throngs, but only a breath away from Piazza San Marco. A leisurely stroll took them to the elegant *palazzo* that served as their home. Many places in Venice claimed to be a palace in a prior life. The age of the buildings foretold countless stories and intrigues that made the stay that much more delightful and mysterious. Minola felt as if she walked the same steps as the master painters, sculptors, and philosophers. Each uneven cobblestone was steeped with history.

The past of the various places always amazed and intrigued her. The canals were clean and not at all odiferous as she had been warned. In fact, little debris could be found anywhere, and with all the tourists, she found that surprising. Venice was old to be sure. Some walls crumbled, were chipped with broken bricks. Others needed paint. Many had graffiti, but somehow, it all added to the allure rather than detracted. She poked her head in every nook and cranny.

Walking into the hotel lobby, Minola looked up at the magnificent Murano candelabra as it glowed brightly and reflected the brilliant light on marble walls and polished floors. The paintings hanging on the walls spoke of centuries of art, forever changing styles still uniquely Venetian.

After acknowledging the staff, they went to their room. Before Peter even locked the door, he had Minola pinned against the wall, kissing her as if his life depended on it. Peter firmly believed it did. He raised her hands above her head and twined his fingers with hers.

"I love you." Peter groaned as he deepened the kiss, and felt her return the embrace measure for measure. As a lover, she gave him everything. He could feel her commitment to him with each stroke of her hand, each caress and whimper. Something intense flared in the pit of his stomach. Panic. Gut wrenching dread. *Why now?* Every day, his love for her deepened. Every day, he wondered how that could be possible. Every day, he was grateful for that great passion. And every day, terror beckoned.

Dazed, he pulled back, his gaze riveted on her face, her red lips, and her cheeks flushed from his kisses and embrace.

"Peter, what is it? Did I do something wrong?" She ran her hand across his cheek.

"God, no. Did you not feel my response? No, my love, you did nothing wrong. Everything's right. Just the old resurrection of dread and fear. Did I mention that you're my world?" He leaned into her.

"Yes. You and Tom Jones. In Paris and in Bath."

"Excellent. Now Venice. I wouldn't want you to become complacent. Minola, you will not get involved in this mess. I have a really bad feeling about this murder."

"If Jennifer is involved, how can I not?"

"You will not," he said emphatically.

"Peter, we have no information, yet, and I will get in touch with her. But in the meantime, could you finish what you started? Make love to me. With me."

Never moving away from her, with her back still against the wall, he took her face in his hands, bent his head, and pressed his mouth to hers. He murmured in a thick voice, "You never have to ask twice." More than kissing her, he caressed her mouth. "You're wearing too many clothes."

"Well...do something about that, Captain." She squirmed against him.

"I plan to, Miss Grey. My pleasure." He nuzzled her neck and then worked on the buttons of her blouse. "How many damn buttons are you wearing?" he muttered, frustrated with his slow progress.

"I'm not wearing any buttons. I'm wearing a sexy blouse with buttons, the one you love. Last time, you said the buttons were perfect and opened one button at a time." She felt his lips move along her neck and gasped in delight.

"Today, I'm in a hurry." He nibbled on her ear and felt her tremble.

"Then stop talking and get to work. I'm very ready for you."

"I know that. That is why I'm in a hurry." He pulled down her Capri pants, still holding her against the wall, unwilling to move farther away from her.

"All I have to remove is that lacy bra of yours." He caressed her breast, and felt her immediate response in his arms. "And the matching panties on your lovely bottom." His hand moved down her thigh as he slid the panties down her legs, and his eyes followed her movement as she kicked them away. He gave a satisfied groan and continued his seduction.

"Very observant of you. You're still fully clothed. I'll have to do something about that." She tugged on his shirt, and then her hands explored the hollows of his back.

"Hmm. Yes, that is an excellent plan. Please. Bed...now." His hoarse voice sounded impatient.

By the time he replied, she had removed his shirt, which he tossed on the floor. Soon the pants followed. He kissed her taut nipples—one then the other—all the while caressing her body. His lips moved over her neck, behind her ear, and finally reached home. Her open mouth waiting for him was sheer bliss. He took her mouth with savage intensity as he felt her body melt against his. Peter didn't wait any longer to enter her, and slid inside in one powerful push. The action of his tongue matched his thrusts inside her body. A moan of ecstasy reached her lips as she climaxed, and he soon followed.

They gazed into each other's eyes, neither one willing to move, savoring the feeling of utter satisfaction and happiness.

"I am home," Peter said softly.

"As am I." Her body felt heavy. Sated. She held him tightly to her and had no desire to leave his arms, her body still tingled from his lovemaking. She relaxed, sinking into his embrace.

Often at such euphoric moments, she was terrified of what the future held. Their past had been turbulent, and murder seemed to intrude on a continuous basis. But in the meantime, he was in her arms, and she in his.

"Peter, I love you. I will never get tired of saying that."

"I'll never get tired of hearing it. And by the way, I love you, too, in case you did not know that."

"Peter…"

"Hmmm…I don't want to budge." He inched a little farther, reluctant to leave her body.

"I don't either. Stay right there with me. Can we sleep like that?"

"Hmm.." His lips curved up in a smile. "I'll see what I can do."

"Please." She moaned as he moved, causing a ripple in her body. "Peter?"

"Hmm…"

"I want you again. I think I'm becoming insatiable." She whimpered against his chest.

"I'm still somewhat inside you, and I'm certainly not complaining." He caressed her neck with his knuckle and spoke. "I do need to rest a little."

Minola massaged his shoulder with her lips, a tender, soft touch to show him she was aware of their intimacy. "I want to go to sleep in your arms—after I shower, that is."

"I can arrange that." He slowly withdrew from her and led her to the shower.

The cascading water washed over them and soothed their bodies, but Peter, impatient to hold her and love her, wasted no time in reaching for her. He couldn't get enough of her. Seeing the water glisten on her body, his hands immediately reached out to cup her breasts firmly in his hands. They fit perfectly. His hands roamed intimately over her breasts, caressing them gently, the rosy peaks grew to pebble hardness. Peter groaned at her reaction to his touch, and bent down and suckled one breast then the other as he heard Minola moan. He reached up and found her mouth, teasing her lips so she would open for his invasion. He pulled her against him, raised her leg over his hip, and entered her with a hard push.

Once inside, he waited a moment to make sure she was comfortable and adjusted to him, and when he felt her move against him, he started pumping into her. Fast and hard. She responded to every thrust, clutching him in her moist heat. The climax was quick and furious. Peter held her against the wall until their breathing returned to normal.

"I love you, Miss Grey."

"I love you so very much, Captain Riley," she murmured as she reached up, cupped his face with her hands, and kissed him passionately, sliding her tongue inside his open mouth.

"God, Minola, I want you again, and I can't. What are you doing to me?" He groaned.

"Showing you how much I love you." Smiling, she stepped out of the tub. He followed her, reached for a towel, and tenderly dried her off. She returned the favor. Once they were ready, they walked back into the bedroom. They lay on the bed, exhausted. Peter turned her so that her back was to him, and he pulled her into his arms and curved his body alongside hers. She was safe in his arms.

"Peter?"

"Hmm…I thought you wanted to sleep?"

"I do." She yawned to prove the point. "But I think that body we found is somehow connected to Jennifer. Can we help her? Would she want us to do so?"

"Probably. Have you forgotten, you're now in the papers? First Paris, then Bath, and finally London. You're a celebrity. You're an artist, as is Jennifer. You have a connection, an old friendship, and you're probably right, a problem exists at the furnace. Now, go to sleep. As the adage goes, tomorrow is another day." He felt her snuggle even closer against him.

"Maybe I can call her and ask her to join us in Venice, dinner at the hotel. That is innocent enough. A friendly visit, nothing more."

"That might work, but it's a big maybe. Depends on how interested the police are in our guests, and us," Peter mumbled.

"I think she couldn't talk when we were together, and maybe when she's away from family and the business, she might open up. Or it could all be a mistake and she's not involved."

"We'll set up a dinner date. Now go to sleep." He leaned over her and nuzzled her neck.

"I love you, Captain Peter Riley." She moved her bottom for a better fit and promptly fell asleep, leaving Peter with a growing erection.

"Damn," he murmured, as he inhaled the perfume she always wore to bed. The scent that he identified with her in Paris. In Bath, she switched to another one. He understood why, as a separation from him. During their tumultuous times in Bath, he remembered she wanted to break away and make a change. She started with the perfume to disassociate herself from him and their problems, something he intended to avoid in the future. At all cost.

Another murder intruded on their time together. This time he was without an advantage. He had no place to start, and out of his element, he fell into a fit-full sleep, holding tightly to the woman he loved above all.

Chapter 3

The bright sun filtered through the gauze curtains and woke Minola. They had made love in the middle of the night, until both fell back asleep from sheer exhaustion. Minola opened her eyes and saw Peter watching her.

"Good morning, my love." He leaned down and kissed her cheek.

"Good morning," she murmured. Still hazy from sleep, she rubbed her eyes.

He smiled as she stretched lazily, her breasts uncovered while she sighed and snuggled closer, giving Peter an involuntary spasm in his groin.

"Two things. Teeth. Coffee." She ran her hand over his chest.

"Stop that, if teeth and coffee are involved. I know the routine. Along the line, I come in third." He pulled the blanket away from her body to allow her to get up and head to the bathroom. He soon followed after calling room service for coffee.

By the time he'd ordered her favorite brew, she was finished in the bathroom and slipped back to bed, nestling into him. She put her arms around his neck and welcomed his kiss.

"So what's on the agenda today?" she asked as she nibbled his chin.

"We have a couple of weeks to get to the bottom of this mystery."

"Why two weeks? I thought we were going to be here for three weeks."

"Yes, well, we are…but I invited our family and friends to join us and celebrate our engagement and wedding. I have everything prepared, or I should say Sally has everything prepared."

"Did you say wedding…in two weeks? How come I didn't know anything about it? Wedding in two weeks?" She shrieked.

"Yes, wedding. That is what usually happens after an engagement. Or was I misinformed?" he groused.

"I knew the wedding would be in Venice, but Peter, there are preparations to be made. People to invite. Shoes to buy. And the prospective bride should be asked. Did I mention shoes to buy?"

"I did ask, and I distinctly remember you saying yes. In Bath, remember?" He saw her nod, and unable to stop himself, he laughed out loud. "Did you just say shoes to buy? Most women, I believe, would worry about a dress. And we did talk about it, and this was a perfect opportunity. And a surprise."

"Well yes, but Peter, shoes…they are important. And I have no dress. Peter, no one assumes a wedding to be a surprise without first informing the bride. There are rules about that. And…and I have no shoes."

"The all-important shoes." His lips curved up. "Well, my love, about the wedding…I talked to Sally, and we came up with this plan. A costume wedding. I have, based on Sally's orders, arranged with that costume shop in the Cannaregio district. The name escapes me at the moment, but I have an address. Sally has all the information. Costumes from the Renaissance period and others. Everyone will have a choice, and masks, an art theme if you will. We'll have the reception at the hotel. Plenty of flowers in Murano vases. I…" He stopped talking when he saw she was crying, tears streaming down her face.

"Minola, please stop," he begged. "I can cancel everything. I know you haven't had any time to plan anything, but I didn't want to waste any more time putting a wedding band on your finger." He tenderly wiped her tears with his finger. "I can cancel."

"Noooo. I'm happy." She hiccupped as a cry of joy bubbled in her voice. "I'm crying because it is so wonderful. Why do I always get so soggy and emotional? You're wonderful. I never would have thought of anything like that. I love it." She leaned into him and kissed him. "I love it. I love you. Change nothing. It will be incredible. Tell me more." She took a deep breath and said, "I have no shoes to wear." She swiped at the tears with her hand.

"Yes, I'm very aware of that. You have no shoes." A wide grin lined his face. "Sally has it all planned, but I don't think she took shoes into account." He rubbed his chin. "On the other hand, she knows you well, so maybe she did. Actually, she is planning everything long distance from Paris. I have been in contact with her, of course, also Becky and Jennifer. Remember, the Castigli furnace will provide the vases that the guests will keep as a souvenir, family and friends only. "

"Family and friends? Who exactly?"

"My parents, sister, the complete Riley contingent, a couple of my friends, and Becky and Kirk. Tracy and Gordon from Chicago are maybe coming, as is Fitzhugh and his wife, David and Ashby, and, of course, I invited Welsey. The hotel knows all. Sally has been in touch with them about the food, and she reserved all the rooms. They will be staying in the hotel. I wanted it to be special and memorable for you," he finished, uncertain if he'd done the right thing. The only defense he had was his love for her and the mystical connection of the vows he desperately needed. She was going to be his. In every way.

"Costumes…how magnificent. I would have never thought of that." She beamed, her eyes shining like the proverbial stars, the remnants of tears still glittering on her lashes. "A masque wedding, instead of a ball."

"Becky is the one that mentioned the possibility to Sally. Saying something along the lines of Venice being the perfect setting, and because the group was small, it would be an ideal, unique, and intimate wedding."

"Peter, I don't know what to say. Thank you. It will be perfect."

"Minola, my love, you forgot to drink your coffee." He leaned over her and kissed her.

"Coffee. I forgot coffee. That has never happened." She reached over to the nightstand and poured Peter a cup of black coffee and then prepared her own brew with hot milk. The steamed milk had been delivered in a carafe, along with the coffee, just the way she liked it. She took a sip, licked her lips, and set the cup down. "Yummy coffee. Is there anything I need to do? Sounds like you have everything covered. Am I really going to be married in a costume?" She took another sip and said, "Do they have shoes?"

"Yes, we're to be married in a costume. We'll buy shoes. You're not getting away from me. All we need to do is pick up our costumes and show up at the appointed hour. The honeymoon will start after our guests leave. Although, I intend for us to have some privacy."

"I can't believe this. I'm speechless." Minola finished her coffee and then placed the empty cup back on the night table with shaky fingers.

"Speechless? That is a good thing. So, my love, what would you like to do today?"

"I want to visit the costume shop, look at my wedding dress, and make sure it fits. If memory serves, according to the map, the Jewish Ghetto is in the Cannaregio district, too. Maybe we can pay a visit. Oh, and a wonderful Romanesque church right on the Grand Canal. I want to stop there, too. And maybe there are some galleries along the way we could stop and visit. And…"

"Miss Grey, we haven't even gotten out of bed yet, and I'm already exhausted."

"Well, in that case, before you become anymore tired, you might want to service your soon-to-be wife." She beamed at him.

"Hmm…now that is an excellent plan."

He made slow and languid love to her, letting her know just how precious she was to him. They rested, showered together, and made love again as the hot water washed over them.

"Peter, what does my dress look like? I must be the first bride ever not to see her dress," she spoke while getting dressed.

"You will have to talk to Sally. She didn't share that piece of information. Remember, I'm the groom. I'm not supposed to see the dress. I just told her to keep mine simple."

"I hope it won't be something in peach, her favorite color."

"Minola, my love, I don't care if it's a potato sack. We'll be married. That is all I care about. Now, I'm hungry. Let's have something to eat downstairs."

On their way out, she playfully pinned him against the door, put her arms around his neck, and kissed him.

"I love you, Captain Riley. Deeply," she whispered into his mouth. "Peter, I'm so afraid something is going to happen. Please promise me we will be together." She felt his hands on her back tighten as he deepened the kiss. She couldn't define her fears, other than she had them. She accepted Peter's job and the danger that came with it. At least that is what she told herself.

"Minola, I don't think I could let you go again and survive. We will be fine."

After a delicious loving interlude, a buffet breakfast, and exquisite coffee, they walked out of the hotel and took the vaporetto to their destination.

The vaporetto, or ferry was an efficient mode of transportation on the Grand Canal and a wonderful way to meet the locals and avoid the day trippers—tourists that arrived by the boatload, literally. They were dropped off for the day and returned to a cruise ship in late afternoon. Minola couldn't imagine not spending at least a few days in this magnificent city.

A tourist at heart, she didn't leave a stone unturned. They took the vaporetto to the Rialto Bridge. As Minola looked up, she sighed in contentment. The famous bridge loomed in front of her. She saw people wave at the oncoming traffic in the canal, and she waved back. Traffic on the canal was vast, and boats were weaving in and out across the water, she was amazed she didn't see any accidents. A magical sight, indeed.

Normally not one for public displays of affection, Minola's attitude changed in Venice. She felt romance and passion with every step she took, whether sipping a cup of coffee in a cafe where the strong aroma made her positively giddy or stopping in a gelateria and picking her flavor *du jour*. Even just going up and down the many bridges, she needed to show Peter how she felt. She took his hand and felt his fingers tighten on hers, his response to her always immediate.

"I read about the bridge. The Rialto is the oldest bridge crossing the Grand Canal. Its origin, in one shape or another, dates back to 1181. The stone bridge as it stands today was completed in 1591, and every visitor to the city visits the bridge. I, too, do my homework," Peter said.

"Magnificent," she murmured as they walked up to the top. "I read somewhere that the design was too risky and it would collapse. But see, today, it is standing strong and is one of the most iconic architectural delights in Venice. Look at the covered ramps! They are lined with souvenirs shops, jewelry, touristy kitsch, and anything else in between. Let's see if I can find shoes. The view is fantastic from the top, glancing down at the canal, or from the vaporetto. I love Venice. What a pair we are." She was blissfully happy, fully alive, and Peter did that for her. She turned to face him and, with her fingertips, caressed his cheek. "I don't care who sees us. I'm so very much in love with you. I just needed to say it." She melted when she saw the heartrending tenderness of his gaze.

"The sentiments are fully reciprocated." He gathered her in his arms and held her snugly against him. "I'm very much in love with you, too," he whispered in her hair. "I think we better see if we can buy some shoes. Now." He heard her giggle. "Nice to know you appreciate my discomfort. Shoes, my love. Let's walk." Peter propelled her forward.

"How about I draw the bridge? And a scene from Piazza San Marco and our hotel. Wouldn't that be a wonderful memory for our friends? It won't take me long, and they'll have three scenes they can pick amongst. Each one would have a different perspective. What do you think?"

"If you have the time. However, I plan on keeping you busy, and let's not forget Jennifer Castigli, a missing glass blower, and a body. And most of all, don't forget me."

"I would never forget you, and I won't let it interfere with our time. This wedding is remarkable and precious to me. I want to acknowledge it."

Hearing her words, he exhaled a long sigh of contentment. "I agree. All I can tell you is that I feel an intense happiness. And an intense physical need to show you that happiness. So let's shop. Please." He took her hand and pulled her toward him. They stopped in a few shops, but did not find any shoes. For the time being, they were carefree tourists.

"I can't buy shoes if I don't know what the dress looks like. No peach. I'm not a fan, but it is Sally's favorite color."

They lingered at the top of the bridge, reluctant to let go of the perfect moment.

"Peter, I think the plan should work." Minola tugged on his arm.

"What plan would that be?" He stopped in his tracks right in the middle of the bridge, bumping several tourists.

"Do you think we should go back to the hotel? Another ferry ride would be lovely about now." Minola loved the watery commute. She was in awe of the history of Venice and the surrounding islands and swore she could hear ghosts rustle in the wind—the past was so rich in art, literature and architecture.

"The plan, Miss Grey? Where we go depends on your plan?" he reminded her.

"Let's invite Jennifer and her husband to dinner at our hotel and see if anything is wrong. Maybe together we might get a glimpse of something unusual, a problem…Make it casual, nothing out of the ordinary, just friends getting together and planning a wedding. Out in the open."

She reached for her purse, took out her cell, and dialed Jennifer's number. The response was quick. "Jen." Minola heard an indrawn breath and then a short silence. "Is something wrong?"

"Yes. No." Jennifer's voice sounded tired.

"Talk to me, please," Minola pleaded

"Only the still-missing employee...he is a friend, and Antonio is concerned. He hasn't called. We checked his home, and he seems to have disappeared."

"I'm sorry. Is there any way we can help?" Minola visibly shivered. This was not a coincidence. She was now sure the body they found was the missing Castigli employee.

"I just need a getaway."

"That is perfect. Would you care to join us for dinner tonight at the hotel?"

"Minola, the police were here this morning. They think they found Julio." Her voice became distant, as if she were a continent away.

"How? What did they say? How did they connect you to the missing body?" Minola spoke softly.

"What? We reported him missing a week ago. They found a body last night covered in glass, and they think he may be ours. Something about the glass, the furnace, and the only missing person report. They will be here soon. Everyone is upset. This is a small operation."

"I'm so sorry. Actually, I called for a reason...eh...my wedding." Minola didn't want to sound callous, but looked for any excuse to get Jennifer to relax and agree to the dinner. She didn't want to discuss anything on the phone.

"I know. Sally has been discussing the affair. It sounds fabulous. And we have enough vases in stock. I can't believe you're getting married. Peter seems like a good man."

"He is a remarkable man, and I'm incredibly lucky." She reached for his hand and felt his fingers curl around hers. "But we wanted to have dinner together at our hotel. Can you make it tonight? I know it is short notice, and your current problems..."

"I would love an escape. I wouldn't mind spending the night in Venice. I want to get away. I need to get away. This is perfect." Minola heard a distinct sob in Jennifer's voice.

"Leave it to me. I'll check if they have a vacancy. How does six sound?" Minola paused. "Jen, are you coming alone or with Antonio?"

"Just me. He's busy, what with the missing employee…just me," she said in a hushed tone.

"We'll eat in the hotel, a fantastic restaurant with a view to match." Minola's cheerful voice belied her concern for her friend. Something was terribly wrong at the Castigli home.

"I can be there by seven," Jennifer replied

"Perfect. See you soon." Minola hung up and turned to Peter.

"I gather the police made the connection and already paid a visit," Peter said as Minola ended the conversation.

"Yes, but the weird thing is, they reported him missing a week ago. Jen mentioned something about comparing the glass shards to the furnace. Do you think they know where we went yesterday?"

"Probably. I certainly would have not wasted time before investigating the people who found the body. The police, for the most part, are the same all over the world. We're in the thick of it, like it or not."

Minola called the hotel, booked a night for her friend, and made reservations for dinner at the same time. "At least we don't have to go to Murano today. She seemed really upset. I'm worried about her. I also think Jennifer and Antonio are having a problem."

"We'll help where we can. I'll call Sergeant Welsey and ask him to pop in a touch early. Let's see if he knows anything."

"It'll be like old times." Minola smiled ruefully.

"Precisely what I didn't want," Peter mumbled as he dialed and heard the familiar voice.

"Sir, is Miss Grey all right?" Welsey asked.

"Yes, Sergeant, she is." Peter smiled and waited for the next question he knew was coming.

"Did Miss Grey find another body, Sir?"

"Yes, Sergeant, she did," Peter replied.

"I see." After a brief pause, Welsey remarked, "I'm due for an extended holiday. Where should I book a hotel?

"I'll take care of the hotel. You'll stay at ours. And thank you."

"Not a problem. I was coming for the wedding, and it has been a while since I've been to Venice. I will be there tomorrow. Miss Grey does seem to have a remarkable talent for discovering bodies."

"Yes, that would seem to be the case. Even in Venice, there are puzzles for Miss Grey to discover. Again, thank you, Sergeant. I will see you tomorrow." Peter gave him the hotel name and address and rung off. He then called the hotel and changed the date of arrival for his sergeant.

"Now, Miss Grey, I want to spend some time with you. Alone. Before our friends invade us. You can decide where we go."

"Remember that old Renaissance church in the Cannaregio district I mentioned earlier. Well, I found out there is an afternoon concert. Will that suit?"

"Anything with you will suit." He took her arm and propelled her toward the vaporetto stop. They boarded the boat once again and enjoyed the commute along the Grand Canal. Minola waved as the boat sped away from the Rialto bridge. She watched as the tourists leaned against the wall of the bridge, looked down, and snapped pictures of the amazing traffic on the Grand Canal. *Beautiful, s*he murmured to herself and sighed.

Minola watched as the boats danced around one another, vying for the quickest way to their destinations. She observed as cases of bottled water were unloaded by hand and empty cases tossed back and caught expertly. A singing gondolier seemed oblivious to the congestion. Oar in hand, he rocked to the flow of the water.

They disembarked at the stop near the Santa Lucia train station and walked along the canal.

The Cannaregio district, with the train station and Piazza Roma where everyone converged upon arrival and departure, was the pulse of the local Venetian life. One could see and hear the suitcases clanking up and down various stairs on either side of the bridges, over the many canals. It almost seemed as if the suitcases were taking the tourists for a walk, tugging at them and trying to reach the many hotels that appeared to flow on water.

The Cannaregio district had a lot to offer a savvy tourist. Among the top sites was the Jewish Ghetto. Minola read a great deal about it. Ghetto actually meant foundry, but the contemporary connotation of ghetto stuck, and today, it was known as the Jewish Ghetto. She turned toward Peter. "Do you know, people were forced to live there until 1527? The history is rich and dark. It evokes a time of the suffering and determination of a people held in captivity. To this day, the area is rich in culture and tradition and even holds a monument to the Jews that died during the Holocaust." She felt Peter take her hand in his for comfort as they continued walking. She shivered at the bleak reminder of the people who perished. The will to survive was felt in every nook.

Children played in a little garden devoid of grass. They visited a temple and listened to a guide tell them that in the olden days the temple was only identified by how many windows there were, so as not to give away the position of the temple and threaten the congregation. They stopped in an outdoor cafe and watched a woman stooped and worn by age lift a trembling cup filled with liquid to her lips, her eyes bright, alive with joy. Her lips curved up a notch, and the lines around her mouth disappeared momentarily. Minola smiled back. People enjoyed an afternoon in the fresh air, but the place was eerily quiet. As they walked along the street, many shop owners nodded and grinned.

After her visit to the Ghetto, a sense of desolation loomed that Minola could not shake. This was not the romantic Venice that all anticipated, but a Venice that remembered and preserved a history of horror, tenacity, and will to survive.

They walked back on narrow and meandering streets to the church. Every step taken was an adventure filled with history.

At the entrance to the church, by the massive doors, a man sat on a rickety wooden chair. His elbows rested on a small scratched table, and a smile lined the wrinkles on his face as he collected the entry fee for the concert. Peter handed him forty Euros for both tickets. He ushered

Minola into the church. "Just how did you find out about the concert?" he whispered.

"I chatted with an artist who is here for the festival. He told me."

"I should have known. Let's rest a bit and enjoy the serenity and quiet." Peter checked to see who else was in the church, and it appeared that mostly locals waited for the concert to begin. In spite of the murder, Peter felt at peace. They sat down in a pew in the back of the church and waited for the concert to begin. The smell of old incense and spent wax permeated the air. Candles flickered, and the dim church lights cast shadows on the walls. The concert began, a slow rhythmic pulse that built to a crescendo. The sound came alive and echoed in the bricks, the very foundation of the church.

The church was well-kept. A few indiscriminate pieces of art were displayed on easels along the wall. They were part of the annual art festival where even churches became galleries, and the displays did not necessarily have to be religious. His hand slipped up her arm, bringing her closer. She leaned her head against his shoulder, closed her eyes, and listened. Contentment and pure joy overwhelmed him. His life had changed dramatically once he admitted he loved her. He was used to affairs with no commitment, an arrangement that was understood by both parties. Everything changed with Minola the instant he met her. His original suspicions notwithstanding, she captured his heart and soul.

Once the concert ended, Minola invariably raised her head to stare at the paintings on the ceiling and the stained glass windows. "A comforting place, not grand by European standards, but welcoming." She spoke softly, afraid she'd be overheard and disturb someone. They walked outside into a still bright, early evening. "Peter, we have about an hour. Maybe we should head back slowly to the hotel."

They took the vaporetto back to Piazza San Marco and their hotel. Enthralled with the square, Minola wanted to savor the ambiance, the sheer abundance of the magnificent place. A short stroll would revive her spirits.

The shopping and restaurants were a tourist trap with prices to match, but not to be missed. From the Doge's Palace, San Marco, and the *Companile* —the tall bell tower— to the expensive jewelers, various gift shops and cafes, and stalls everywhere, each step reflected the bygone era of romance and mystery. Minola allowed herself the luxury of a momentary escape to the past and imagined the passionate intrigues of Casanova, who had roamed the dark and narrow streets of Venice. Once told the canals reeked, she couldn't smell anything other than normal everyday life: The scent of Italian cooking permeated the area, roasted garlic and onions, fresh roses as she walked by a flower stand, and a deep rich smell of chocolate that had her mouth water. The familiar aromas, most people took for granted. She had a whiff of perfume someone wore as she passed them by. The daily life of a city teeming with people.

Loud voices filled with excitement, children shrieking with joy, peddlers selling their wares, and glasses clanking revived her spirits. She walked by a cafe and smelled the rich aroma of freshly brewed coffee. Minola inhaled deeply and smiled. The allure of the city captivated and enthralled her, but she couldn't stop the sudden shiver that ran through her body.

Holding hands, they walked in silence back to the hotel. Minola wondered how life had changed for her in seemingly a short time. She left Chicago to study and paint in Paris, became involved in murder, fell in love with an Interpol man, and helped solve a crime. With Peter by her side, she travelled to Bath and became involved in another murder. Now traipsing through the continent, she arrived in Venice to marry, and instead, she found a body, most probably another murder. This time she was not alone, but with the love of her life, Interpol Captain Peter Riley, a man obsessed with her safety. A man who almost let her go to keep her safe. *I hope we survive this latest tragedy.*

She immediately felt shame for her selfish thoughts and sorrow for the loss of life. As before, she wondered at the callous way a life was taken without regard. What made people go over the edge? Her experience had been that rage, along with greed and desire for power, always played a part in the crime, and this time most likely would not be different. The most elemental reasons to kill and destroy always focused on material gain, passion, and jealousy. Her simple reasoning was to do without if she couldn't afford it, walk away if betrayed and make a clean break—after all, that was precisely what she had done. *Except that doesn't work for everyone.*

While living in Chicago at the start of her career, sometimes she bought paint before food. Minola smiled and remembered she always had some change leftover for coffee. Hard times, but she managed. She had dear friends and didn't miss much else. She lost herself in her art and books. Mysteries were the preferred escape. A simple and satisfying life.

With her eventual artistic success and since meeting Peter, her life changed drastically, but she didn't. Her values and needs were the same as before. Except now, Peter was the center of her universe. She gained more friends, and her life was richer because of them.

Chapter 4

The lobby of the elegant hotel welcomed them back. A huge bouquet of flowers rested on a gigantic marble table in the center, and the aroma of fresh blooms permeated the lobby. Deep plush couches and small low tables surrounded by luxurious chairs were perfect, restful corners for sipping a drink or simply waiting for someone. The massive rug on the ancient well-worn marble floor was old but not ragged and added a level of coziness to the opulent lobby. Murano chandeliers and sconces lined the walls, along with magnificent glass lamps on the tables that cast warm and soothing shadows.

One could sit down, order coffee, and relax in peace and solitude, away from the continuous and tumultuous crowds at the Piazza San Marco. The hotel located only a few steps away was a haven of tranquility.

Once in the room, Minola sat down on the bed while Peter ordered her favorite brew. She was addicted to coffee, and no matter time of day or night, coffee soothed and revived her spirits. She watched as he cradled the phone and turned toward her. "Peter, what do we do?"

"As far as?" he asked pointedly.

"The body, Jennifer, and our involvement?" She took a deep breath and, for a second, closed her eyes.

"We're waiting for Jennifer. We'll talk to her and take it from there." Peter sat down next to her and put his arm around her shoulder. "We will be fine. I learned my lesson and won't let you go again. That is a promise." He ran his hand up and down her arm in a tender caress.

"How did you know I was worried about us?"

"Because I know you. And it is obvious to me." He got up off the bed when he heard the knock. Checking the peep hole, he opened the door. Minola's coffee was served just how she liked it, in a thermos and very hot, along with a pitcher of steamed milk. Peter poured her coffee and watched as she sipped the brew, licked her lips, and took another sip. He smiled when he heard her murmur *yummy*. "I will not let anything happen to us. That is a promise I must and intend to keep. We're in this together, although at a great disadvantage."

"Good. I intend to make sure you keep that promise." She patted the spot next to her on the bed. As soon as he sat down, she gave him a light kiss on his cheek. "What do we have to do to make progress in this investigation?"

"I need to make nice with the local police, but first, we have to make sure the body is that of the missing Castigli employee. If it is, we have a reasonable cause for butting in. Helping out a friend and I could be useful to them, the usual drill." He shrugged his shoulders and said, "However, an ongoing corruption investigation surrounding the local police might present a slight problem. They may not take too kindly to anyone from Interpol at the moment."

"Why didn't you tell me before?"

"Didn't see a point, had other things on my mind. You," he whispered.

Minola leaned into him.

"Besides, you didn't expect to get involved in a murder here. I'm so sorry. I should have left well enough alone."

Biting her lip, she looked down and away from him.

Peter wouldn't allow the separation. With his fingertips, he lifted her head up so that she gazed directly at him. He kissed the tip of her nose and whispered, "You, my love, have nothing to be sorry for. We'll work it out. Notice I said *we*."

"Duly noted. Peter, I just thought of this, but the Castigli family is an old one and I think really wealthy. If they want our help and let the local police know, we already have an in. Money talks."

"That it does, Miss Grey, but they will resent my involvement. I'm an outsider interfering with their investigation. I'm with Interpol, and with our involvement, we'll have proven that money talks. The resentment will be far reaching. The Castigli family will have to reach out to the police, and of course, that presents a certain risk as well."

"I know. Are you going to keep calling me Miss Grey after we're married?"

"I certainly am not. You'll be Mrs. Riley," he replied adamantly, his voice soft but firm. "Except your professional name is well-established. That might present a problem if you change it."

"No, it won't. The art should sell, not my name. Mrs. Riley, it is. I rather like it, Captain Riley." She saw his lips curve up in a smile.

"Good." He sighed, stood up, and pulled her straight into his arms.

"You do know we didn't make it to the costume shop, and I have no shoes and haven't seen my dress."

"Yes, I know. Tomorrow is another day." He bent down and was about to kiss her when a knock on the door interrupted any intentions he might have had. He swore under his breath and went to open the door. Jennifer Castigli stood outside the room. Peter moved out of the way to allow her in. Her eyes were red and puffy, and she seemed distracted. "Jennifer, please come in." Peter closed the door and motioned for her to sit down.

Minola jumped off the bed and walked over to hug Jennifer. "What's wrong?"

"Everything," was the tearful reply. Jennifer slumped down on the small couch. "Everything," she repeated.

Minola put her arms around her friend. "Is it Antonio? Has something happened?"

"Antonio has been distant. Detached. Almost as if I have no place in his life and he's single again." She hiccupped and continued. "We don't talk anymore. I can't reach him. He won't allow it. He's distant and preoccupied."

"Is it the business?" Peter asked.

"I don't know. Business or not, we haven't talked. All I know is it started about three months ago. Most nights, he doesn't even bother to come home. I don't know where he stays. And well, Julio…he's still missing, and the police have been asking questions. I think they found him, but won't say." Jennifer rubbed her hands together, and when she saw Minola watching her, she stopped, looked at her friend, and closed her eyes.

"What do you suspect?" Minola asked gently.

"That Antonio is having an affair. What else can I suspect? He's probably gone back to his first love. They grew up together. She's Italian, and I'm an American."

"Are we talking about Pia Deniccali?" Minola asked.

"Who else? The families are lifelong friends, although you'd never know it by the acerbic tone of the conversation when they are together. At least lately. Something happened."

"What do you mean?" Minola asked.

"Antonio is curt, angry, even defiant. I heard them when I was in the furnace last week. I don't think they knew I was even there."

"Jennifer, I know this is difficult for you, but under the circumstances, you need to tell us everything. Why do you suspect Antonio of duplicity?" Peter asked.

"What a quaint word, Peter…Because he's been spending his time, his nights, elsewhere. Not in our bed. Whenever I went to the furnace, they were together in his office, huddling…whispering. Do you know that feeling when you walk in and the conversation stops and people draw apart, as if caught? Well, that has happened too many times lately. I'm offered no explanation, just a shrug as if nothing was wrong."

"Did you try talking to Antonio? Let him know how you feel?" Minola asked.

"Yes, I did. Several times, all to no avail. He either ignored me or told me it's my imagination. Now, he just doesn't even bother coming home."

"Was there a problem with Julio? Anything you remember might shed some light on the current situation." Peter spoke softly. He didn't want to cause any further pain, but he wanted to know if the missing glass blower and Antonio's disregard for his marriage were somehow related. He couldn't possibly imagine betraying Minola, physically or emotionally. It was an impossibility. He'd never pull away from her ever again. Yet the persistent fear for her safety always lurked. Peter wondered if maybe something was going on at the furnace that involved both families and the end result was Julio's death. He needed to learn more about the glass business and intricacies involved.

"Jennifer, we'd like to help." Minola looked up to Peter for confirmation, and when she saw him nod, she continued. "I can't believe Antonio would ever betray you. I saw how much he loved you."

"Things change, feelings change, and passion fades," Jennifer replied, tears smearing her mascara.

"I don't believe it. He wouldn't." Minola reached for a box of tissues and handed it to her friend.

"What world are you living in? Must be the newly engaged world where everything is perfect." She pointedly looked down at Minola's ring and shrugged her shoulders.

Peter saw Minola wince at the bitter words, and he stepped in. Helping a friend was one thing; tolerating Minola being hurt was quite another. "I think that is enough," he said brutally, a shadow of annoyance crossed his face. "We'll help, but I will not have Minola hurt in the process. She does not deserve it." He covered her hands with his own.

"I'm sorry." Jennifer whimpered.

"I'm fine, all right." Minola felt cherished and protected. She ran her fingertips over Peter's arm, a light, tender caress that acknowledged his care. "I agree, we're newly engaged but we have had our share of problems and never once did we betray one another." The only problem they had was Peter's obsessive fear for her safety and the resulting issues with lack of communication, something that was important to Minola. Peter grudgingly was learning how to respond.

"I've seen it with my own eyes, and besides, both families wanted the marriage between Antonio and Pia. He married me instead. His family was never happy about it. Antonio went so far as to accuse me of spending too much time with the hired help."

"Julio?" Minola asked.

"Yes, but I was learning from him—nothing more. He was a master at design, blending colors and blowing. His *incalmo* technique, the way he fused glass, was brilliant. And he's more than a hired hand."

"How did Antonio come to suspect an affair?" Minola saw her friend cringe. "I'm sorry, Jennifer, but if we're to help, we need to know everything."

"That's just it. I don't know anything. Maybe he saw us together, but then he never asked what I was doing. He didn't even notice my new work. I could say the same thing about him. Pia spends more time in his office than she does at her own place. I've seen them together."

"It's obvious there is something wrong, and it has to be related to the furnace. Peter took some pictures of a mound of glass. Can you somehow identify the colors?" Peter handed her his phone, and Jennifer gasped as she stared at the colorful glass display.

"What do you see?" Minola demanded.

"The deep blue gray hues, cobalt pearl as I call it. Ours—Julio recently perfected it from an old formula he found somewhere. Julio and I worked on it for many hours. You have the deep blue, and the gray sort of rides on top yet blends together. On a large piece, the iridescence is fantastic. He started at the Deniccali Furnace. Maybe the colors on that glass thing are close. We tried to come up with a new blend. I worked so hard with Julio, and Antonio didn't even care to see it. I just don't know anymore."

Minola bent down and stared at the display. "Beautiful combination," she murmured and ran her fingers through her hair to hide her agitation. She knew a body lay beneath, covered by that stunning ray of colors.

"That's enough for now." Peter reached for his phone then moved closer to Minola. He could always sense her distress.

"Peter, why do you have a picture of that? Where did you get it?" Jennifer asked.

"Minola found it while we were cruising the Grand Canal, and she thought it intriguing. Do you know anything about it?"

"Really nothing, other than the striking colors. I'd have to see it. It does look like scrap. Never occurred to me to use it like that. The colors…"

"Well, now we know that it possibly came from your furnace," Minola said.

"Maybe. I would never think to do something that big with the leftovers. But when you think about it, you could make a lovely piece of furniture from it—a table top, maybe a stand, even decorative bricks, anything really. Something to consider going forward. We've used the discarded pieces in inexpensive jewelry. Interesting possibilities," Jennifer replied thoughtfully.

"Let's take a break and go to dinner." Peter extended his hand to Minola and felt her grasp his fingers, and he relaxed. She had a touch that soothed, no matter the circumstances.

The restaurant was ablaze in light. Beautiful chandeliers and sconces cast shadows on walls. The crisp, cream-colored tablecloths and small bouquets of flowers on each table, along with candlelight, provided the perfect romantic ambiance. Peter wanted an intimate dinner with Minola and not a discussion on potential adultery and murder, but he understood Minola's need to help.

Once seated and wine was ordered, Peter asked, "Jennifer, tell me when you noticed a problem with your husband?"

"A month, two, more. It's my fault, I didn't really pay attention. The new project took all my time, and I… my fault he went to Pia." The desolate tone left no doubt of her despair.

"Jen, it could be something entirely different. You don't know for sure that he went to Pia. Maybe like you and Julio, they were working together, and you misunderstood," Minola tried to comfort her friend.

"I don't think so. He's been distant…everywhere," murmured Jennifer.

"The only way we're going to find out is to become involved…" Minola responded matter-of-factly.

"Minola, did you not notice the chilly reception we received from the police? We can't just jump in." Peter's voice was calm and steady as he gazed at Minola, willing her to let go of the investigation. Fear for her safety drove him to distraction.

"I noticed, but…"

"There are no *buts*. We have nothing to go on." Peter's words were cool, but his tone had a degree of warmth and concern.

"I know that, but doesn't it always start that way. You collect information, make your charts, dig for information, and solve the case." Minola winked at Peter and smiled.

"When I get arrested for interfering with an ongoing investigation, you can bail me out. Better yet, we'll probably be married in jail." Peter sighed.

"I'd marry you anywhere. Just thought you should know." Minola took his hand in hers and wrapped her fingers around his.

"I know what you're trying to do, and as always, it worked." Peter lifted her hand to his mouth and ran his lips over her knuckles. "We'll see what we can find out. Were there any issues at the furnace? Is the business slow? Anything?"

"I was never involved in the business. I've been on the creative side, but Julio was involved in both. I really wasn't interested. All I wanted to do was blow glass. Come up with different colors, textures. Nothing else." She blinked twice and stared at Peter. "What is it that you're not telling me? You're with the police. What is it? Did you find Julio?"

"First and foremost, you must keep your wits about you. We found a body. Whether it's Julio—that, as yet, is undetermined." Peter spoke quietly.

"A body? Under that glass blanket you showed me—a body?" She visibly shuddered.

"Yes. The police are investigating, but we don't have the identity of the victim, yet. And I'm not sure the police will be in any hurry to confirm it for us, either."

"Jen, you can't really discuss it with anyone. I don't want this to lead to your house anymore than it already has," Minola stated.

"Well, we can't just sit and do nothing. Julio had a family, his mother and sister. They're worried sick about him."

"He wasn't married?" Minola asked.

"No, and no, I didn't have an affair with him, if that is where you're going with this."

"I wasn't," Minola replied softly. She felt Peter's fingers caress her hand. He was her own personal pillar of strength. She watched Jennifer acknowledge the gesture. "That's the first thing the police will look at."

"I'm sorry, Minola. In my defense, I haven't been myself." She raised her hand slightly and twirled the wedding ring around her finger. "Julio and Pia were an item a long time ago. She goes after every man, eligible or not. She's a consummate flirt and really, really good at it. They all fall for her. I think she felt betrayed when Julio came to work for us, and no one betrays her."

"Why did he?" Peter asked.

"I heard talk of making him a partner, but Pia's brother felt he wasn't ready, and her father considered him an outsider. In that family, you had to prove your lineage goes back centuries, or you're an outsider. I guess he got tired of waiting."

"So it could be said that Antonio stole Julio from his competitor?"

"Yes, probably, but the families have been friends for centuries. That lineage thing again."

"We've been at this for a while. Let's eat and relax. We'll pick this up again later."

They ordered their food, and for a while, everything was forgotten but the delicious classic Venetian fare and wine. Minola's favorite dish was cuttlefish cooked in black ink over spaghetti. Peter ordered fried sardines smothered in caramelized onions, cooked with raisins, pine nuts, and vinegar. Jennifer chose another classic dish of white corn polenta cooked with tiny gray shrimp.

"I had another thought. That huge hunk of glass—it may not have been all remnants. It would take much too long to collect and store. It could have been a work in progress that shattered, and someone saved the pieces and used them," Minola supposed.

"That is a distinct possibility," Jennifer replied.

"I did notice that the center of that pile, the blue grey color, was perfectly finished, and the pieces were larger and cut evenly. The rest was rugged, and the pieces looked like...well, like discards. How would we be able to find out?" Peter asked.

"Not easily, I'm afraid. And certainly not without drawing suspicion. I don't remember seeing anything like that at the furnace. It would have been rather obvious," Jennifer replied.

"Unless someone wanted to hide it," Minola corrected.

"Well, we know it must be connected to a furnace. We know there are three families involved: Pia's, yours, and maybe Julio's. We know problems existed with management. Until we find out who was under that blanket, everything else is pure speculation. Something else to remember, there are other furnaces in Murano. We narrowed things down to two furnaces for simplicity, but..." Peter speculated.

"Yes, all of that is true, but the police were already working on the missing person. And it looks like they probably tied it together just like we did. I'm convinced Julio is buried under that glass. We just need to prove how, why, and when. Not necessarily in that order." Minola took a sip of water, set the glass down. *How did things go so wrong for Jennifer? What happened to them?*

"Of course, why didn't I think of that? So simple." Sarcasm dripped from every word Peter uttered.

"I knew you'd see it my way." Minola's lips curved up in a big grin as she shook her head. His sarcasm did not escape her notice. "So what do we do first?"

"We can skip the preliminary investigation and just report to jail. I'm convinced we're going to wind up there, might as well make it sooner than later," Peter replied.

"Do you two always work like this? I've been reading the local society pages, and you seem to be rather a good investigative duo."

"No, not always. Sometimes we even argue. And Peter doesn't communicate well, and that leads to further trouble."

"I don't…Arrrgh. You, my love, have once again reduced my vocabulary to practically nothing. You don't think you're going to get away with this, do you?" Peter tried for levity to ease the tension and allow Jennifer to get her emotions under control. He relaxed when he saw her smile.

"Peter, whether you like it or not, we're in it already. Jen needs help, a person is dead, and…" Minola blinked and focused her gaze on Peter. She knew he'd understand.

"And yes, I know when I've been outmaneuvered." His voice was resigned, the battle lost, as he knew it would be. "Let's call it a night. We need to confirm the identity of the body before we can do anything else. I'll call the police tomorrow, but cannot appear overly anxious. In the meantime, we'll need to pay a visit to the Deniccali furnace and see if we can find anything out." Peter asked for the bill.

"Jennifer, you'll need to talk to Antonio, this time about Julio." Peter stood up and extended his hand to Minola.

"I'd rather not, not yet." Jennifer's voice shook. "I'll go to my room. Thank you for booking it for me. I'm a little tired."

"Not at all. We can have breakfast together, if you'd like." Minola offered.

"No, thank you. It is a lovely invitation, but I need time alone. I have some thinking to do. We'll keep in touch. Most likely, I'll see you in Murano. Have a good night, you two." Jennifer waved and walked out of the restaurant.

Minola waited until Jennifer was well out of earshot then spoke. "Peter, maybe I can stop at the furnace and say I'm checking on the wedding vases or want another tour of the furnace for some kind of research I'm doing. This way I can ask questions without arousing too much suspicion. Doesn't it sound like a good plan? I have a reason to go."

"By all means, it is reasonable, but there is no *I*. We're going to do it together." Peter grasped her hand firmly in his and waited for her response. He didn't know if she'd be angry, but he knew he wasn't going to let her go alone. She'd have to live with his obsessive fears. Just as he had to learn—and in fact, was still learning—to live with her insatiable curiosity and lack of concern for her own wellbeing.

Minola leaned toward him and whispered, "Peter, you are the love of my life. I can't even begin to tell you how I feel about you. The depth is profound. I show you every time we make love. I'm fully aware of you every second I'm awake. It may not appear that way to you, but it is the truth. Even when we're asleep, I seem to cuddle closer to you." She took a deep breath and continued. "I understand your fears. They are mine, as well. I accept your job, because that is a huge part of who you are, but my concern for your wellbeing is always there. I understand how you feel. I really do. I just don't want it to undermine our daily lives." She looked at Peter then at her hand still firmly clasped in his. The touch of his hand was suddenly almost unbearable in its tenderness.

"It won't. I won't let it. I promised you that, but you have to allow for a certain restraint on my part." His arms encircled her, one hand in the small of her back. He felt her soft curves mold against the contours of his body. She fit so perfectly. "I love you," he whispered into her hair. "I always will."

"Do you realize we're standing by our table in the restaurant discussing something so intimate?" Minola asked.

"So we are. I hadn't noticed. You do that to me," he said in a husky whisper.

She murmured in his ear. "Let's go to our room. We can discuss our wedding. Suddenly, I can't wait to marry you. That is a commitment I want to make."

"We'll do a lot more than talk about it." He gazed at her speculatively and escorted Minola out of the restaurant.

Once in the room, he locked the door, took her in his arms, and ran his lips over her mouth then asked, "Minola, what was that all about? What are you nervous about?" He spoke gently and waited for her answer.

"You know me too well," she responded.

"I know you intimately. Now, let's sit down on the couch and chat." He patted the seat next to him in invitation.

"Antonio and Jennifer were so in love, and look what happened to them. She's spending a night in one of the most romantic hotels in Venice, alone. She thinks Antonio is cheating on her and no longer wants her. I saw them together when they married. They were deeply in love, and now…they are far apart and can't even talk to each other." She hiccupped, and her eyes filled with tears.

"They are not us. I wouldn't allow that to happen to us, and I know you wouldn't. You've reached out to me when we had issues. When I pulled away from you, you waited. Granted, it took a great deal to convince you, but you stayed. We learned from our mistakes, just as they will have to learn from theirs. If Antonio in fact is having an affair, we'll be there for Jennifer, and they'll have to work it out. But I will never, never betray you. I will be faithful. That is a promise I can easily make." He pulled her on his lap and wrapped his arms around her waist. "I am deeply, passionately in love with you," he whispered, his breath hot against her ear. He then reached for her mouth, and the kiss, when it came, was slow and thoughtful. He felt drugged by her response. His hand shook when he touched her face and held it gently. "I can't wait for us to be married."

"You always know what to say and do. Thank you, Peter, for loving me."

"It is the easiest thing I've ever done. The hardest has been being away from you. I will not let anything happen to us."

"I won't, either. But I do want to help Jennifer. I want her as happy as we are. Can you call the police and see if maybe they found out something new?"

"I will do so. The sergeant is scheduled to arrive tomorrow. Perhaps he can help. He often has contacts where least expected. Here is the plan for tonight. I want us to shower, make love, and sleep."

"Sounds wonderful, especially the *make love* part. Let's go shower. Oh, before I forget, I want to see the Doge's Palace tomorrow, visit the costume shop where my wedding dress is being held hostage, and buy shoes. And we need to go to Murano to visit Antonio Castigli. And.."

"Minola, my heart, I'm already tired, and we haven't even started. .Shower, love. Now." He gently pushed her off his lap, took her hand, and propelled her toward the bathroom. Usually bathrooms were tiny in European hotels. This one allowed quite a bit of room for comfort.

The hot water washed over them, and Minola relaxed against Peter. She put her arms around his neck and pressed herself closer to his wet body. He loved her like this, uninhibited, water dripping from her face and hair, her eyes filled with passion and love for him. All for him. He needed her as he needed the air he breathed. He pulled her against him and felt her eyelashes flutter against his cheek. Sheer euphoria overtook him. He was humbled by her love. Her lips were moist, and he couldn't resist. His mouth covered hers hungrily.

Minola's skin tingled when he touched her. The sybaritic experience of the flowing water over their bodies and Peter's exploring hands and mouth was almost too much to bear. She moaned and felt his lips sear a path down her neck and shoulders. She shuddered as her hands lightly traced a path over his back. Caressing him at every opportunity, she whispered, "I love you."

"Your love is fully reciprocated." He touched her nipples and felt them firm in his hand. His mouth covered hers hungrily, as if he hadn't loved her for a long time, the need was so great. "I want to love you in bed and fall asleep in you." Groaning he turned off the faucet, reached for a towel, and dried her off before himself. He led her to their bed, laid her down in the middle, and quickly joined her. He brushed a gentle kiss against her forehead and then moved his mouth over hers. "I'm very much in love…" The words of love were smothered against her lips. Then his mouth seared a path down her neck, her shoulders, and moved back to capture her mouth once again. She was ready for him, and he slipped inside her. Home. He made slow languid love to her, filling her completely, and left her in no doubt how he felt about her. She buried her face in his neck, and he felt a breathless kiss there as his hands lightly traced a sensuous path over her body. They slept locked together.

Chapter 5

Tired of waiting for information, Peter took matters in his own hands. While Minola worked on a Venetian landscape, Peter headed to Murano. Under the pretext of helping Antonio Castigli, he paid an early morning visit to the Deniccali Furnace. Peter was escorted to the office and asked to wait a few minutes. Dario Deniccali walked in first, and he was followed by Pia, who slammed the door behind her. Peter could only assume they were not used to being summoned.

Pia stood perfectly still and eyed Peter as if he were a piece of meat, cold and calculating. She reminded him of Alexis Yardleigh, an ex-fiancée who left him for a wealthier and titled man. It was not a great love story, and he gave thanks for her swift departure. Pia dressed as if ready for a photo shoot with a figure most men would covet. Nothing, not even a whisper of hair, was out of place. Another reminder of Alexis. He glanced at Pia and didn't react. Her eyes constricted to a flicker. She obviously assumed most men would want her and knew instinctively Peter did not. He could see her fury at his dismissal of her many charms. Pia Deniccali was someone to watch.

Peter didn't waste any time. "I'm here on behalf of the Castigli family and Julio Divini."At the mention of the name, Dario's eyes narrowed, and he shrugged. Peter explained the missing employee and his past with the Deniccali family. He showed Dario his credentials and waited for a response. Pia continued to stare at Peter.

"How may I help you? What is this about?" Dario's voice was icy cold. "He no longer worked for us. This does not concern us."

"Perhaps not directly, but I believe you have a connection. Can you tell me a little about his work here? Did Julio have any family secrets that he took with him?" Peter's hint hit home. Dario's hands clenched, his lips thinned in anger, and he waited a second too long to respond. Pia Deniccali just stood there and watched. She didn't give anything away.

"That is insolence. We do not allow mere employees with family secrets. Where did you hear such a preposterous thing?" Dario thundered.

"There are rumors, you understand, and I'm trying to help. I heard that at some time he was connected to your family and was more than a mere employee." Peter's hints worked. The man's bitter cold voice could have frozen a river.

"I cannot help you. Pia was romantic with Julio, but even she would not share family affairs." He turned toward his sister, who did not betray any emotion and did not reply. Her silent and immovable stance and her continued fascination with Peter were eerie.

"He was missing. Is he dead? How did he die?" Dario demanded.

"As yet, we don't have all the details. I wanted a head start, and your family does have a link to Julio." Peter deliberately included himself in the investigation and made it sound as if he's involved. As the old adage went, *in for a penny, in for a pound.* If something was wrong at this furnace, he now became a target. "If there is nothing else you wish to share…"

"We have nothing to share. We are not involved," Dario advised in a dry, even voice.

"Thank you for your time." Peter reached into his coat pocket, handed Dario his business card, and watched as Dario casually threw it on his desk. Pia was dismissive and didn't even glance at the card. The bait was now set. He smiled ruefully and wondered if he was the bait.

He was convinced the family was involved. Based on his first impressions, Dario was capable of a great deal more than murder. His office was packed with family history, paintings, photographs, and designs. It spoke of centuries of tradition in glass making—a history

Dario valued and would not easily destroy. Given how careful the police were of antagonizing the old families, Dario probably thought he could get away with anything.

Peter strolled along the Murano Grand Canal and sensed, rather than saw, that he was being followed. He turned toward a small street, stopped in front of a souvenir shop, and saw a man's reflection in the window. Back on the main street, he continued to the vaporetto stop, and again, he had company. He had no idea why, other than Dario was curious, and that, in turn, made Peter curious.

The vaporetto moved smoothly on the canal, and once they were closer to Venice, Peter relaxed and enjoyed the ride. He never tired of the scenery around him. At the San Marco stop, Peter waited for the man who followed him. "Is there something I can do for you?" The man appeared shocked that he'd been caught, or was he?

"*Scuza? Che cosa e questo?*" Surprise etched his face, except for his shrewd eyes, which thinned in suspicion and matched the coldness he'd seen in Dario's.

"You know quite well what this is. I do not speak Italian, but I'm going to assume you speak English. Everyone else so far has spoken English quite well. Please remind Dario and Pia Deniccali that I'm with Interpol, and if they need to speak with me, all that is needed was a phone call. Dario has my card." Peter saw a slight hunch of the shoulders at the mention of Pia Deniccali. He stared the man down, waited a second, then walked toward San Marco, and became lost in the tourist throngs. It would be impossible to follow him. Peter didn't want to lead the man to the hotel, although that would not present a problem for a resourceful individual. Connections were everywhere. Why was he followed so soon after leaving the furnace? An open tail, easy to spot, but what prompted the action?

Peter headed to the hotel and Minola. He missed her, and he'd have to tell her what he'd done. The fact that he didn't inform her beforehand might present a problem.

He found her sitting at the desk, drawing. She looked up when she heard him come in, and he heard her indrawn breath. She stood up, went straight into his arms, and asked, "What happened?"

Peter shared everything and watched as she closed her eyes and stepped away from him. He couldn't stand the separation and pulled her back against him. "I'm sorry, my love. We weren't getting anywhere. We don't even know for sure it's Julio. The police aren't talking to us, and I'm convinced that is his body we found. A nudge, that is all. I needed to do something."

"Obviously more than a nudge! You were followed. And… you went without telling me. What if something happened to you?" She trembled in fear.

"I had my cell."

"Who were you going to call, the local police? What if I had done what you just did?"

"Point well-taken. I would be furious." He kissed her hair and mumbled, "Don't ever do what I just did, I beg you. I'm a policeman and am trained." He held her tightly and promised to be careful.

"You're not bullet proof. You're also the love of my life, Peter. Please don't…" She smothered the rest of the sentence against his chest and clung to him as if she never wanted to let go.

The rest of the day Peter spent with Minola. He called the police, who were less than forthcoming, and he took a phone call from Dario Deniccali, who apologized for having Peter followed, let him know that he verified Peter's credentials, and now believed Peter was in fact with Interpol. But the conversation offered no other insights. Peter thought the call was strange and marked it in his notes. He suspected it was Pia who had him followed. After all, the man following him showed alarm at the mention of Pia's name. Not so with Dario.

Chapter 6

The following morning brought with it the realization that their friends were in serious trouble and, somehow in the midst of everything, she was to be married. Minola didn't want anything to interfere with her wedding, but she couldn't ignore the problems they faced, either, like Peter's arbitrary decision to go on his own.

The clanging phone woke her out of her reverie, and she automatically reached for Peter first. She found him fully awake, staring at her, and grinning. "What? I need coffee," she said and snuggled closer against him.

"I think you need to answer the phone first. It's on your side, and in case you missed the noise, it's still ringing." Peter pulled her closer to him.

She almost dropped the handle when she felt Peter nestle against her. "I need coffee," she mumbled.

"So you do," replied Peter, running his thumb deliciously up and down her arm.

"Miss Grey?" The voice at the other end spoke. "I'm on my way and can bring coffee."

"Sergeant Welsey, is that you? I'm sorry, not quite coherent. No coffee yet, but I'm sure it will be delivered soon. Thank you."

"I just wanted to let the Captain know I'll be at the hotel in about an hour."

"I'll tell him. Have you had breakfast yet? If not, please join us at the restaurant. They serve it on the patio. The view is magnificent, and

61

the food is exquisite. Coffee-the coffee is delicious, too. We'll see you in an hour. I need coffee."

She heard the sergeant laugh and say, "Thank you, Miss Grey."

Minola replaced the receiver and glared at Peter, who was now laughing out loud. "What?" she demanded.

"You didn't even give the poor man a chance to answer. He may have already eaten."

"Well, the view is stunning. I'm sure he'll at least have a cup of coffee or tea. Speaking of which, where is my morning brew?"

While Minola complained about her missing coffee, a knock on the door indicated room service's arrival with the obligatory coffee, along with hot steamed milk.

"You wish is their command," Peter replied, as he put on his robe and went to open the door. He signed the receipt and poured Minola her coffee, just the way she liked it. He watched as she took the first taste, licked her lips, and swallowed another sip.

"Hmm, I could get used to this," she murmured satisfied. She licked her lips again like a contented kitten.

"What do you mean *could get used*? You are used to it. I think if it were a choice between coffee and me, you'd actually choose coffee," he grumbled and poured himself a cup.

"You." Minola swiftly got out of bed, took the cup out of his hand, and kissed him. "I'd choose you. Anytime. Anyplace. You. Always you." She kissed him again, and with hips swaying, she returned to bed and her half empty cup of coffee.

"That's better." Peter was satisfied with the result as he watched her saunter back to her brew. "Since you invited Sergeant Welsey to breakfast, we need to get dressed and actually meet him at the restaurant."

Minola finished her coffee, jumped out of bed, and beat Peter to the bathroom.

"We didn't make love this morning. That is also part of our routine," Peter grumbled as he dressed.

"So now I'm a routine." Touching her lips to his in a slow drugging kiss, she explored his mouth. Her tongue played havoc with his. She kissed him with a hunger she didn't know she possessed, and it left her breathless. Slowly, she pulled away, then swayed into his arms, and heard him groan.

"Not a routine, but a desperate need. A desperate desire." He shuddered at the passion she aroused in him.

"Much better, and I feel the same way." She caressed his cheek with the tip of her fingers. "We need to meet the sergeant." She took a deep breath, opened the door, and walked out.

Once in the restaurant, they sat down, and coffee with steamed milk appeared almost simultaneously. Minola poured Peter a cup and then filled her own demitasse. The breakfast was a buffet with an omelet station, an international cheese selection, various cold cuts, breads, pastries, fruit, and the usual hot dishes. Minola's favorites were the cheeses and the fresh breads, from croissants to assorted rolls and baguettes.

Minola gazed at the Grand Canal and the early morning traffic. Gondoliers picking up guests from the hotel, water taxis, delivery boats filled with boxes and other sundries, and the vaporettos all seemed to be waltzing in an orchestrated dance of avoidance. She watched in fascination.

The sergeant's approach startled Minola. "Good morning, Miss Grey, Sir. I haven't been here in a long time." He sighed wistfully.

"Good morning, Sergeant. Thank you for joining us. Coffee or tea?" Minola already reached for the coffee when she heard Peter roar. "What did I do?"

"You didn't give the man a chance to reply."

"Oh. Apologies, Sergeant."

"Not at all. Coffee will be fine. Thank you, Miss Grey." Welsey replied.

"Breakfast is a buffet, and I'm famished. Let's eat and talk." Minola was already moving her chair out of the way when Peter stood up and helped her up. "Thank you, Peter." She brushed her hand against his, and as always, Peter acknowledged the caress by clasping her hand in his. Minola waited until everyone had the plate full before she spoke. "We have our food. Now we can discuss the murder."

"The Captain told me you found a body. I do have a contact here. The son of a local prominent businessman and I went to school together. We kept in touch. I called him this morning, and we're to meet for an espresso later this afternoon. He is rather influential in the high *Venezia* social circles. I asked about the local police, and he would be able to give us a contact and offered his help. He's a barrister and opted out of the police force."

"You have been busy. Thank you, Sergeant. What is his name?" Peter asked.

"Gio…Giovanni Bruloni."

"Bruloni as in the real estate Bruloni? That prominent Bruloni family?" Peter asked.

"Yes. Do you know them?" Welsey looked down at his plate.

"Not personally. They own a few treasures in Italy and the rest of Europe. I didn't know they lived in Venice." Peter leaned back in his chair and waited for Welsey to continue.

"They own a *palazzo* in Venice. The sister lives here as well…with Gio and their father." Evan Welsey found the napkin on his lap rather interesting and refused to make eye contact.

"The sister, Sergeant?" Minola watched as his cheeks turned bright red. "What is her name?"

"I believe it is Adriana. She went to school in England."

"Hmm. You believe?" Minola quipped. "Let's invite Gio and Adriana to dinner."

"Just like that?" Peter asked.

"Absolutely, the sergeant is here on holiday, sort of…and this would be a lovely way to get some information on the local police." Minola reached for a croissant, put a sliver of Stilton on the back of her croissant, and took a bite. "This is delicious, an excellent Stilton. Frankly, I'm tired of calling you 'Sergeant'. May we use our names?

Peter, Evan, and Minola. Are there any objections?" She looked at Peter and saw him smile and shake his head.

I...Miss Grey..." Sergeant Welsey stumbled.

"Very well, then I'll start. Evan, we've been through a great deal together, and we have become friends. You're attending our wedding. You're my friend."

"The lady has a point, Evan," Peter spoke empathically. "I think we can forgo the formalities."

"Now that we have established the niceties, let's meet Gio, and Evan...I suspect you'd like to see Adriana." Minola took a sip of her coffee.

"I'll call Gio. In the meantime, I need details, whatever you have." Sergeant Welsey pointedly ignored Minola's obvious matchmaking attempt.

Peter outlined everything he knew to date. "We need to confirm the identity of the body. If it is not Julio, then we can marry and celebrate," Peter spoke with quiet emphasis. "So arrange for dinner as soon as possible, today would suit, anywhere in Venice or the hotel—the food is formidable. Minola and I are going to spend the day sightseeing."

"Perfect. I received a text from Sally. They're arriving tomorrow. It'll be just like old times." Minola heard Peter growl when she rubbed her hands together.

"That's what I'm afraid of," Peter groused.

After breakfast, they said goodbye to the sergeant and took the vaporetto to visit Minola's wedding dress. The elegant shop served as a museum as well. Centuries old costumes were on display and copies available for sale or rent. Minola gasped when she saw the selection. "Peter, I feel as if I entered the world of Casanova. These are magnificent. Look at the masks and the brilliant colors. The feathers on some of the masks are huge, and so vibrant."

"I think Sally selected a mask for you, too, one that will match your dress."

"Peter, I'm not wearing a mask. I'm not hiding from you. It's important to me that you understand and won't mind."

"I never assumed you'd be hiding from me, Miss Grey. I don't want you to wear one, either. I want to see your face when we take our vows." Peter touched her back in a gentle caress.

"Thank you. I'll opt for flowers in my hair. This is such a strange and untraditional wedding. My maid of honor selected my dress. I'm not even sure anyone else is standing up. Robert is your best man." She felt blissfully happy and alive and couldn't wait to marry the man standing next to her. "Other than the best man and maid of honor, I have no ideas about the wedding. I know nothing about the food, flowers, nothing. Is that normal?"

"It is for us. And there are two best men... you forgot my brother-in-law, Edward. This is going to be rather unique. Do you care? We're going to be there. So will our families and friends. That is all that is important. Sally wanted you to enjoy the art festival, and after Bath, she wanted us to have some time alone together."

"I know. I want our guests to be well-fed and have a good time."

"Sally is organizing everything. They'll be well-fed. She wouldn't let me interfere, either," Peter said indulgently. "Everything will work out. It'll be perfect."

They waited patiently until Minola saw the woman carry her dress and hang it on a door. It was covered by what looked like a linen tent. "Thank you. I would like to see the dress, if I may?"

"*Si*. The *Signorina* has not seen her dress before?" the saleswoman asked, surprise etched in her voice.

"No, my friend has arranged everything." Minola turned toward Peter and said, "I'm sticking to some traditions. Chief among them, you're the groom, so you cannot see the dress. Please go."

"You're seriously asking me to leave after bringing me here?" he quipped, his voice filled with happiness.

"Yes, please wait for me at the cafe down the street. Shouldn't take more than twenty minutes. We'll have an espresso."

"We can have all of the costumes sent at the same time. Sally took care of all the measurements." Peter's eyes locked on hers, his gaze tender. "I'll see you at the cafe." He waved as he walked out.

"I'll try the dress now, if you please." Minola anticipated the unveiling with dread. She didn't know what Sally had chosen, and their tastes were rather different. Sally's favorite color was peach, and Minola loathed peach. As she watched the dress appear from underneath the expansive cover, Minola noted the color was a deep ivory, a bit more opulent than Minola would have liked, but it fitted the *Carnevale* spirit Sally had in mind. Minola heaved a sigh of relief. *I can live with that.*

The dress had a square cut neckline and empire waist etched with lace and gold thread. The full, flowing sleeves had the same gold and lace design as the bodice and added a buoyancy to the design, but the floor length dress flowed simply and was not outrageously full. *I rather like it.* "Is there a place I can try it on?" Minola saw the woman point to a curtain.

The dress fit perfectly. "Thank you." Minola took out the hotel business card, handed it to the woman, and asked that everything be sent together. As the woman nodded, Minola thanked her once again and walked out.

Peter was sipping his espresso when Minola approached him.

"So how was the dress? To your liking?" He stood up, pulled a chair out for her, and, at the same time, motioned to the waiter to bring another espresso.

Before she sat down, she gently brushed her lips against his and then lowered herself into the chair. "Yes, it fits perfectly, and no peach anywhere. Delivery will be tomorrow. I'm going to try the shop near the hotel for the shoes. I want something simple. Really simple."

"We'll get your shoes. Let's finish our coffee and head to Murano. I'll check with the sergeant to see if we, in fact, have a dinner engagement tonight and at what time." Peter took out his cell and spoke with Evan Welsey. "Fine, thank you." Peter ended the call. "Dinner tonight with Gio and Adriana at the hotel. This should prove rather interesting. If I didn't know better, I'd say our friend Evan is smitten."

"I know better, and he is. He blushed when he talked about her. He has been withholding information, and that simply won't do. She went to school in England, hmm."

"Minola, stay out of it. He can handle himself," Peter warned.

"Of course he can, but we're in Venice. Romance is in the air, and…"

"There is no *and*. There will be no matchmaking. And while I'm at it, Ashby and David, as well. Leave them alone." Ashby was Peter's friend, and David handled Minola's show in London and helped out in Bath, too. The art world was a small one, and David and Ashby had been friends—and Minola suspected more than friends—but neither was willing to make a move. David was not one to settle down, but maybe Ashby was the woman to do it.

Chapter 7

The thirty minute vaporetto ride took them to Murano. Once on the island, a short stroll took them to the Castigli furnace on what passed as the Grand Canal in Murano. One side of the entrance to the furnace was roped off. A glimpse along the long hallway showed a few large platters, and the utilitarian ceiling light brought the glass to life; the colors seemed to dance and swirl. The main entrance led directly to the store—aisles of glass vases, assorted lamps, and African woven baskets made from glass, all exquisite.

Many colors and shapes, along with geometric paper weights, and other souvenir *must haves* lined two large tables alongside the entryway to the store. Inexpensive trinkets, earrings, rings, pendants, and bracelets made from glass beads, easily packaged and affordable, were loaded on the tables. A counter with glass enclosures housed more expensive jewelry, beautifully finished, with colors that matched the artist's palette. The store was simple, yet elegant.

Minola raised her head and saw chandeliers hanging above. The lights lit up the walls and cast shadows on some of the glass below. The traditional Romanesque and Baroque style pieces, demonstrating that too much was never enough, likely required professional cleaning for the many lines and curves intricately flowing in the design. Many contemporary geometric chandeliers hung along with the others and once again. An array of color was reflected everywhere.

One modern design caught Minola's attention. She accidently bumped into Peter as she kept staring up at the ceiling. She apologized and said, "Peter, see the cobalt blue chandelier, the cube one? I didn't notice that one before. Look at the prisms, two colors blended. The result is fantastic—stunning. I've never seen anything like it, with just a touch of clear glass. In the center is ice glass—the process includes immersing the glass attached to a blow pipe in a bucket of water. The shock produces the cracks. The effect is magnificent." She felt Peter pull her in the circle of his arms. "I think that is the color Jennifer was talking about. In a large piece like this, it is spectacular, almost translucent, yet it shimmers. Brilliant." A tinge of wonder could be heard in her voice as she continued to stare.

"You're going to get a stiff neck if you persist. I agree…beautiful. Let's see if Jennifer or Antonio are in." Peter walked toward the cashier and asked to speak to any Castigli family member. At this point, it didn't make any difference who he spoke with.

The wait was not long. Peter saw Antonio approach them.

"*Ciao.*" Antonio's voice was deep and mellow.

At that exact moment, Minola turned and said, "Antonio, how are you? I'd recognize your voice anywhere."

"Minola Grey? Minola, is that you?" Antonio hugged her in welcome.

"Your English has improved a great deal, you're practically a native. Alas, my Italian is limited to *buon giorno* and *grazie* and, of course, the ever eloquent *ciao.*"

"*Ciao, bella.*" Antonio laughed out loud and asked, "Jennifer's influence. Why didn't you tell us you were coming today?"

"I…we spoke with Jennifer, and…"

"I see. She didn't mention anything about you being here today, but we've been rather busy…" Antonio's voice trailed off, and his brows furrowed.

"Of course," Minola replied softly.

"Peter, it is good to see you again. You're a patient man."

Minola turned toward Peter, leaned against him, and said, "I'm so sorry. Peter, this is Antonio, but you've met before."

"Yes, indeed, we have met. As you know, I'm only her soon-to-be husband." Peter extended his hand and felt it shaken vigorously.

"Welcome. Please excuse me for a moment." Antonio walked outside and left them to their own devices. A few minutes later, he returned. "Let's go to the office." Antonio led them past a wooden double door where the narrow hallway was lined with exquisite etched glass panels. Minola couldn't help but stare and then run her fingers over the deep cuts. The geometric patterns reminded her of Picasso's cubist period. Minola was a sucker for geometric patterns.

She suddenly remembered the office in Paris where the carpet had similar shapes. The main color was a rich burgundy, along with a thick opulent texture. She shivered at the memory. It seemed so long ago and yet not. Paris would always be close to her heart. That was where she met Peter and fell deeply in love. That was also where she became involved in murder for the first time.

They followed Antonio along a long narrow hallway. On the walls hung various pieces of glass, odd shapes, and colors. Some deeply etched pieces were on the floor leaning against the wall. Minola couldn't help but stare. She saw a few vases made with thick glass, layer upon another layer of seemingly floating glass. She recognized it as the *vetro sommerso* or dip-overlay method of blowing glass.

Antonio noticed Minola's interest. "Some of these are sample pieces. You'd be surprised what people do with glass these days. We have requests for Murano shower doors...Now there is someone with too much money, but we always and eagerly comply. Business is business," Antonio said matter-of-factly.

They walked past the work area, and Minola was able to identify the main furnace—the crucible that held molten glass, the glory hole, used to reheat glass that was being worked on—and the annealing or drying area used for cooling the glass slowly, so that it wouldn't shatter or crack.

"All so beautiful." Minola followed Antonio through another set of glass doors and waited as he motioned for them to sit down. The office was utilitarian at best. Four comfortable chairs joined one long, scratched wooden table that needed polish. A well-used, dented filing cabinet completed the decor, and everywhere one glanced, glass beckoned. An old dimpled bucket was filled with shards, several thick square colored glass pieces leaned against the wall, and even the scarred table was covered by colorful, elongated pieces. Minola stared at three hanging chandeliers. "Amazing," she whispered.

"They are beautiful, aren't they? They were just finished and actually are sold. They'll be packed tomorrow. In the meantime, they are safe hanging from those hooks."

"Who did these? Magnificent. I love the one in the store, the cobalt blue one. The work is amazing. Is it new?" Minola asked.

"Julio, our master blower created that one. I just hung it in the shop yesterday. If you look closely at the colors when lit, you can really see the iridescence. Such a soft reflection on walls. A wisp of gold leaf and...But I suspect you did not come here to admire our glass. I just called Jennifer," he added.

"I thought you might have. I'm sorry, Antonio. You know I love glass. That is not a pretense. But we do have another reason for our visit. And it has to do with Julio. At least, we think it does. Peter..." Minola turned toward Peter.

"Minola found a body off the Grand Canal in Venice, and it could be Julio. At least, it may be a distinct possibility." Peter didn't waste any time with formalities. He took out his cell and showed Antonio the glass sarcophagus that covered the body. "Does the glass seem familiar to you? Is it from your furnace?" Peter watched as Antonio seemed mesmerized by the photo.

"There is a body underneath that?" He visibly trembled. "It might be ours. The colors are familiar, but that is a lot of glass. I have no idea where it came from. We empty the buckets daily, and most often reuse the pieces for inexpensive jewelry. Sometimes we add the shards to vases, glasses, even trays. Very little gets wasted. We sometimes also give them to another furnace, but this is a big piece." Antonio rubbed his chin in frustration. "I just don't know."

"Another furnace? Who?" Peter asked.

"The Deniccali Furnace, and also some of the smaller ones that do little touristy trinkets. We can produce large pieces, but…"

"I see. Why would someone create something like that?" Peter asked.

"Again, I don't know. I'd have to see it, and under the circumstances, I'm not sure I want to. Some of the colors seem familiar, Julio was working on some replica glass daggers from the middle ages."

"How is that significant?" Peter asked.

"The colors are familiar. The customer wanted gold tip daggers. I remember those things were sharp. Julio kept them in a safe. There's quite a bit of gold in those daggers, both the tip and the handle had it. They used the rich cobalt blue mix, but gold was always a factor. It enriched the design and gave it a certain crackling sparkle. Jennifer and Julio were working on a few projects together."

"You do get some strange orders. For some reason, I just thought of vases, chandeliers, and inexpensive charms." Peter hesitated then continued. "You knew Jennifer was working with Julio."

"I know everything my wife does. She may not think so, but I'm aware of everything." Antonio's voice was low and without inflection.

"Would you care to define that further?" Peter asked.

"No, I would not." Antonio abruptly turned toward Minola and asked, "I remember you love coffee. May I offer you an espresso? Peter, how about you?"

"Yes, of course. I never turn down an espresso. Thank you," Minola replied.

"I accept as well." Peter was puzzled. Antonio seemed incensed, his body rigid. Whether with Jennifer or him for asking about Jennifer and her work with Julio, Peter didn't know, but there was something extremely wrong at the Castigli furnace.

"I'll be right back." Antonio closed the door behind him, and that left Peter alone with Minola.

"What just happened here? He has an espresso machine on the counter against the wall." Minola pointed to the spot and shook her head.

"I wish I knew, but I think maybe we overstayed our welcome," Peter replied.

Antonio walked in with a tray that held three espressos and a few dark chocolate covered biscotti and some macaroons. He set it down on the table and handed Minola the cup first.

"The machine here needs repair," Antonio stated as if he'd overheard Minola.

"I see. Thank you." She took a sip and licked her lips to make sure she got every bit of the delicious crema that topped the espresso. "Yummy. Antonio, we weren't prying. It's just Jennifer is worried, and frankly, she appeared to be terribly unhappy." Minola thought Antonio needed to get his temper under control. She'd bet anything the espresso machine was in working order, and he just needed to cool off. *He's angry, but with whom? Us or Jennifer?*

"Why should she be unhappy? I'm not the one having the affair."

"Who said anything about an affair?" Minola asked.

"She spent hours with Julio, to the point where I didn't see her at all."

"Antonio, please forgive the intrusion in this personal matter, but she mentioned the same thing about you and Pia." Minola spoke quietly.

"Ha," Antonio gulped his espresso then waved his arm in anger. "Pia saw them together, and they weren't blowing glass. Now, I have had enough of this."

"Antonio, you can't possibly believe Jennifer would betray you. What exactly did Pia see?" Minola asked.

"Suffice it to say she saw them together, and I have no wish to relive my wife with…" Antonio glanced down at a note left on his desk. "Please excuse me for a moment." He opened the door with a bang and walked out.

"Wow. That could give him a motive for murder. The jealous husband kills the lover. I don't believe it for a second," Minola closed her eyes for a moment.

"You may not, but the police will. He's unnerved. You'll have to reach him. We need details on what happened the day Julio went missing."

"Peter, how do we help them?"

"The easiest and simplest answer is we find out who was killed, how, and why."

"Easy for you to say."

"Not easy at all. Remember we have no resources here and are on our own," Peter reminded her.

"Where did Antonio go? He should be back by now."

"I know as much as you do. Let's go back to the shop. He may have forgotten about us, and he is decidedly angry." Peter stood up and glanced at the note, but before he could read it, he heard footsteps and Antonio coming back.

"My apologies, but I needed to check on a shipment." He walked over to his desk, picked up the note, and put it in his pocket before sitting down.

"Antonio, we're trying to help, but you're making it extremely difficult. Jennifer is a friend."

"I apologize." Antonio sat down and looked directly at Minola. "What is it you want to know?"

"Tell us about Julio, what he did here. What was he working on? How does Pia fit in?" Minola asked.

"You don't want much, do you? Julio joined our family about two or three years ago. He wanted more responsibility, and I was more than willing to give it to him. He is a master at his craft. He had an old formula for that blue grey color, and he could do wonders with it. There is nothing he can't do with glass and design. The last night he was here, he worked on the daggers, and then I assume he went home. He kept his own hours. We all do. Pia was at some time attached to Julio, but she had family issues. He then courted a friend of Pia's. It became serious, and of course, that did not go well with Pia or her family. A bitter disagreement within their ranks ended the relationship. I do not know anything else. Other than Jennifer and Julio together… that is."

"Antonio, how can you so easily believe that of your wife?" Minola asked.

"I was given rather specific details." He shrugged his shoulders in resignation.

"By Pia? You so readily believed her? She may have had a reason to say what she did. You can't convict Jennifer without…have you talked to her?" Minola glanced at Antonio and felt he was reliving Jennifer's supposed infidelity. Minola was convinced he still cared about his wife.

"Yes, I can, and no, I haven't discussed it with her. What, do you want me to give you the graphic details of my wife having sex with my employee?" His voice was brutal and cold.

"Stop it, Antonio. Think about what you're saying," Minola replied sharply.

"I know precisely what I'm saying," was the curt reply.

"Is Jenny here? Can I speak with her?" Minola asked.

"She's at home. She's inconsolable. After all, her lover has disappeared."

"Antonio, I don't for a moment believe…Thank you. I'll call her." Minola leaned forward in her chair, her voice was full of entreaty. "We're trying to help. When was the last time you saw Julio?"

"Two weeks ago, he and Jennifer were working on something new. She was rather excited about the project. She spent a lot of time in the furnace with him. I did see some beautiful new blue shades and a new style of chandelier using some of the leftover pieces we had. Various sizes of elongated colored glass held together by a glass ring. A rather unique and stunningly modern take on the classic chandelier." He rubbed his chin in agitation and continued, "I haven't seen any of the work. I've been otherwise occupied."

"Have the police been back? Have they inspected the furnace? Asked any questions?"

"Yes, they were here yesterday, looked everywhere, but said nothing. We're an old, established family, and of course, they were very cordial."

"I see. Thank you," Peter replied.

"I'll call Jennifer." Minola wanted to hug Antonio, but saw his hands clench around a glass paperweight and decided against it. "Goodbye, Antonio."

Peter opened the door for Minola and stopped for a minute. "Let me give him my business card, just in case he wants to get in touch. I'll see you in the shop."

Peter walked back in and closed the door behind him "I'd like to buy that blue chandelier hanging in the gift shop for Minola as a wedding present. Can you arrange it?"

Antonio raised his eyebrows, surprised at the request, and relaxed. "Yes, of course. You have excellent taste. The last thing Julio completed, his final masterpiece. He didn't want to sell it."

"Actually, Minola saw it and fell in love with it. She couldn't take eyes off the piece. She…at any rate, here is my home address." Peter took out his wallet and handed Antonio a credit card. His personal thoughts about Minola were just that…personal.

"That is quite a gift. Have you room for it? It is rather large." Antonio was shocked that Peter could afford to pay for the piece.

"I'm sure Minola will find a spot." Peter accepted the card back and gave Antonio his business card. "In case you need to talk, or something comes up. Jennifer and Minola are friends, and I'd like to help. I have no jurisdiction here, but can offer support if needed."

"Thank you." Antonio extended his hand to Peter.

This case became stranger by the second. A thriller in the making and waiting to be written; a gruesome murder, adultery—at least perceived adultery—old families battling for supremacy, and replicas of ancient glass daggers thrown in for good measure. Peter found the glass daggers a curious addition.

He saw Minola in the shop staring at the chandelier he'd just bought for her. She was mesmerized by the light reflected on the ceiling and walls. A slow swirling fan on one side of the room allowed the long glass panels of the chandelier to dance a slow waltz, and the gentle and elegant movement dazzled Minola. "I love this one," she whispered, more to herself than Peter.

"You'll get a stiff neck if you keep this up," he murmured in her ear.

"It is a stunning piece. Do you remember Jennifer said something about that cobalt grey color? Take a good look. See the short pieces right in the center? The color is superb, almost alive as it shimmers. Does it seem familiar?" Minola asked.

"It certainly does. Some of the pieces match the sarcophagus. We need to take a closer peek at that glass blanket."

"Peter, I wonder…maybe requisitioned by a customer? Antonio indicated Julio and Jennifer were working on something special. Maybe that was it."

"No, I don't think so. Remember Jennifer denied any knowledge of it, unless she was lying. Parts of the coffin were quite beautiful and artistically done. The mosaics were laid out in a specific pattern, but only the center was finished, the piece that had the cobalt blue. The edges were just shards randomly assembled and fused together. Maybe it was supposed to be something else, or maybe it started as a work of art and then was botched for some reason. At the moment, all is pure conjecture."

Minola reached for her cell and heard Jennifer answer on the third ring. She listened for a couple of seconds and then put her cell away. "She's on her way here. It'll be just a few minutes."

While they waited for Jennifer, Peter wanted to tell Minola the chandelier was theirs and was grateful when he heard the door open and Jennifer walk in. He didn't want to destroy the surprise, but he wanted to share it with her immediately. She turned his life upside down, and he wouldn't have it any other way.

Jennifer walked over to Minola and embraced her friend, while at the same time nodding to Peter. "I was on my way here. Need to work on some things Julio didn't finish."

"What was he working on?" Peter asked.

"Well, we had a commission for a hundred replicas of ancient daggers. Julio only completed ten, and they disappeared. I can't find them, and they haven't been delivered. They were magnificent and sharp. Dangerously so."

"Were they stolen? Are there any ancient daggers still in existence?" Peter asked.

"Yes, as a matter of fact, Pia's family has a few in a vault. They are quite rare and rather expensive. I haven't seen them, but know that they are a prized possession for the family. Their claim to fame for centuries, supposedly blown by ancestors. That is how the Deniccali Furnace gained its fame. That, and the assassins using those daggers to eliminate enemies of the state and anyone else who either stood in their way, or simply ordered a murder for hire. Quite the business. A family business if you will. At least, that is the legend. Fascinating history. I imagine the Castigli name has a similar history, although not quite as old." Jennifer took a breath. "I can tell you based on the limited research available, the daggers Julio produced looked authentic. He had some old pieces of paper that he often referred to while working on the daggers."

"Do you have any pictures we can see?" Minola asked.

"We had pictures from his research, but they, as well as the replicas, are gone, along with the old papers. He kept the daggers and the photos, everything in the safe. All rather hush-hush. Originally, Julio reached out to Pia so he could see the real ones, but she wasn't interested in showing any of the ones they own. She was unhappy with Julio."

"Do you think she'd show us?" Peter asked.

"Maybe, if Antonio made the request. Certainly not if I asked," Jennifer replied.

"Somehow, I think the daggers are significant. His murder…"

"Are you saying it's Julio?" Minola asked.

"I think so. I don't believe in coincidences. There are too many connections here." Peter's voice was silky. He didn't want to frighten

Jennifer. "First, let's see if we can get a positive identification and find out how he was killed. Then we can ask Antonio for help."

"He might not be willing to do so," Jennifer managed to reply through stiff lips. She didn't think he'd do anything to help her.

"He'll do it for you. You're his wife," Minola interjected and saw Jennifer's eyes tear.

"Did you work on the daggers with Julio?" Peter asked.

"Yes, a little bit. I selected the colors. They were all gold tipped. Spare no cost, that is what the client wanted. We didn't even meet the client, arrangements were made through the secretary. When you think about it, it seems rather strange now, but perfectly fine then. I didn't know they disappeared until recently."

"We'll sort it out," Peter offered comfort.

"Jenny, call if you need us. We're going back to the hotel, but we'll keep in touch." Minola hugged her friend.

Once outside, Minola took a deep breath to release some tension. "I hope Evan will have some information for us. Dinner should prove interesting."

"No matchmaking," Peter said adamantly, and to take the sting out of his words, he twined his fingers with hers and grasped them possessively. They walked along Murano's Grand Canal toward the vaporetto station.

Murano was a working island. Much of the charm and romance that was Venice was missing. However, the galleries and furnaces, along with the glass museum, and the many tourists shops, and galleries made it a shopping paradise. The long and often violent history, the extreme need for secrecy even today, and the utilitarian streets and canals gave an impression of guarded mystery and concealment.

"Peter, do you know that the history of this island goes back to the Romans? The glass blowers were all moved here from Venice in the 13th century. The powers that be were afraid of fires, afraid that Venice would burn down. After that, Murano became famous. The glassblowers became the elite citizens, marrying into Venice's most powerful families. They were the rock stars of their time."

"Rock stars? What do you know about rock stars?" Peter chided. He knew she occasionally liked soft rock, but tended to prefer classical music when she worked. Of course, it depended on what she working on. He knew her better than he knew himself. His fingers tightened around hers.

"I don't live under a rock. I pay attention. The Beatles…need I say more."

"No, indeed not." Peter laughed out loud. She had such power over him, and yet, she was totally unaware of it.

"Good. I'm just saying the history is amazing, I read quite a bit about it. What I haven't read anything about are the daggers and the assassins. If they were so famous, there must be some information available somewhere. Why isn't there?"

"I do not know, but may I make a suggestion? When we return to the hotel, I want to spend some time with you, just you. Then we'll have dinner, and tomorrow, we'll come back here, and you can visit the museum. Maybe we'll learn something about the elusive ancient daggers. We can visit a few more furnaces and see if the processes are really all that different."

"First and foremost, loving you would be perfect. I am ready…always, Peter. The rest sounds positively delightful."

"I know you're always ready for me, and you can't possibly know what that means to me." He stopped mid-stride, lowered his head, and gave her a hard swift kiss. Then, hand in hand, they took the vaporetto back to the hotel.

"I feel the same way. You always respond to me. I'm incredibly lucky." Minola watched as the vaporetto slid on the water, the movement at once rapid and soothing.

They were able to find a seat and relax for the next thirty minutes. She scooted closer to Peter and asked. "At dinner, maybe we should ask Gio if we can meet with the police."

"I had every intention of doing precisely that. This will be messy. There are too many variables. We have a glass coffin, missing glass daggers, two old families, and, according to Jennifer, at least one of them familiar with death and assassinations, supposedly using those or similar glass daggers."

"Do you think that still goes on today?" Minola asked.

"What? The assassinations? Of course they go on. Some are rather good at the killing business, and in a sense, it is rather ritualistic, whether poison, guns, or daggers are used. And, yes, it is treated as a business," Peter said.

"I have read somewhere that the dagger was inserted and then twisted to cause maximum damage. The tip remained inside, with little external bleeding. What I don't remember is whether fact or fiction. Were there any autopsies done in the sixteenth century? I would have thought not." She shuddered at the gruesome statement.

"Autopsies go back a long way. I believe the first studies of disease along with corresponding dissections were performed as far back as three hundred BCE. In the second century CE, Greek physician Galen of Pergamum was able to relate medical complaints to what was found upon an open examination of the body. Here is a bit of trivia, *autopsia* comes from the Greek word and means 'the act of seeing for oneself.' Hence autopsy."

"I didn't know it went that far back. I do know that centuries later Leonardo da Vinci and Michelangelo furthered the science by examining and dissecting bodies."

"Indeed. The history is long. Odd, I should remember this, but all history helps in an investigation, not all the time, but all is somehow related." Peter ran his hand through his hair and wondered the turn his life took, from the cold and often brutal side of his professional life to his loving and passionate personal life.

"I understand. Look at the lack of history of the daggers, or I should say the missing history of the daggers. It would help immensely if we had some sort of background, other than hints and innuendos," Minola replied.

"That is a perfect example." Peter smiled. She so easily picked up on the essentials. "In the meantime, we'll do what we can to help. However, let's concentrate on us for a little bit," Peter whispered, his breath hot against her ear. "I want to spend time with you and not think about anything else."

She moved against him. "Peter, you're my everything. Always. Thank you for making this a little easier."

"You do know I'll always try to make you happy? I think this is our stop." He helped her up, and they waited to disembark. Peter had an uneasy feeling they weren't alone, but didn't want to frighten Minola. He didn't see anything out of the ordinary, but kept his guard up.

The short stroll to the hotel was a delight, centered in a small square. The area brimmed with boutiques, artists selling their work, and an old Romanesque church, a short walk to Piazza San Marco, yet far enough away from the tourists. The location was perfect. Minola walked over to the small bridge across from the hotel and looked down at the water flowing in the canal. Mesmerized by the movement, she leaned forward, hoping to discover the secret of the magic she found in Venice. She closed her eyes, and she swore she could hear a gondolier serenading his passengers.

Hand-in-hand, they walked to the hotel. After the visit to the Castigli Furnace, Minola had an even greater appreciation for the work involved in creating the sconces, chandeliers, and glass table lamps that decorated the opulent hotel lobby. They were all exquisite and all from Murano. The deep plush carpet silenced any footsteps, at once elegant and intimate, and as always the scent of the fresh bouquets of red roses at each table permeated the lobby.

Venice held her enthralled. The magic and mystery seemed elusive and, today for some reason, terrifying. "Peter, promise me we'll share everything. You won't hold anything back. I don't want a dark moment where you're afraid and fear for my safety and push me away. Promise me we'll work together. Always."

He spun her around to face him. "What is it, my love? What is worrying you?"

"A feeling of evil I can't shake. I don't know how to describe it. This murder seems so ritualistic. The glass enclosure, the daggers, all meant to send a message, but to whom?"

"So far we don't have enough information to do anything, but I promise you we'll be together. I could never send you away again, anymore than I could stop loving you." A pledge he intended to keep.

Chapter 8

"Peter?" Minola whispered, drowsy from their lovemaking. She burrowed farther into his arms. The bed, once neat and tidy, was now ruffled and well-used. She pillowed her body against his and never wanted to move.

"Hmmm…" he answered and curved his body against hers to get closer still. "What…better yet let me guess? You have daggers on your mind."

"Oh, that is positively scary. You know me much too well." She caressed his face, the touch at once sensual and tender. "There is a great deal of information available online about Murano, Venice, glass, and furnaces, and yet nothing about ancient glass daggers made anywhere near Venice. They make new ones, but they're just tourist trinkets, certainly not lethal."

"I know you intimately." He gazed at her face and exhaled a long sigh of contentment. "But before we get ahead of ourselves, let's find out how the murder was committed. First, we need to pick up the clothes lying all over the room. We were a bit in a hurry. We have a dinner engagement." Peter looked down at the mess they made and smiled, happy beyond measure.

"Yes, we were. I always am when it comes to loving you, and you always reciprocate—I love that about you…among other things." She relaxed, sinking into his cushioning embrace, her head pillowed on his chest. Her hand once again brushed his face. Then she felt his kiss. His mouth sent the pit of her stomach into the now wild and familiar swirl.

Peter heard her moan and deepened the kiss, and his declaration of love was smothered against her lips. He released her and took a deep breath. "I can't seem to get enough of you." Something intense flared in the pit of his stomach. "All I can say is I'm very much in love with you."

"That is a wonderful thing. I always want you too. And I love you so very much. We're well-suited." She whispered and brushed her lips against his, slipped out of bed, and headed straight for the bathroom. She knew Peter would be right behind her, and he didn't disappoint.

"I love you, Miss Grey." Every time his gaze met hers, his heart turned over in response. Every time he looked at her, or thought of her, he felt warmth and a sense of peace consume him. The act of loving her was an exquisite pleasure, and he gave thanks for the everyday life he shared with her.

Peter turned on the shower and let her go in first, and soon followed and swung her in the circle of his arms. As the warm water cascaded over them, he couldn't let go. She buried her face against his throat. He felt her warms lips run sensuously against his skin. His hand took her face and held it gently, and watched as she reached up, and parting her lips, she raised herself to meet his mouth. He smothered her lips with demanding mastery.

She moaned as she felt his kiss, it left her mouth burning with fire. He pinned her against the wall and entered her fast and hard. She gave herself to him, and responded to his passion as she always did. Fully and equally. A generous lover, he waited for her, but the interval was not long. "I love you so very much." She gulped the words as she tried to catch her breath.

Peter touched his forehead to hers and paused for a few seconds before he could speak. "At the moment, I can't even..." He couldn't quite catch his breath, his voice hoarse and uneven.

"I know. It frightens me, this euphoric feeling, this unbelievable emotion that sometimes feels as if it is strangling me. Is this normal?" Minola asked.

"I no longer know what is normal. All I know is, no matter the panic or fear I occasionally succumb to where you are concerned, it is all worth it."

"Panic, fear, Peter? Why?"

"You safety is paramount for me. You find bodies everywhere we go." He turned the water off and got out, took a towel, and proceeded to dry her off, a tender touch that was more of a caress. He felt her sway toward him.

"I have to return the favor." She reached for a towel and did the same, running her fingers over his skin. "I have to make sure you're dry."

"Neither one of us will stay that way if you keep this up. I shall have to retaliate, and then we're going to be late." He caressed her cheek and bent down to give her a slow and thoughtful kiss.

"What was it you said about being late?" She buried her hands in his hair, pulled him closer to her, and locked herself in his embrace. She kissed him with a hunger she didn't know she possessed, even now as close as they'd been. Minola was still surprised and shocked at her primitive reaction to him and the fear that their time together was somehow threatened.

"What is it, my love?" Peter whispered in her ear. He could always sense when things were not well, when she was too frightened to voice her emotions and fears. "What are you afraid of?"

"Peter, sometimes I feel so…" She swallowed. "How do I describe this…This happiness. This tremendous love I feel for you. I can't even tell you or explain it—other than to say I love you. There is so much more behind the words. Peter, I feel as if I'm losing myself in you. I'm so much in love with you that it frightens me." She clung to him in desperation.

"I understand more than you think." He caressed her back, knew he had to offer comfort. "I feel the same way. It is at once exhilarating and terrifying. Why do you think my obsessive terror for your safety played such a huge part in our differences? I can't seem to let you go, for fear you'll be hurt." He took a deep breath. "Just because I promised an equal partnership doesn't mean the terror is far behind. It is not, but I'm working on developing your trust. I need to touch you constantly, know you're there. I need to love you, a constant demand from my body. All I can tell you is we have something unique, and I will do anything and everything to keep it. We will be fine." He kissed the tip of her nose. "I love you as I have never loved before. We will be fine." He reached for his robe, tied it securely, then found hers and helped her put it on, and murmured in her ear. "We'll be fine."

Before Minola could respond, a knock on the door interrupted her. Peter went to answer and saw Sally and Robert Jones standing there, smiling. "We're early. Let us in. And as the saying goes, there is room at the inn. You're stuck with our early arrival. I missed you." The exuberant and pregnant Sally walked in and hugged her best friend. "Oh… did I interrupt something? I'm sorry…"

"You did no such thing. We were just going to get dressed. Sit down, you must be tired." Minola returned Sally's embrace. She then turned toward Robert and hugged him as well. After Peter, they were her lifelong best friends. "Okay, spill. Why are you here early?"

"Well, I thought about your dress, all the preparations, and the fact you have no shoes…" Sally stopped when she heard Peter roar.

"Sally, I'm glad you're here to save the day. Minola has been lamenting the lack of proper shoes. I'll call and add two more to the dinner reservations. This will be quite a party.

"Party, what party? And why wasn't I invited?" Sally demanded.

"An unintentional party…sort of, and now you're invited." Minola pulled Sally aside and explained the dinner arrangement, the fact that the sergeant had a love interest, and the reason for the dinner.

Peter heard Sally shriek in excitement. "Stop right there, you two. We're going to dinner to get information about a murder…" Peter tried to interrupt and knew the attempt to be futile. When Minola and Sally were together like this, there would be no interruption. He, for one, was happy they arrived early. He worried about Minola. She didn't often display her fears, although he knew she had them.

He remembered the attacks on him in Bath and how strong she was, yet the attacks terrified her. Her bravery was almost his undoing. He even went so far as to idiotically reject her. Deny her. He thought it would keep her safe, and the end result was not what he'd anticipated. Peter swore never to let anything interfere with their relationship.

"Murder?" Sally screeched. "You found a body, didn't you? Where? What happened? Why wasn't I notified? I should have been here to help. Sit down, and spill everything—don't leave anything out." She rubbed her hands in glee.

"You're rather bloodthirsty. We were in a gondola, and I saw this glass thing…" Minola proceeded to tell Sally everything she knew to date.

"Wait a minute…you were in a gondola with Peter, and you saw something other than Peter. What is the matter with you?" Sally teased.

"My sentiments precisely. That's what I tried to tell her, but no, she insisted I go and look," replied Peter.

"Stop it, both of you. We have a problem, hence the dinner tonight." More information was relayed to Sally about the Castigli furnace, the police, the missing apprentice, and the wealthy Italian socialite who'd captivated Sergeant Welsey. "You'll meet her tonight. Where is your room?"

"We're on the floor below—nothing close to you until tomorrow, our scheduled arrival. What time is dinner? I'm starving—eating for two." Sally rubbed her tummy protectively.

"More like four." Robert said indulgently. He would never deny Sally anything. She was the love of his life.

"Pregnancy suits you. You're glowing. We'll meet you in the lobby for some milk," Minola suggested.

"The only way you're going to drink milk is if coffee is attached to it. We'll order a bite and wait for you. Hurry up." Sally hugged her friend again, took Robert's hand, and led him out the door, but not before she blew a kiss to Peter. "Thank you for making her so happy." Sally slammed the door behind her.

"Pregnant, and she still has the force of the Energizer Bunny." Minola smiled, turned toward Peter, and cupped his face in her hands. "She's right. You do make me happy. Exceedingly so." She touched her lips to his, a gentle massage that left her reeling. A shiver of desire raced through her body. "We better change," she whispered in his ear.

"Yes, before we start to make love and won't be going anywhere." They dressed quickly and went down in search of their friends. They were easy to spot, sitting in the lobby. Both were sipping milk and nibbling on assorted biscotti.

"Let's go eat, but these are really good." Sally took another cookie.

Once seated in the restaurant, Minola watched for the other guests. First to arrive was Sergeant Welsey. His dark blue suit fit as if tailor-made for him. As he approached, Minola realized the stark white linen shirt and a bold red and blue silk tie made it stand out. She could practically see herself in his Italian loafers; they shined from the polish. There was more to the Sergeant than she originally suspected. For some reason, she always observed what people wore and whether the ensemble was pleasing to the eye. It must be her artistic sense of color selection, and it came naturally to her to observe people. How did he meet the wealthy socialite? Mere acquaintances didn't begin to describe their relationship. Minola was sure there had to be more. She'd never seen him so spiffy, and his shoes positively gleamed.

Evan watched her progress and grinned. "I remember you like shoes."

"Indeed. That was the second thing I noticed about Peter. The first was his face. Wrinkled suit and worn loafers. Exhausted beyond measure, he looked as if he hadn't slept in twenty four hours, and he had been decidedly displeased, a grim expression on his face..."

"You're not going to bring that up, are you?" Peter asked.

"Of course I am..." Minola stopped when she saw a stunning woman approach them, simply dressed in the typical little black silk dress that fit as if molded to her curves. And she had plenty of those. Killer black suede stiletto heels completed the outfit. Eyes as black as the night, with hair to match pulled tightly in a bun, Minola thought she just stepped out of a magazine cover. She wore no jewelry. She didn't need any. The effect was at once startling and mesmerizing. Minola couldn't stop staring. She imagined painting the stunning woman, a pale shimmer of ivory as the background, and the focus would be on the face and body. Draped in silk, she would make the canvas come to life.

Adriana walked toward them, her eyes riveted on Evan. Her lips curved in a smile that showed perfectly even white teeth. The woman was striking and seemingly unaware of herself, her focus directed solely on Evan Welsey.

"Good evening. I hope I'm not late. Gio met with a friend. He'll be here shortly." Her voice was low and pure seduction.

Evan Welsey stood up and almost knocked his chair down. "Adriana, it is a pleasure to see you again." Welsey murmured in a soft voice. He then introduced everyone at the table, and pulled out a chair for Adriana. She sat down gracefully like a swan gliding on water.

"Thank you, Evan. It is, as you put it, a pleasure, and thank you for the invitation to dinner." Adriana turned toward Minola and spoke, "I'm familiar with your artistry, Miss Grey. It is quite beautiful. Gio owns a few pieces and is quite captivated by your work."

"It's Minola, and thank you. That is indeed a compliment. How do you know our sergeant?" Minola asked.

"Ah…Evan, Gio, and I were at school together in England, and we have remained friends." She looked at Evan, and when he acknowledged the statement and bowed his head, Adriana turned toward Sally and congratulated her on the pregnancy. "Gio told me a little bit about this case, and I know the families. The man Gio is meeting is an old friend and a carabiniere." She spoke quietly, but raised her eyes sharply when she heard Evan speak, his voice harsh.

"You will not get involved in this. Never, do you understand?"

"*Scusi*? Sorry…" Her tone was as soft as velvet, yet edged with steel. "If a friend is in trouble, I will stand by them, Evan. You should know me well enough for that."

"I do. Precisely why I do not want…"

"You do not want…You have no right…" Adriana's indignant voice bristled.

"Oh, oh, be careful." Minola's lips curved up, and to break the tension, she said, "Evan, you sound just like Peter. Orders and demands won't go over well. Surely you must know that by now."

"Yes, indeed I do know. I also know we must be careful."

Sally, not to be left out, joined in the fun. "Actually, this sounds just like the other times, except now we have more help."

"Yes, because we need more help. We have no information, no leads. We have absolutely nothing, except that is…a body and, of course, more help," Peter replied.

"Sarcasm, Captain Riley?"

"Sarcasm, Miss Grey," was the quick reply.

"Adriana, are you living here permanently?" Minola asked.

"No, I went back to school in Cambridge." She felt Evan staring at her and lowered her eyes to avoid his penetrating gaze.

"You have not mentioned that you're living in England." Evan Welsey was visibly angry. His hands were clenched and his voice cold.

"We have not kept in touch." Adriana's voice was steady and calm.

"That is not my fault. I …" Evan's response was swift.

"Adriana, do you know how late Gio is going to be?" Minola wanted to break the thick atmosphere that surrounded them. Obviously, some history that neither wanted to share existed between them, and Minola used the hovering waiter as a distraction. She also knew Sally was hungry and wanted to order at least an appetizer to tide them over.

"Please let us eat and not stand on ceremony. It will not be the first time that Gio is late, and he will understand," Adriana replied. "I'm rather famished, too.

The waiter noted they were ready and took their salad orders, along with a bottle of wine. A basket filled with fresh bread arrived even before the waiter finished.

"This bread smells delicious," Sally chimed in as Robert served her a piece. She took a bite. "It is a little drier than what we're used to."

Once her salad has been served, she used the bread to soak up a little of the dressing. "The bread is excellent."

"Yes, bread is used to absorb the sauces, that is why it is dry, not stale." Adriana responded.

"Tell us, Adriana, how well do you know Evan?" Minola asked sheepishly.

"We were close at the University. My family is rather blustery...outspoken. Evan..."

"I joined Interpol after University. I'm not Italian," Evan interrupted grimly.

"Odd, I did notice that about you." Peter's lips curved in a smile.

"What Evan meant to say is that my family wanted an Italian for me, and Evan decided to agree with my father," Adriana spoke quietly.

"I did no such thing." Evan's voice was husky and uneven.

"Yes, in fact, you did. You left without a word," Adriana said quietly. She turned when she heard even, purposeful footsteps and saw her brother approach. She stood and hugged her brother. "Gio, let me introduce you to everyone."

Gio returned the embrace, glanced at Evan, and then focused on Minola. "Miss Grey, I'd know you anywhere. I have a few of your paintings. They are magnificent." He helped Adriana sit down and extended his hand to Minola. "It is, indeed, a great pleasure."

"Thank you, and please call me Minola." Minola glanced up, accepted the handshake, and stared at his perfect, chiseled face. Beauty must run in the family. High cheek bones, eyes black as coal, black and curly hair, and two perfect dimples that appeared to smile at her. The man didn't look real. She shook her head as if to clear the cobwebs. His was an unusual male beauty, but she wouldn't know how to paint him. Maybe as a Roman God, but she didn't do period pieces. The oddest sensation frightened her, more so because she didn't understand it.

"Thank you. That is gracious of you," Gio answered smoothly. After the introductions were made, Gio finally sat, took a sip of water, and surveyed everyone.

Adriana saw Minola's reaction to Gio and spoke, "My brother is quite handsome. Yes?"

"Yes. Astonishingly so. Beautiful, in fact, just as you are," Minola agreed easily. "But I would not know how to paint…My apologies, I often react this way to people I just meet. The first thing that comes to mind is a blank canvas, paint, and setting. The only exception was when I first met Peter. I knew exactly how I wanted to see him on canvas. Rather immediate and amazing for me. The one and only time." She remembered vividly her reaction to him. The moment she set her eyes on him, she was captivated. "In fact, I started that same evening, worked most of the night, and finished the outline. The rest took time." She turned toward Peter, smiled, and heard his indrawn gulp.

"I remember your reaction to me quite well," Peter replied softly. The love for him that shone in her eyes took his breath away.

"And yours to me." She laughed out loud at the memory. "Now that we've all been introduced, let's look at the menu, order the entrees, and then we can chat."

That silenced the murder discussion for a while. Sally selected a roasted vegetable pizza, one of her preferred pies, and this one was exceptionally well-prepared in Venice. The veggie slices tended to be big and perfectly roasted. Minola ordered black pasta. The rich and earthy iron flavor of the cuttlefish ink was quickly becoming her favorite dish in Venice. Adriana chose rice and peas, another traditional dish. Peter and Evan opted for the creamed cod, and Gio picked clams with parsley.

"What a lovely sample of local cuisine, well, except for my pizza." Sally raised her head. She was still perusing the menu, and Robert smiled as he watched her. "What? I'm eating for two, and the salad was small." She gently rubbed her belly.

"Your pizza is also traditional, sometimes served with big chunks of grilled vegetables. Eggplant is popular. It is a good choice." Adriana laughed when she saw Sally still perusing the menu.

"Yes, we know you're eating for two. You can taste my pasta."

"No, thanks. No fish for me."

"Now that we've ordered and wine has been delivered, let's get down to business."

"Are you in a hurry, Minola?" Gio asked.

"In fact, I am. I'd like to be married without a murder investigation lurking in the background, and Jennifer is a friend, and we'd like to help." Minola said.

"Yes, I understand perfectly," Gio replied.

"Thank you. Do you have the identity of the victim?"

"Yes, I do, and yes, it was Julio Divini, the Castigli employee."

"Well, at least now we know. How was he killed?" Peter didn't like the way Gio was staring at Minola.

"Ah, you come directly to the point. That is most unusual. He was stabbed once in the heart, and he bled out. The cut was larger than the dagger—it seems as if..." Gio glanced around the table. "Let us just say a rather brutal act of fury and a professional job. At least, according to the policeman I met with. Half the dagger was imbedded in his heart. The rest was placed carefully on his chest. The police are puzzled. It seemed ritualistic."

"That is odd. It is exactly the way I described it, without even seeing the...just the placement of the sarcophagus. Do they know where the dagger was made?" Minola asked.

"Again, you go to the heart of the matter. The murder weapon was old. They do not know how old, but old. I saw a picture of it, hard to identify the age. The aim, however, was perfect."

"Interesting...old dagger. I wonder if anyone is going to claim it?" Minola asked.

"No one has claimed it as yet. Even damaged, I suspect it is valuable. I know both families involved, and I would say the dagger belongs to the Deniccali family. It is probably five or six hundred years old. I have seen one similar. I cannot tell you it is the same as the one in the picture, but if I were to place a wager...I know the Deniccali collection. They will not claim it if the crime points to their door. Old families, old money, old secrets, old traditions, and all that..."

"Do you know Pia Deniccali?" Minola heard an indrawn hiss from Gio.

"Yes." He instantly changed the subject. "Wealthy and old families in Venice hold a great deal of power. We need to tread lightly, their connections run high. I say this not to frighten you, but make you aware of limitations and certain constraints we'll meet. But then my family is older, wealthier, and more powerful." Gio grinned and brushed the front of his shirt with his fingertips as if to eliminate invisible lint.

"We?" Minola ignored the pointed, but valid, assessment of Gio's family. She didn't get the sense he was boasting, but rather that he stated the simple truth.

"Yes, I want to help." Gio replied.

"Yes, because we need more help." Peter's mouth curved up a notch.

"Ah, you deride my involvement, but so far I'm the only one with local connections. Those rich and old families of Venice—we're one of them—you won't find better help. You certainly won't get much assistance from the carabinieri at the moment, at least not without my involvement." Gio grinned.

"That is certainly true. I will not deny it," Peter answered.

"Gio, you are a wealth of information. Anything else?" Robert asked.

"I have more."

"Well, please, don't keep it to yourself," Minola quipped.

"Normally I would not, but our food is here." Gio watched as the plates were set on the table. "We can enjoy our meal and then discuss the murder." Even though a bottle of wine already rested on the table, Gio ordered a bottle of his favorite wine, an Amarone della Valpolicella, the intense dry red wine from the Veneto region.

"Excellent choice," Peter murmured.

"I see you're familiar with our wines," Gio responded and took a sip of his wine, and nodded his approval. The wine then was poured for everyone except Sally. She settled on a bottle of Pellegrino, the Italian sparkling mineral water.

"I do my best. It is quite good." Peter took a sip.

"Yes, it is one of my favorite local wines, even with fish," Gio replied and raised his glass to toast Minola. "The food is excellent, the company good, and the location is *perfecto*."

Minola observed Gio's delight in the scene in front of him. He watched as the gondoliers maneuvered the traffic on the Grand Canal. The dimly lit Church across the canal, the gondoliers, water taxis, and vaporettos one could wish for, vying for a spot, and the ancient buildings that seemed to float on water added to the ambiance. He smiled at the view, and took a sip of his wine. She understood his attachment, his beautiful Venice. She never tired of the view either.

Mesmerized, Minola watched as soft candlelight flickered on the table, and over the railing she saw a gondolier help someone board. She heard the water lapping against the gondola. In the distance, a tenor sang a Neapolitan love song, and the echo, rich and vibrant, floated over the water. "It is stunning here. I don't think I want to leave." Minola twirled the black pasta on her fork, contemplated the magic of the canal and Venice, and smiled.

"I am happy you like Venice." Gio sipped his wine, obviously enjoying himself.

"I really do. And I love the food. Black pasta is a particular favorite. While we're eating, maybe we can discuss the reason we're all here," Minola said.

"I thought I was here for a wedding. Yours," Sally quipped.

"So did I," Peter responded, a tender gaze locked on Minola. "Ours." He couldn't hide the love he held for the woman sitting next to him.

"I know, and that is why I'm here, too…but it became a bit complicated."

"Fair enough. We shall continue with the murder while we eat." Gio longingly stared at his plate filled with fresh clams and sighed. He preferred to savor his food. "If we must. Julio apparently was killed not quite in the traditional manner of the assassins. Good amount of blood surrounded his body. The police do not know where he was killed, but they know he was killed and brought over in a boat. The blood trail ended at the pier. No trace leading to the house along the pier. As the saying goes, the investigation is ongoing."

"I see. Do the police have anything else? Possibly the owner of the house?" Peter twirled the glass of wine and watched the dark liquid drape the inside of the glass. Like a rich thick coating that slowly dripped down, the wine had legs.

"Not that they are saying. Nothing other than conjecture. I will have to ask. They suspect a professional job that was meant to leave a message to someone. They're running DNA and all the other necessary tests, and they're waiting for the pathology report. No fingerprints on the dagger." Gio explained.

"They have a huge sarcophagus that could possibly shed some light. There must be some evidence left on that piece of glass. And the dagger is damned interesting. If, as you say, it is that old and rare, why destroy it? Why not use one of the copies Julio made? I am convinced the theft and murder are related." Peter replied.

"That may be, but we...the police do not know who stole the copies. Because we don't know who took them that is why the police suspect perhaps a warning. Or maybe retribution." Gio answered.

"To whom? Why?" Evan Welsey asked.

Gio took a bite of his clams, swallowed, and spoke quietly. "That is an excellent question, one for which I do not have an answer." Gio turned toward the sergeant and asked, "How are you, Evan?"

"Fine, thank you," was the stiff reply.

"You look well. Interpol must agree with you."

"Indeed," Evan responded.

"I have been trying to find some information on the legendary assassins that used the glass daggers, and I can't. It seems to be a known fact, yet no documentation exists to back up these supposed *facts.*" Minola raised her head and gazed at Gio. As an artist, she marveled at the perfectly chiseled cheeks, the perfect nose—in fact, everything about him was perfect.

"Ah. They are legendary and a well-kept secret. That is why not many people know about them. Here is a quick summary of the tales of the assassins…the daggers were manufactured especially for them, and even back then, they were prized possessions. Each dagger had a tiny identifying mark on the handle—a crest or a signature, if you will—identifying the assassin's guild they were made for. At least that is the legend," Gio spoke absentmindedly as if he remembered something. "The glass blowers kept the client list a secret, for obvious reasons, a matter of survival, you understand. Each family had a sort of coat of arms on the handle, nothing big, but enough to identify them. The tip was left in the body, and the rest of the dagger remained with the assassin as proof of a completed mission. That sometimes gave way to lies, and further proof of the deed was required. This particular dagger as yet cannot be identified and, therefore, could not point to the assassin or the family business involved."

"Fascinating legend. Remarkable in fact, if as you say this has been going on for centuries. In this case, that means the police can identify the owners of the dagger," Minola said.

"Only if they know where to look and had the code. The marks are small and hidden, and the coat of arms were known only to the assassins and, in this case, may have been removed since the dagger was left with the body. Or there may not be one," Gio replied.

"This is an unbelievable story. Are you helping the police?" Minola asked.

"I'm going to work with the police to help us. This is an interesting case, but first, I want to learn more," Gio stated.

"How detailed were the pictures? Were you able to identify any imperfection in the glass to indicate the mark was removed?" Peter took a bite of his fish and waited for a reply.

"No, not easily visible. Not yet. If the dagger was truly an antique, I don't know if it would be easy to remove the identifying mark without leaving a blemish, and we don't have any way of proving which old guild or family it belonged to. Remember they were secret, and the marks were coded. It is known I have an extensive glass collection, old and new, and my interest in this case is not at all suspicious. When the time comes, I can be most helpful. At the moment, I did not want to draw any additional attention."

"Why are these assassins so mysterious that no one knows of their existence?" Sally asked.

Gio smiled. "Rest assured, certain people know. It is a matter of survival. It is a lethal profession, extremely well paid even today, and anonymity is paramount, because they sometimes travel in the best social circles. Most of the killings today are attributed to natural causes or accidents. Generations of perfecting their skill, as in any profession. Daggers are no longer used, except in ceremonial killings, as perhaps in this case, or possibly a warning. Daggers were used as a lethal symbol of power and domination. Today, such a way to kill would certainly draw attention to the glass world."

"You make it sound almost...I'm lost for words here...casual, acceptable. That is frightening." Minola shuddered.

"That may be, but you read about murder, atrocities of every kind, on a daily basis. It is not any different. It is a business, brutal to be sure, but a business nevertheless," Gio replied calmly.

"You're telling us that it is still going on?" Robert's fork clattered against his plate.

"Yes, it is, and in the best of families."

"Do you mean that the Castigli family is a bunch of assassins?" Minola asked.

"I do not know, and cannot speak for the Castigli or the Deniccali family. I only know that is it still going on." Gio took another sip of wine, then gracefully set the goblet down, and gazed steadily at Minola.

"That is truly evil. I don't know what else to say." She returned his gaze and was uncomfortable with his penetrating stare.

"That may be, Minola, but it is nevertheless a reality," Gio replied.

"It is difficult to accept. Tell us about Pia Deniccali. What do you know about her?" Minola watched as Gio flinched, looked down, and refused to meet her gaze.

"Nothing to tell. She's an accomplished glass blower and a superb business woman."

"Gio was once engaged to Pia. It did not end well," Adriana responded.

"Adriana, do not…" Gio's face reddened in anger, but he said nothing else.

"She seems to get around," Minola murmured under her breath.

"You assume Julio's death was a warning. If so, to whom?" Peter appeared to be casually moving the food on his plate, but he was totally aware of Gio's fascination with Minola, and he did not like it. His reluctance to discuss Pia Deniccali, on the other hand, had Peter curious. The intrigues ran deep in the old families of Venice.

"Another good question, one I cannot answer. I do not know. The history is long between the two families. That is where you'll find your answers. As for me, I'll keep in touch with my friend and report back," Gio's gaze now totally focused on Peter. "That is what you want me to do, is it not?"

"What I want is direct access to the police, but at the moment, it is unavailable to me," Peter replied.

"Yes, I'm also aware of that." Gio's lips curved up a bit. "I can introduce you to my friend Matteo Ciconti. He's high enough in the organization that there won't be any questions and low enough to investigate the murder without much risk, and of course, he's been assigned that particular task. What you do after the introduction will be entirely up to you. "

"That will suit me fine. Thank you."

"So now what do we do?" Minola asked.

"I would recommend we finish dinner and then go to the *piazza* for a drink," Adriana said. Her voice was soft and seductive.

"That sound like a wonderful idea." Minola watched as Sergeant Welsey squirmed in his seat. He was obviously uncomfortable with the suggestion.

"Evan, do you remember we were going to come here on holiday? And then you had more pressing matters to attend to." Adriana spoke in a hushed tone that was an obvious rebuke.

"I remember." Evan gritted his teeth.

"It does sound quite lovely." Adriana frowned at Evan's noticeable discomfort.

"The Cafe Florian is always a must for the tourists and some locals. It is old, fashionable, and rather formal," Gio commented. "The cafe dates back to 1725 so you see, by American standards, it is quite old." A hefty cover charge was applied to sit down to listen to the band. For the most part, they played international pieces rather than just Italian ones, a welcome to the tourists that usually filled the piazza to capacity. It cost a small fortune to sit down and order anything to eat or drink, but the incomparable setting was well worth it. "It is a tourist trap to be sure, but the venue is magnificent." Gio was understandably proud of his city.

"Peter and I enjoyed our time there, and the coffee is quite good. Is there anything else we neglected to discuss about the murder?"

"Do the police have any suspects? I know it is early in the investigation, but…" Peter asked.

"It is a little comical, but Matteo did mention a certain Interpol Captain and his rather curious artist friend. That wouldn't be you two by any chance, would it?" Gio asked innocently. "Not that you're considered suspects. They mentioned possible sabotage, corporate spying, persons of interest—words like that were bandied about."

"Minola, you sure know how to get into trouble," Sally laughed.

"Believe me, had I but known, but the glass…so glorious. Families have skeletons in their closets. That is life. These families, though, seem to have real skeletons in their closets."

"We're discussing families that go back five or six hundred years, often times more." Adriana leaned back in her chair and relaxed. "I will agree with you, Minola. The sarcophagus is most intriguing. I'm sure it is significant. There are so many mysteries and secrets that surround the furnaces in Murano. I'm also an avid collector of blown glass and have bought a few pieces from the Castigli and Deniccali furnaces. They're both creative and innovative where glass is concerned."

"I have visited the Castigli furnace, and their work in incredible. I still cannot believe the things that can be done with glass," Minola granted.

"I agree, and you must remember there are secrets to glass blowing techniques, design, color blending, and all things glass. Secrets that some would kill to protect." Gio leaned back in his chair and seemed to relax.

"Are you warning us off?" Sally asked.

"No, not at all, I am just letting you know that the stakes are high." Gio turned toward Minola. "Murano is the place for glass, and Venice apparently is the place for romantic weddings. Are you sure you want to go through with yours?" Gio asked.

"That is a strange thing to ask someone you just met."

"My apologies, but I'm quite fascinated by you—your work captivates me—and I was curious. I assure you there were no other intentions."

"Gio doesn't trust easily, and always found it best to test people he would befriend or work with. Experience taught him that, and how people respond in adversity is a good way for him to tell." Adriana defended her brother.

"Apology accepted," Minola responded easily. She was surprised at what she felt was a personal, inappropriate, and rather intimate question. She cherished her privacy, especially her relationship with Peter, and to have a stranger discuss it made her uncomfortable and even a tad angry, but she trusted Gio. She understood his need to test people, considering his wealth. Something about his demeanor, his apparent honesty touched her. "To answer you, more than anything I've ever wanted. And please understand that I do not ever discuss my personal life." Underneath the tablecloth, she placed her hand on Peter's thigh and felt it grasped by him.

"I did not mean to imply anything by it. I was merely curious why you would engage in a murder investigation and plan a wedding at the same time."

"An excellent question." Peter laughed to lighten Minola's discomfort. He tightened his grip on her hand and felt her relax.

"I'm not going to win this one, am I?" A small curve lined her lips. "To be fair, my marvelous and original wedding was planned by you and Sally." She turned to Peter, smiled, and continued. "All I had to do was pick-up my dress and buy shoes, which— by the way—I have not yet done." Minola heard Adriana laugh.

"Let me remedy the shoe situation immediately. I will take you to my favorite shop. I'm sure you'll find a pair there. What is your dress like?"

"I won't give the details away. Suffice it to say it is a period costume and not peach."

"Well…" Sally exclaimed. "Just because I love the color peach…"

"Sally selected my dress. How she did that, I do not know."

"I called and talked to them, that's how."

"That again is most unusual. You are a remarkable woman, and it rather fits your attempt to help your friends." Gio nodded, satisfied with the answer.

"Yes, she is that." Peter's lips thinned in irritation.

"Thank you." Minola whispered, her gaze first directed at Peter then Adriana. "I would like to extend an invitation to you and, of course, you, Gio. It'll be a surprise for all of us, except Sally and, to some extent, Peter."

"That is certainly original. I accept, and I'll speak for my brother as well. He would not miss it." Adriana saw Gio nod in confirmation.

"Original…that is one way to put it, but yes, it is. I'm truly blessed to have Peter, Sally, and Robert in my life."

"I have some invitations left and can send them to you." Sally was speaking directly to Adriana and Gio.

"*Grazie*, that would be lovely." Adriana opened her small metallic purse covered with what appeared to be pave diamonds and extended her private card with her address on it to Sally. "Where is the wedding to be held? At a furnace?"

"No, I wish I'd thought of that. Here at the hotel." Sally saw Adriana's purse and exclaimed, "That is an exquisite evening bag."

"Thank you. A birthday gift from my father."

Minola heard an indrawn breath from Evan Welsey and asked. "Is something wrong, Evan?"

"No, not at all." He turned toward Adriana and asked, "When did he give it to you…the year I went back to London?" The bitterness in his voice could be heard by all.

"No, Evan," Adriana replied softly. "Last year, a significant birthday for me. My father recognized the error he made, but you did not stay long enough to find out." Adriana eyes filled with tears, and she blinked them quickly away.

"You missed her engagement, too." Gio swirled his glass of wine and watched the wine gently drip down the glass.

"Engaged? Bloody hell…to whom?" was his swift reply, Evan glanced down to her hand to see the ring. He expected one at least the size of a large grape. He was surprised to see no ring on her finger. In fact, she wore no jewelry at all. He heaved a sigh of relief.

Gio watched his progress and finally said, "Do not worry, Evan. It was of short duration. She would not agree to the merger, and father learned his lesson."

"There seems to be a lot going on here. Are you all right?" Minola spoke to Evan.

"Yes." Evan was curt. "My apologies. I did not mean to be rude."

"No need. I understand." Minola wanted everyone to be as happy as she was, and she was convinced Evan and Adriana had a long history together and, she hoped, a promising future. "Adriana, let's set the date for shoe shopping."

"Tomorrow soon enough? The three of us can have lunch and chat." Adriana smiled as she saw Sally rub her hands in joy.

"Sally will buy out the store," Robert replied indulgently. "Please don't let her. We have no room, and we're not moving to a larger apartment until after our baby is born," Robert pleaded, and peals of laughter accompanied his remark.

The dinner ended with Gio promising a breakfast appointment with his friend Matteo, the location to be determined later, and shoe shopping for Minola and Sally.

The short walk to Piazza San Marco allowed Minola to think about Adriana and Evan. They had a combustible past and still cared deeply for each other. Rather than paint a Venetian scene as a gift, she was going to draw their likeness. Evan would get Adriana's and Adriana Evan's. Minola smiled and saw Peter raise his eyebrows and glance at her with suspicion. He took her hand and they walked to the cafe.

Chapter 9

Peter's early breakfast meeting with Matteo and Gio was scheduled far away from the crowds, locals, and tourists alike. Discretion truly was the better part of valor. They did not want to draw attention to their meeting. A secluded cafe on one of the narrow streets in Venice that screamed mystery and intrigue did the trick. A fitting venue for what they were about to discuss.

Peter arrived first, ordered coffee, and waited for his guests. He had no idea what this meeting would resolve, if anything. There were hidden depths within the old Venetian families. *Why did Gio seem afraid or, or at best reluctant to discuss Pia Deniccali, what is he hiding?*

While waiting for Gio and his friend, Peter thought about last night's dinner and the break at the piazza. It ended at the cafe. The murder was not discussed once. Gio made a particular effort to avoid any mention of it or his connection to the Deniccali family. He concentrated instead on the history of Venice and its current issues with the sinking of the city, and the large cruise lines that visited daily. The real or perceived damage they caused, and how they seemed to disrupt the Venetian way of life, while at the same time relying heavily on the income the cruise ships and tourists bring, and of course how politics played a large part in the lack of progress.

Peter's wait was not long. Gio strode toward Peter, his hand extended in welcome. The handshake was firm and steady. The man was comfortable with himself and self-assured. "Good morning, Gio. Thank you for arranging this meeting."

"That was not a problem. Do be careful. Matteo understands why you're curious, but he's also a carabiniere," Gio warned Peter and rose when he saw his friend approach them. "Matteo, meet my friend Peter Riley. He and Evan work together."

"A pleasure." Peter shook hands with the man and was struck by Gio's mention of Evan Welsey. Sergeant Welsey had been keeping secrets, and that wouldn't do at all. "Thank you for meeting us. I was surprised to hear that you have met Sergeant Welsey. May I ask how?"

"*Si.*" Matteo glanced at Gio for confirmation. When he saw Gio nod his approval, he continued. "The sergeant was a friend of the Bruloni family, and he helped with a small issue while he stayed with the family. He solved a case."

"I always knew the sergeant was discreet, but I didn't know quite the extent and depth of that discretion." Peter saw a gentle smile line Gio's face. "Is it a secret or may I know about it?"

Gio hesitated, took a sip of water, and responded, "An issue with my engagement to Pia. Evan helped dissolve it. Pia likes power and men, not necessarily in that order. Prior to my engagement to Pia, she also slept with Julio, our victim, and continued to do so during our engagement. Her father did not approve of Julio, and she thought she could have both of us. I did not approve of that arrangement. Before you say anything, it is a small world. She tried a little blackmail, and Evan put a stop to it." Gio finished casually, as if he was talking about the weather."

"Blackmail? And you didn't think to mention that earlier? You have a connection to the murdered man."

"I did have a connection, but it no longer existed. Let me explain the situation to you. Matteo is aware of all. No love lost between us, no great passion, a business proposition sanctioned by our fathers, not by us. Pia wanted everything on her terms. I disagreed with that arrangement. She is a beautiful woman and did not appreciate the fact that I begged off. She knew of the intimate relationship between my sister and Evan and tried a little blackmail, even threatened to tell my father. As you can surmise, Evan requested a secret relationship because my father would not have approved. Evan did not want to cause any problems between Adriana and her father."

"In your father's eyes, Evan brought nothing to the table," Peter said.

"Yes. My father would not recognize character, even now...well, maybe now, Adriana taught him a lesson." Gio eyed Peter speculatively. "Evan did receive an inheritance upon the death of his parents—a car accident. He is not poor by any means, but certainly not nearly as wealthy as my family. Of course he's not Italian and not in business. In that sense, he brought nothing to our table."

"Let me guess. Rather than be blackmailed, Evan went to your father and told him the truth."

"Again, yes. My father told him the relationship must end or he would banish Adriana out of his home. Evan knew Adriana loved her home and her father, and he didn't want to cause her any undue pain. What Evan failed to understand was her uncompromising love for him. He left without telling her why he did so. He thought it would be easier for her."

"Blackmail averted, and Pia furious at the end result."

Gio nodded in agreement. "Rather simple, but yes. My father soon after arranged a marriage to another powerful house in Venice. Only by this time, Adriana knew what had happened. I may have let a few things slip. She told my father she would leave if he chose to continue. He did, and she left—went back to school in England. Only recently, my father...as Americans say...came around. My father miscalculated her devotion to the family power, and he couldn't afford to lose her business acumen. She's brilliant, scrupulous to a fault, and will always be honest with my father. His would have been the greater loss. Hence that rather ridiculously expensive purse for her last birthday. Adriana uses it to remind her of what is important in life. For her, that is Evan. Even today, she still cares. And she is independently wealthy in her own right, thanks to our mother." Gio took a deep breath and continued. "Evan is a good friend, foolish and proud, but a man of excellent character. I don't think anything else needs to be said."

"Evan is indeed an excellent man with great character. You do realize Minola will play the matchmaker." Peter waited for another cup of coffee to be set down and took a sip. Along with the coffee came a selection of biscotti.

"I certainly hope so," Gio replied easily and turned toward Matteo. "Now, Matteo, the murder if you please."

"The cause of death was the stab wound. The dagger had no fingerprints. We are waiting to learn the age of the dagger. There are no identifying marks at all on the weapon. Anywhere. We don't know where he was killed. The trail of blood stops at the edge of the canal. We don't know why he was left there, and we do not yet know where he was killed. No one is saying anything, and until we learn more, there will be no questions for the Castigli or Deniccali families."

"Is that normal? He was connected to both families. How can there be no questions?" Peter shook his head in disbelief. *How are they going to learn anything if they're afraid to anger the families involved?*

"At the moment, that is normal here, and everywhere else as well." Matteo replied.

"In that case, off the record, we have an in with the Castigli family, and you, Gio, with Pia Deniccali. I met the woman, and I did not impress her."

"Strange, all men impress her. That may not be the case, Peter. I cannot be of help with Pia. She will not give me the time of day," Gio announced smoothly.

"And why is that?"

"Because I left her at the altar and lived."

"Hmm. You did not say you left her at the altar. She is still holding a grudge?" Peter asked.

"I have not spoken to her in three years. I know the woman, and yes, she's still bitter, and that one holds a grudge. Only because it was not her idea. I warned her I would not be in church. She persisted, thinking I could not possibly give her up. I could and did," Gio said simply.

"Well, in that case, we have Antonio Castigli. He's a friend. One she apparently trusts, or at least she's working with him."

"In this case, you do not need me?" Matteo was ready to leave.

"Yes, we do, Matteo. It would be simpler for you to investigate on your own, but I'm involved in this case, and we will work with Captain Riley."

"Thank you. As the investigation progresses, we'll need access to lab reports and any information that may cross your desk. From what you indicated, it won't be because suspects or persons of interest will be interviewed, but in a murder investigation, stranger things have happened." Peter glanced at Gio and saw him smirk.

"I think, Peter, that you understand how things work."

"In reality, we all tend to be rather cautious when handling delicate situations," Peter said.

"How diplomatic of you." Matteo's voice was as dry as dust.

"I've been told it is one of my specialties. That is how I wound up in Paris," Peter replied.

"I have done a little research on you and Miss Grey—that is where you met, is it not?" Gio asked.

"Research...why may I ask?

"I always want to know the people I deal with. You and Miss Grey, Paris, yes?"

"Yes, that is where we met. Since you have already done your research, you already have the answer. Now, shall we get back to the issues at hand?" Peter was not about to discuss Minola and their life together with anyone. "We have a body, we have a dagger of unknown age, and we have two wealthy and powerful families that are obviously involved but will not be approached by the local police."

"At the moment," Matteo added.

"At the moment," Peter repeated and smiled. "Gio, I need all the information you have on Pia Deniccali, her family, as well as the

Castigli group. Any innuendos, past history, any difficulties, financial issues, anything at all." Peter saw Gio nod in agreement.

"Miss Grey can help with Jennifer and Antonio," Gio suggested with authority.

"Yes, she can, but I want the gossip, hints of impropriety, things Jennifer will not share with Minola. Lest you forget, they're friends."

"I will help in any way possible. I would like to see this crime solved," Matteo said.

"I believe you. We'll keep in touch." Peter took a sip of his now cold coffee.

"This is a good place to meet. I know the proprietor, and it is secluded." Gio was a careful man.

"Thank you, gentlemen. I appreciate your time. Matteo, I assume you're still in charge of this investigation?" Peter asked.

"*Si.*"

"That is good."

"Perhaps I should mention one more thing." Matteo rubbed his chin with his fingers.

"Please." Peter replied.

"I do not know if it is important, but the glass cover included three gilded daggers. They were not melted but were in fact perfect. They were on his body and formed a triangle. They may or may not be old. We're waiting for test results."

"That is interesting." Peter was not about to mention the theft of Julio's daggers or even their history to Matteo. "A ritual of some sort."

"Indeed. Are there any suspicions within your ranks, Matteo?" Gio asked.

"No. They're looking closely at the daggers because rumors persist about it being a show of power as in the old days. In today's time, it could be considered an assassination and the daggers a warning and maybe a message to certain families. But why three and in the form of a triangle?" Matteo asked.

"How would anyone have found out about the warning? The police have not released any information that related to the murder. Who is to be warned? There most likely is a reason for the staging of the body, and it could have been significant to the victim—more of a symbol of betrayal rather than a warning," Peter replied.

"If we look at old times, as Matteo put it, there would be a notice given to the family paying for the assassination. There were ways to communicate," Gio commented.

"How would that be done?" Peter asked.

"A souvenir from the murder would work, anything that would identify the deed as having been done. The traditions and tales are rich in the telling," Gio replied.

"Odd that we can't find any of those tales anywhere." Peter saw Gio shrug and smile. "What kind of souvenir?"

"A piece of clothing, rest of the dagger, a piece of jewelry…something the victim would not part with willingly, anything would be accepted as proof." Gio's gaze rested on Peter.

"That is all I have for you." Matteo heaved a sigh of relief.

"*Mille grazie,* Matteo. We will keep in touch." Gio nodded to acknowledge Matteo's efforts. He understood the difficulties Matteo would encounter in his investigation.

"Once again, thank you, gentlemen." Peter had a bit more than before, but he still had no idea where to go from here. The meeting over, the men stood up, shook hands, and went their separate ways.

Peter wondered at the machinations of the powerful and wealthy, but given his background in psychology, he was not at all surprised that everyone was fair game, including the children. Gio and Adriana were strong, willful, and it would appear ethical. Their father greatly underestimated them. Did Bruloni do anything else to help his cause along? Peter walked back to the hotel. He needed to clear his head and figure out exactly what to do next. At least they were not alone. Now Peter had an inside track to the investigation. *Do I trust everyone and accept them at their word? I do not think so. This went a little too smoothly. What does Gio Bruloni stand to gain from his involvement? I can understand Matteo's desire to solve this crime. Is there more to Matteo than the genial and helpful police officer on friendly terms with an exceedingly wealthy and powerful family?*

Chapter 10

While Peter had his meeting, Adriana, Sally, and Minola went to an exclusive shoe boutique where every shoe was handmade in Italy. Adriana was welcomed as a treasured friend. Given her superb taste and pocketbook, Minola was not surprised they fawned over Adriana. Shoes were everywhere Minola turned, artistically displayed on colorful glass tables.

Adriana was immediately greeted with *"Buon Giorno, Adriana."*

"Buon Giorno, Katarina. I have brought you new clients." Adriana smiled and sank down in a royal purple overstuffed couch. The leather was exquisite, and Adriana sighed as she sank farther into the luxurious sofa. An espresso appeared instantly at the small glass table next to the couch. The glass was etched then painted in various hues of deep ivory, tan, and beige. A sliver of the purple that matched the couch ran through the center. Minola stared at the table as if mesmerized. An offer of coffee was extended to Minola and Sally. Minola, addicted to the brew, immediately agreed. Sally chose orange juice.

"How can I help?" Katarina Ivanov asked, her Russian accent thick, but she spoke English well.

"Shoes...we need shoes," Sally replied, giddy with delight. She loved to shop, and adored shoes.

"In that case, you have come to the right place. We have many, and all made in Italy, and we have excellent service. I even deliver them to my clients at home or work, when necessary," Katarina said proudly.

"That is really unusual and wonderful customer service." Minola found three pair, one that fit the dress to perfection—a pale ivory pump with a small gold bow, one pair of leather sandals embellished with colorful stones she could wear with everything, and a pair of black suede heels. "I have never owned anything quite this luxurious, nor have I ever paid such a fortune for them. Ouch."

"They are beautiful, will always be stylish, and most importantly they're comfortable. They are well-made and will last. You will not regret your purchase." Adriana chuckled.

"I'm sure they will last. The few collection pieces I have, I bought at a consignment shop at a great discount." When Minola saw Adriana frown, she quickly added, "A resale shop." Minola was sure Adriana never heard of a resale shop, much less shopped in one. "The few designs I really liked, I had to hunt many stores until I found them. I shop sales. There are no sales here." Minola ran her hand over the glass table, and because of the etching, she felt grit like fine sand under her fingertips rather than the smooth feel of glass. Tactile and gorgeous. "Beautiful table," she whispered to no one in particular.

"Yes, it is. From Murano, in fact from the Deniccali furnace. I own two pieces. Their furniture is unique and a relatively new market for them. " Adriana was proud to introduce Murano's treasures to her new friends.

"The tables are unique. Maybe they should sell them, too, and I love the shoes."

"That is an excellent idea, and you will enjoy the shoes. You picked well. And I think your Peter will love to see you wear them."

Minola smiled at the comment. "Sally, on the other hand, bought six pair, all the while complaining about swollen ankles."

"Well, see." Sally extended her feet. "They are swollen. I'm pregnant. Speaking of which, I'm also hungry."

"We'll stop for lunch and feed you two." Minola leaned down and gently rubbed Sally's belly then whispered. "I bet you're really hungry. Your mommy spent a long time picking her shoes." Minola saw tears brimming in Sally's eyes and hugged her best friend. "Let's find a lovely spot and have lunch."

Adriana watched the exchange with surprise and envy. "You must be great friends."

"Yes." The reply was simultaneous and in stereo. They looked at each other and burst out laughing.

"I have no such friends. Evan was the only..."

"You now have us. Adriana, whatever happened between you and Evan—he is a good and honorable man. Give him another chance. He deserves it, and more to the point, he desperately wants one."

"You just met me." Adriana spoke quietly, hoping against hope that was true.

"Yes, but I happen to be good with faces, and I observe well. He couldn't take his off you. I saw the same reaction from you, although you were a little less obvious. You belong together."

"It is not that simple."

"Nothing worthwhile ever is. I firmly believe in that old and trite but true saying."

"He must make the first move. I cannot. I would rather live thinking he cares than find out for sure he does not. I'm a coward when it comes to Evan."

"Believe me, I understand." Minola remembered her time in Paris and Peter. She did exactly the same thing. Now she realized the massive mistake she made, but back then, no one—including Peter—could convince her otherwise.

"I need food—lots of food." Sally glanced at Minola and knew exactly what Minola was reliving. "Did I mention I'm hungry?"

"Yes, yes, you did, at least once," Minola gathered her bags and Sally's, thanked Katarina, and they walked out. Minola squinted at the bright sunshine. The blue sky was lined with streaks of white, there was a small canal directly in front of them, and plenty of foot traffic. Minola took a deep breath, and her voice rang with joy. "I love Venice. And I have shoes. Thank you, Adriana."

"My pleasure. As you can see, I cannot resist shoes, either." Adriana extended her shopping bag filled with four pairs of sandals. "The outdoor cafe down the street serves a most excellent pizza."

"That is terrific," Sally chimed in.

The al fresco dining in Venice was plentiful, and the restaurant fit the bill perfectly. White tablecloths, comfortable chairs, and pots of colorful flowers added to the ambiance. The waiters all wore black with white aprons and were eager to serve. Another restaurant a few feet away vied for the patrons. Once they sat down, their waiter told them the restaurants were owned by the same family, but served different food, and that a friendly competition for customers existed between the two restaurants.

They ordered grilled calamari for Minola and Adriana and a salad for Sally, along with a large pizza, wine, and juice for Sally. Her eyes widened when she saw the huge size of the pizza. "Good thing, too. Remember, I'm eating for two." Sally winked at her friends.

"We know, and later, we can have gelato, so leave room. Adriana, Gio was reluctant to talk about Pia. What can you tell us?"

"I do not like her. I was happy when Gio ended the relationship, and I think she's spoiled and dangerous when she doesn't get way."

"Would she kill if crossed?" Minola asked.

"I cannot say, but she comes from a hard family. Her brother, Dario, is more determined to succeed than Pia and just as ruthless a business man, and she has a younger sister Carina who is different, a scholar, and keeps to herself. A lovely, shy, and bright young woman who most often has a book in her hand and keeps away from the business and, for the most part, from the family as a whole. Gio was captivated by her, but stayed away for fear that Pia would make her life miserable."

"That certainly is interesting. I wonder why Gio never mentioned the rest of the family last night?" Minola took a sip of her sparkling water.

"Gio is a private and a rather cautious man. He doesn't trust easily," Adriana answered.

"But you do. Why is that?" Minola asked.

"I have been blessed with good and honest friends. Gio, for a short time, became involved with people who saw nothing but his money. And of course Pia. He learned the hard way and became distrustful and careful in the choices he made."

"So now we know the Deniccali family is ruthless and opportunistic. What can you tell us about the Castigli clan?" Sally asked.

"They are not that different from the Deniccali family, except that Antonio is an only child, the last of the family. He hoped he and Jennifer would have a child together, but that has not happened. Of course, rumors of a relationship between Antonio and Pia were many, but nothing since he married. At least, there are no rumors. I heard that Pia had a relationship with Julio at about the same time. It is difficult to keep track of all that was being said."

"The woman must be remarkable." Sally swallowed a bite of pizza. "Yummy food by the way, and this place is wonderful."

"I met Pia at the Castigli Furnace, but she ignored me. She is charismatic and quite beautiful, but cold." Minola shivered at the memory.

"Yes, she is all that, yet Evan was totally unaware of her considerable charms." Adriana lips curved up a little. "I found that remarkable, but after meeting Captain Riley, I suspect he wouldn't react, either."

"Peter met her, too, and he didn't mention her allure, and Evan was oblivious to her magnetism because he had you. He deeply cares for you, and if I could glimpse that in just one evening, surely you must know it." Minola took a bite of the calamari and licked her lips. "Fresh and delicious. I have to bring Peter here."

"I may have mentioned earlier, I'm a coward and insecure when it comes to Evan, and I stand by that."

"Adriana, give him a small way in. He'll take it."

"I will think about it. Now, what else can we do?"

"Dig into the background of both families, their customers, where they go, what they do in their free time, types of meetings, who they socialize with. That is where you'll be most helpful, Adriana. Any information will help. There must be a link somewhere. We just have to find it," Minola said.

"Have computer. Will research," Sally added.

"I think, in this case, it will be more like legwork. They seem to be a rather secretive bunch," Minola replied.

"What do you mean legwork? We're going to follow someone?" Sally asked.

"We'll start with Pia. See where she goes and what she does on a daily basis," Minola replied.

"That could be dangerous." Adriana paused and rubbed her neck. She knew the people involved. "It will be unpleasant if we get caught."

"There are also three men to contend with, namely Peter, Robert, and Evan. When they find out what we're up to there will be trouble."

"Do we have to tell them?" Sally nibbled on her pizza.

"I promised Peter we would share and not hold anything back. I will not go back on my promise." Minola was adamant on that point. It would feel like betrayal.

"I made no such promise to anyone, and I travel in the same circles, and I know Pia. It will be easier for me to be at the same places," Adriana replied.

"If you were to do that, I would lose a cherished friend. Evan would never forgive me. We do this together. Sally, except for you. You will stay out of sight and record everything. Use the computer and see if you can discover something else. Sometimes the most innocent statement prove most interesting. Even an innuendo could be of help." When Minola saw that Sally was about to object to the plan, she stopped her. "You're pregnant. You cannot be involved and be seen as part of the investigation—that is a deal breaker. You stay out of sight or we don't do anything. I mean it." Minola's voice was firm.

"Fine. I'll be your secretary. Just know that I disagree. In Paris, I was your assistant while you played reporter and artist. I think I've been demoted. That is not how it should go. People, good workers, should be promoted, and I'm good. Hmm."

"Dully noted, next time you'll be promoted, but may I remind you that you're pregnant? Adriana, can you find out where she'll be and we can go together? If necessary, you can introduce me and tell her you commissioned me to paint your father's portrait—any story will do."

"*Si.*" Adriana waved her hand in the air in excitement. "*Bueno.* Excellent, my father would love it. Please do it."

Minola laughed. "I did not mean to solicit work from you, just that it would be a good excuse, one I've used before."

"Does not matter. I should have thought of that the moment I met you."

"You do realize a project like that takes time, and I'm to be married and want a long honeymoon with my soon-to-be husband."

"Whenever you finish will be fine. There will be no time constraints. We can also say Gio and Peter are long time friends, here for the wedding, and that we're guests. She won't question it because Gio never shared his work with her, but she knows of his police background. It all fits."

"You forgot one teeny, tiny detail…the men," Sally reminded them.

"Oops. Yes, we did," Minola said.

"So?" Sally asked.

"So what?" Minola replied.

"What are you going to do about it?" Sally persisted.

"We'll cross that bridge…" Minola's lips curved up in a smile.

"Not good." Sally laughed.

"You two will contrive something. I'm sure of it."

"That does not speak well for us." Sally rubbed her tummy. "I think we're full."

"Wrap up the rest. You'll be hungry in an hour." Minola had never seen Sally happier.

"It speaks well for you. You are creative, and you both care." Adriana smiled, grateful to the two women. They just met, and it felt as if Adriana had known them for years. Things like that did not happen often, but when they did, they should be treasured. She never took a gift for granted, especially one of true friendship.

"We'll start by visiting the Deniccali Furnace. I really love glass and want to compare the difference between Castigli and Deniccali. We won't hide the fact that Jennifer and Antonio are my friends." Minola hoped they'd remain friends.

"Peter will see right through your plan, as will the other two." Sally replied.

"They will, but as before, they can't keep us out." Minola shook her head, anticipating the lecture from Peter she knew was coming.

"I'll arrange a morning meeting at the Deniccali furnace. I'll have to buy something." Adriana sighed heavily and then burst out laughing. "They are unique. Wait until you see some of the tables and shelves. They do not have many furniture pieces, but what they do have is all original and quite beautiful. Pia started the furniture pieces for Katarina, and the demand grew."

"How could a shoe salon afford such expensive furnishings…never mind, I just remembered how much I paid for my shoes." Minola's lips curved up in a smile.

"I'm sure she didn't pay full price for the table. Katarina and Pia are friends, and I think Pia even invested initially in the shop. Pia told me about it, maybe as long as six years ago. It is a quality product, and Pia always wants to make more money."

"Speaking of quality, what are you going to buy Peter as a wedding gift? Inquiring minds want to know." Sally asked.

"I already did."

"Well? Really, it's like pulling teeth. It was not a rhetorical question. I want to know. Geesh."

"If you must know, I bought him a horse."

"A horse? Are you kidding me? A real horse, as in alive? Barn and all that?"

"A real horse, minus the barn. A horse Peter has been eyeing for quite a while. You know he loves horses."

"I know he loves horses. It certainly is a unique gift. Does he know?" Sally asked.

"No, of course not. It was meant to be a surprise."

"What kind of horse?" Sally demanded.

"How should I know? A horse. He wanted it desperately, and when he was told the horse has been sold, he was so disappointed I almost told him I bought it."

"Where is this horse? Not going to be at the wedding, is it? With you, I never know." Sally bubbled with joy.

"At home, and Mr. Dobbs is taking good care of him. Maybe I made a mistake. Who gives a horse as a wedding gift? Mr. Dobbs thought it was remarkable. But I don't know if that is good or bad? Mr. Dobbs doesn't really say much…Didn't really think about it until now. Adriana, Mr. Dobbs is Peter's friend and handles everything at home."

"I see. What a magnificent gift. It is quite wonderful." Adriana spoke softly.

"I wanted something special and unique," Minola murmured, afraid she may have made a mistake in her choice of gift, but Peter really wanted that horse. *Too late now to worry about it. And I have a portrait of his family as backup.*

"Well, you certainly succeeded. All I gave Robert was a gold watch. How did you arrange it?"

"I called the seller, told him where to deliver the horse, called Mr. Dobbs told him what to expect, and as always he replied 'very well, Miss Grey', and that was the end of it. We were already here when the horse was delivered."

"That's Mr. Dobbs, a man of few words, and nothing surprises him." Sally smiled.

"He is a gem. Let's get back to business…Adriana, please arrange something for tomorrow, if possible. I find the Katarina and Pia connection rather interesting, but then, everything about this case is interesting. I suspect everyone and everything."

"Not at all. It is a small community, and connections are made at social events. Katarina is well-versed in attending these events and meeting the wealthy. You noticed she's a rather striking blonde, many curves, and an exotic accent that appeals to many men. Evan met her and was unimpressed." Adriana closed her eyes for a moment.

"I know how it all works, but I've never been good at it and am always surprised that it really does work," Minola replied.

"You'll see for yourself. I'll be your guide. I have an excellent plan. It is safe and could prove useful. I will throw an engagement ball for you at our home and invite the Deniccali and Castigli families and anyone else I can think of. We can observe and learn something, and we will have fun at the same time. I can arrange everything quickly."

"I think that is an excellent suggestion, and I suspect no one will say no to you." They exchanged cell numbers and promised to meet soon.

On the way back to the hotel, Minola thought about her incredible life. She was blessed with a good man who loved her beyond reason and whom she loved equally well. She had many acquaintances, but few cherished friends, and that is as it should be. She suddenly turned toward Sally. "You're my sister, and I love you like one. Thank you for being here."

"Min, is anything wrong? I love you, too. Always have."

"No, everything is perfect. It is rather scary, isn't it?"

"Yes, in fact, it is. I feel the same way. Must be Venice. It is spectacular, and ever since you left Chicago, our lives have not been the same. It has been exciting, romantic, and just plain terrific. And I thank you for bringing such joy and adventure to my life."

"It is amazing. Everywhere we traipse, there are centuries old footsteps that we follow. I always get goose pumps when I think about it," Minola said.

"I also know you're worried about the murder, and Peter's reactions."

"I am. He doesn't say much, but I know he's afraid more is to come. Such a callous and brutal murder. As if taking a life was a matter of course. That is frightening."

"We'll help our friends. I think Gio Bruloni has a lot of pull."

"Yes, I suspect he does, but why? What does he stand to gain? And I don't want Sergeant Welsey hurt in the process. He's still in love with Adriana."

"I think she's a straightforward person, and I suspect she loves him, too. Pride is rather difficult to overcome, especially in romance. We'll hope for a happy ending." Sally took Minola's arm, and they walked back to the hotel. The meandering narrow streets lined with boutiques, restaurants, cafes, and the ever present tourist shops lifted their spirits. The gelaterias made Minola smile—she loved the huge assortment of choices. She never ordered anything sweet in the restaurant, because she knew she'd end up with a scoop of gelato.

The uneven cobblestones, the frequent bridges that crossed the small canals, the clanking suitcases lugged by exasperated tourists, the people who lingered atop a bridge and looked down to the canal below, and the waiters beckoning the tourists to eat in their restaurants, it all spoke to the vitality and pure romanticism that was Venice.

Minola thought about her wedding in this remarkable city filled with art almost everywhere she turned. Venice celebrated art at every opportunity, and that made her feel accomplished and her talent appreciated. Peter certainly made her aware of herself as an artist. She was lucky in that she could paint whatever she wanted. Her work sold well, and ever since Paris, she could pick and choose her portrait commissions. She couldn't abide cruelty of any sort, and she saw it all too often since meeting Peter. From one point of view, she was grateful to see life from all sides, yet she felt profoundly saddened that so much malevolence existed in the world.

After walking for a couple of hours, they stopped at the stairs of a small canal where a few women were sitting down on the steps of a bridge. Coffee, a bottle of wine, and sandwiches lined a stair. They were discussing linguistics and art. Minola and Sally took part in the lively discussion. It turned out that the women were in Venice to participate in the art festival and found a common interest in linguistics. Meeting strangers in exactly such circumstances was always a valued bonus to her travels and somehow redeemed the other violent extremes she'd come to experience since meeting Peter.

Back at the hotel, Minola stood in front of the entrance. She said, "Look how beautiful this building is, quite old and gracious. Peter couldn't have picked a better place. I want to come back here every year." Minola gazed at the structures that seemed to float in water, and in fact, most first floors were used to access the buildings. No one lived on those floors. Many were at water level or sometimes below. In spite of the flooding issues and sometimes dire circumstances, the effect was mesmerizing and magical.

"So do I. Let's go have a bite to eat and savor the beauty of the Grand Canal from the perfect vantage point—the restaurant at the hotel. I need food."

"Excellent plan. I told you you'd be hungry soon. Let me call Peter to let him know we're back. I need coffee, and it's delicious here." They entered the opulent lobby. The fresh scent of flowers at every table welcomed Minola home, and a sense of pure joy assailed her senses. *I will not worry about the future, but cherish the present.* She savored the rare, brief moment where everything was right with the world.

Chapter 11

Peter realized he loved being in Venice. No matter what the future held, it would be with Minola, and above all, that was what he wanted. There was joy in her discoveries, a lighter more carefree step in her walk, and she laughed more. He fell more deeply in love with her each day. *How can that be?*

Paris brought her into his life and changed it forever. He spent many summers on holiday in Bath with his family and considered it his home away from home. In Bath, he lost himself. His obsessive fear for her safety almost cost him his greatest love. He became more aware of Minola and loved her beyond measure, but communication issues persisted. Venice offered solace, beauty, and a new closeness with Minola that he treasured. He had made monstrous mistakes in his relationship with her. In Venice, so far, he turned everything around and was sharing, communicating with her, and including her in his life on all levels. However, a dark and evil presence interfered with the joyous occasion.

The murder intruded on their life, but he knew Minola and her need to help her friends. He was to be married in a few days, but in the meantime, he had a job to do. Venice somehow soothed the soul, maybe because of the beauty of the surroundings or maybe because so much rich history existed in each narrow street that he had yet to discover. Every step seemed to have a story to tell. Before he met Minola, he never would have thought about that. He would go about his business. Now he stopped and took stock of everything. She showed him Bath as he'd never seen it before. She made Paris come alive for him. How remarkable his life had become, all because one artist entered his life in Paris and never let go.

He learned as much as he could about the history of glass and the various guilds, or unions in modern terms, that allowed the industry to flourish in Murano. The Guild of Glassmakers, *Ars Fiolaria,* was established in 1224 and helped Venice reach the pinnacle of glass artistry. By the time the businesses moved to Murano in 1291, they were renowned, and to insure they would remain in Murano, some artisans were murdered to keep them from leaving with their secrets and to show others what would happen should they even think about leaving and betraying their craft to others. Another covert reminder of the assassin guilds, yet he couldn't find anything in print to specifically point them out.

Peter read about the guilds and the important part they played in the past. The efficient and organized unions were oftentimes brutal. He was sure the assassin guilds existed as well. How could such a business stay hidden through the ages? How did they function in this day and age? What were their rituals? His speed increased. As always he was eager to see Minola. He smiled as he thought of her wedding shoes.

Peter entered the lobby and headed straight to the restaurant. Most likely she'll already be sipping coffee. Her addiction to the brew was legendary. He grinned as he saw her wave to him. She'd found a perfect spot along the railing overlooking the Grand Canal. Her smile dazzled him. *I can't take a breath without thinking about her.*

Minola ran up to greet him and hugged him. "I have coffee, and I have shoes," she exclaimed happily, leaned into him, and whispered, "And I love you so very much."

His lips curved up in a wide grin. He kissed the tip of her nose and murmured, "I love you deeply and passionately. And we're in a public place and I can't do a thing about it at the moment. And you're going to tell me something, aren't you?"

"Yes, later. And I know we're in a public place, but I wanted to tell you I love you .Venice is pure magic. Did I mention I have shoes?"

Peter laughed out loud. "Yes, my love, you did. Tell me what happened. Did you learn anything?" He sat down and ordered coffee and a salad.

Sally had already eaten her leftover pizza and leaned back in her chair for more comfort. "You two need some time alone."

"We're fine, and you are family. Sit and relax." Minola said.

"We really have the most exciting adventures. Who would have thought our lives would change so dramatically?" Sally lovingly ran her hand over her belly. "We have Paris, Bath, and now Venice together, and a baby on the way." She was brimming with joy.

"You're exhausted." Minola watched Sally's head slump down as she closed her eyes. "You should be tired after all that shopping and walking."

"You're also exceedingly happy, Sally." Peter watched her sway as she fought with exhaustion and the desire to stay and enjoy the view, and most probably the murder investigation.

"Yes, I am," Sally replied smugly. "I'm staying; the nap can wait."

"We had a lot of fun. Peter, are we doing well? Are you happy, even with everything going on?"

"Yes, even with everything going on, I am happy. It is such an innocuous word for what I really feel, but there it is." Peter tenderly brushed a strand of hair away from her face, took a sip of his coffee, and asked again, "How was your meeting? Did you learn anything?"

"Yes."

"Well, are you going to share? Other than shoes, what did you find out?"

Minola watched Sally rub her eyes and shared everything she heard, and Peter did the same.

"I'll have more once I visit the Deniccali furnace and maybe a couple of social events where I can see Gio and Pia together. You should have heard Adriana discuss their relationship. Pia thought she could marry Gio and continue her affair with Julio."

"That gives Gio an excellent reason to commit murder, except you indicated that it was not a love match," Peter replied.

"But it would still rankle, wouldn't it? I mean, she was cheating. Romance or not, that would not sit well with someone as…how shall I put it…as confident as Gio," Sally asked.

"Speaking as a man who has been through something similar, I would say the ego would be bruised, but there would also be a sense of relief. Now, that being said, we're assuming that Gio did not care. What if he secretly did?" Peter's affair with Alexis Yardleigh was in the past, and he could honestly say his heart was not involved. His body was. Time had come for him to marry and she was willing. Minola on the other hand was an entirely different matter. When he met her, all his senses became involved to the point where he couldn't remember any of his previous affairs. She was his life. She was his everything.

"An excellent point." Minola nibbled on the biscotti that accompanied her coffee. "I still tend to take people at their word. At least now I wait until proven wrong." Minola watched as Sally's lids slowly drooped down over her eyes.

"Sally, you're exhausted." Minola nudged her friend.

"What? I've been listening. Just resting my eyes." Sally opened her eyes, blinked twice, and said, "I arranged a dinner tomorrow. There's this lovely restaurant near San Marco, al fresco dining and a stunning view. If you like, it'll be one of the restaurants we'll go with family and friends. On that note, I'm going to excuse myself and visit with my husband, or most likely take a nap." Sally motioned to the waiter to get the check, and Peter waved his hand indicating he would take care of it. Sally got up, hugged Minola and Peter, rubbed her tummy, and waddled out of the restaurant.

"I missed you." Peter ran his fingers against her cheek. He could not stop touching her. It was as instinctive as breathing for him. "What would you like to do?"

"I want to show you my all important shoes, and I want to show you just how much I love you," she whispered in his ear and felt a tug on her arm as Peter pulled her up and propelled her forward to the elevators.

He could think of nothing better to do than make love with Minola. There would be time later to delve into the remarkable history of Murano glass and the intrigues that often led to murder, apparently even today. The legends were legion in the mysterious ways glass could be designed, shaped, and blown. The mystique was deserved and preserved.

Once in the room, Peter slammed the door shut and pinned Minola against the wall. "I missed loving you." He ran his lips against hers then made love to her, his need as swift as hers.

"Peter," she moaned after they lay down on the bed. She cuddled into his arms. "Is it supposed to be like this? Where I think about you all the time? Want you at all times."

"I can only assume yes, because that is how I feel as well." He pulled her closer to him.

"I can't even imagine another man with me. How could a woman in love cheat on the man she loves? And vice-versa."

"I cannot imagine nor do I want to imagine you with someone else. There will not be another as long as I draw breath." He tucked a few strands of hair behind her ears and nibbled on her neck. Peter couldn't control a fueling anger at the possibility of Minola with someone other than him. He never thought he was capable of rage at the thought of betrayal, but now he knew he was capable of extreme fury, passion, tenderness, and violence—everything rolled into this emotion called love. Except this was far more than mere love, this all-encompassing roller coaster sensation that he tried but could not define. He knew it bordered on obsession, and he would live with that.

He also realized and understood that Minola would never betray him in any way. He trusted her implicitly. What he didn't trust was her ability to keep her beautiful nose out of trouble.

"There will never be anyone but you. Promises like that are made frequently, but hopefully, you know me well enough to realize I speak the truth." His breath hot against her neck.

She felt him shudder as her feather light kisses reached his mouth, parting her lips she raised herself to meet his kiss. His demanding lips caressed hers. Her moan was swallowed by the kiss. She took a deep breath and ran her fingers along his neck in a tender caress. "I can't imagine what it will be like to be married to you. We're already so close. How else will it change?"

"I'll nag you more about your safety, and I'll call you Mrs. Riley, since you decided to take my name, which by the way I'm grateful for. It is a personal pleasure, and I thank you. You're well-established under your own name. I know what it is costing you."

"Not costing me at all. My art should sell, not my name. I'll love being Mrs. Riley. Peter, there is something we haven't talked about— and I want to…" She didn't know how to approach the subject. Peter never mentioned it, yet he should have.

"What?" he demanded. He didn't like where this was going. She rarely hesitated in talking to him, and when she did, he knew trouble would soon follow.

"A—a…" she stammered.

"Tell me."

"A…a pre-nuptial agreement. I want your attorney to draft something up." She heard his soft hiss and knew he was not happy with her request.

"No."

"What do you mean *no*?"

"Which part of *no* did you have a problem with? No."

"Peter, be reasonable. You have a great deal at stake here. You're from an old English family. What difference does it make? I'm the one requesting it. You need…"

"I need to marry you, make love with you and to you. I need to share everything with you, and that means everything I own, all my worldly goods. There will be no agreement signed by me. I do not need one." It never occurred to him she'd go this far to try and prove to him she loved him. He already knew that. *Damn Alexis Yardleigh and her avarice.* His past was catching up with him.

"Peter…I…" she mumbled and bit her lip. She wanted to make sure he knew she was marrying him because she loved him, not his money.

She wanted to distinguish her relationship with him from the one he had with Alexis. It was crucial to her he know the difference. She never wanted him to doubt her.

"What did you do?" He shook his head and looked at her speculatively. She bit her lip and drew blood. With his finger, he gently wiped it away. "What did you do?" he asked again. This time his voice was soothing.

"I talked with Rebecca and used her attorney in Chicago to draw up an agreement, just in case you didn't agree. It simply states that you retain all your property even after marriage, and all your financial matters are to remain yours prior to our marriage. There, I said it."

"I will not sign such an agreement, and without my signature, it is worthless."

"That may be, but on my side, it stands. Peter, I am deeply in love with you. I don't know how else to tell you, or show you. I feel this is right. If we have children, then that will alter the agreement, but…"

"I have proof of your love, every second of every day. Every time you touch me. Every time we make love. I don't need anything else." He blinked and swallowed hard. She never mentioned children before. It came as quite a shock. He wanted them desperately with her, but wasn't about to bring it up until she did. He'd take her on any terms. "Children? You…" He was blindsided by her statement and couldn't quite focus.

"Do you not want any? I thought…I'll agree to whatever you decide. I'm fine with anything you want," she answered and blinked back tears that threatened to fall. It seemed as if they hadn't discussed much about their married life, their future together. Did most people? She was new to this side of a relationship. She assumed that more often than not children were a result of marriage. Otherwise, the couple would decide that before marriage. She and Peter never talked about it. What else should they discuss? Did they just fall into a relationship? *No, we worked hard, both of us. With the complications, some almost to the point of a break-up, the path was not smooth, but we made it work.*

"We apparently have not communicated well at all." His voice shook with emotion. "I want our children. How could you think not? I just followed your lead. I didn't think you wanted any, and I wasn't about to put any undue pressure on our commitment to one another. I want children with you, but I want a life with you at any cost." He brushed his knuckle against her cheek and watched as she tried to keep the tears from falling. "I love you and want you on any terms. Never doubt that, but having children will only add to our joy and fulfillment. I watch you with Sally and how happy you are for her. I want that for us." He wanted to make sure she understood his total and abiding love for her. "Now, let's discuss that silly agreement. I trust you, and there will be no need for any agreement on my part. You may do as you please, as long as you understand my signature will not be going on that piece of paper." In this case, he knew Minola would persist, no matter how he felt about it. She knew of his past history with a money grabbing ex fiancée, and she was trying to let him know she wasn't one…as if he didn't already know that.

"Peter, it'll make me feel better." She smiled and changed the subject. "Now about my shoes." She went over to the bag and modeled the shoes for him.

"They're lovely." He sighed in contentment and searched for another bag then asked. "Where are the rest of them?" He heard her laugh.

"Sally…they're with Sally. She practically bought every pair." Minola took a deep breath. "Adriana travels in lofty circles. Peter, I'm afraid for Evan."

"She does indeed. She comes from an incredibly wealthy family, but Evan has a sense of honor, and if he loves her, it is because of Adriana, not her money. I believe she trusts him, but really hard to say after only seeing them together one evening. What are our future plans with the Bruloni family?"

"Adriana will host a ball for us and invite all the suspects, and she is planning a visit to the Deniccali Furnace tomorrow. I'll call Jennifer now and see if anything has changed." Minola picked up her cell and placed the call. She heard a quiet voice answer. "Jen, I just called to say hi and see if anything has changed."

"You mean, other than the break in at the furnace? The back door was jimmied. I don't think anything was stolen. I think just some old papers that were in the safe…or someone was searching for the gold that Julio had. I don't know. The daggers were already stolen. Other than the gold, not much else left to steal. He kept his things in a small office near the big drying room. We have a safe there. Wait, he had some old formulas in there, too, but the safe was intact. Who would do this?"

"Did you open the safe and see if everything was still there? Maybe someone else needed whatever was in there?"

"There are only two blowers and one assistant, and they would not touch the safe. They wouldn't do anything without telling me." She hiccupped and swallowed hard.

"Did you call the police?"

"No."

"You should have called them."

"I'm afraid. I don't know if the papers in the safe were Julio's or they belonged to Pia Deniccali. He had this ancient pattern, for lack of a better work, formula, whatever, that he followed, but I just couldn't get it right. He was rather secretive. He kept it hidden in the safe. He also had a hiding place under the floor board in the office that Antonio uses. He kept some of the gold there. This crazy secrecy is all part of this business. He was always afraid someone was going to steal his design, process, blending. I'm like that, too. You become paranoid and feel you're being watched. Except in this case, Julio was right." Minola heard a deep breath. "I feel like I'm being watched, too, and my husband couldn't care less. The earlier theft, why would someone steal replica daggers? I can understand the formula, and I can understand the gold, but the daggers? Makes no sense. Someone knew of the hiding place. Do you think this is all related?"

"As Peter would say, I don't believe in coincidences. Call the police, and call us if anything else happens…and Jen…talk to Antonio. Tell him how you feel."

"I'll think about it. You're lucky with Peter. Enjoy it while it lasts."

"Call me if you need to talk." Minola ended the call and told Peter everything. "Jennifer seems lost. She and Antonio had such a loving and passionate relationship. What happened to them? She told me to enjoy what we have while it lasts." Minola choked on the words.

"She'll have to put her house in order." A shadow of annoyance crossed his face. Minola was hurt by her friend, and that he could not tolerate. "It will not happen to us. We will not let it. We'll try and help her. Then she can decide if she wants to continue and be your friend or merely an acquaintance." Peter took Minola in his arms and held her. "The theft of the daggers bothers me. I need to talk to Matteo and Gio."

"This is a mess."

"It is a bloody convoluted mess. I hope she calls the police and tells them everything."

"I am so sorry for getting us involved," she mumbled against his shoulder. Then she raised her head and touched her lips against his in a gentle caress. "Peter, could we go for a walk, just the two of us?"

"Anything you want to do." He grabbed the hotel key from the table and escorted her out the door. They walked down to the narrow street lined with small boutiques and restaurants packed with tourists.

Minola came to a stop in front of a gelateria and bought two scoops of coffee and double dark chocolate gelato. "That is perfect."

"I thought coffee made things perfect. Now gelato, too."

"You make things perfect. Always. Coffee and gelato are an added bonus." She smiled, offered Peter some of her gelato, and watched as he licked the double dark chocolate and smacked his lips. She ran her finger intimately against his mouth, seemingly to remove a touch of chocolate, but the caress was to let him know she cherished him.

"Thank you for that." Peter's gaze locked with hers, and the searing love he saw in her eyes took his breath away. "And the gelato is delicious."

"Peter, so much is going on here, all twisted and somehow related. Pia really sounds dangerous, but it could be our interpretation of what we heard." Minola took a breath.

"It could all be innocent. It looks as if someone is manipulating this investigation, and throwing things at us. I wonder how much the police know. This murder is giving me a large migraine, not just a headache." Peter rubbed his forehead. He was not kidding about the migraine.

"What if the formula was a code somehow for something?"

"Considering we have the assassins lurking in the background, the vitriolic animosity between Julio and Pia, and the stolen daggers? Anything is possible." Peter took her hand in his, curled his fingers around hers, and they continued to stroll back to the hotel in silence.

For Peter, the case proved interesting, and as always, the cop instinct took over. A murder had been committed, and a murderer had to be brought to justice. As a cop, that was the simple answer. That was why he became a cop in the first place. He understood that justice must prevail. He was not a simpleton and realized that was not always possible. More often than not, politics prevailed and raised its ugly head, but for him, justice always fought for supremacy, and he always did what he could to make sure it won.

Once Minola entered his life, everything changed. Her safety, her protection, his love for her prevailed. He cared about justice and would serve the cause for as long as he lived, but she was paramount.

He was ready to let go of Interpol. Peter knew he needed to discuss it with her, and he also knew she would feel responsible for his choice. He had to somehow convince her that was not the case. He even thought about assuming a police role in his home town to make things easier for her.

They returned to the hotel, and Minola grabbed her satchel and said, "I want to paint a scene, the small canal not far from the hotel. You remember the place where I saw that one single dim lantern shining over the water? The light is perfect now. I won't be gone long."

He didn't like it, but he had to show her he trusted her—she was not his prisoner. "Don't forget your cell."

"I have it, and I won't be late. There are plenty of tourists and locals still out. I'll be fine, back in a couple of hours." She kissed him and left.

The walk was short. She found the perfect spot on the bridge and started drawing. The scene was magical. That one beam shone bright in the dusky light. Others were muted. An empty gondola leaned against a wall, and laundry hung on a line. The water glowed from the reflecting light and was as still as the night. Not even a shimmer could be seen or a ripple heard. Minola's fingers flew over the sketch pad.

Suddenly, she felt uneasy, as if someone was waiting and watching, but she saw no one. She realized she'd been gone longer than anticipated and knew Peter would be worried. She took out her cell and called to let him know she was on the way back. Minola gathered her belongings, stepped down the bridge stairs, and started walking on the narrow arched alley. Faintly lit, the shadows seemed to follow her. She was uneasy, and every sound resonated in her ears. Every uneven cobblestone a pitfall. She hadn't felt that sensation before, but now she was on alert. Minola had no idea why until she heard light persistent footsteps behind her. The speed increased and without thinking, she began running. Out of breath, she stopped for a second and was met only by silence. A cat meowed in the distance and then total and complete silence, an eerily quiet moment. She stood perfectly still and listened; the hush was deafening.

So many meandering streets where someone could hide caused her imagination to soar. Maybe someone was going home and turned into one of those dark alley that often passed for a street. She sighed in relief. Then she heard the footsteps again—slow, methodical, meant to frighten her, and they damn well succeeded. Minola took off again. The footsteps resonated in her ears. Out of breath, she continued running until she had to stop and breathe. *Why didn't I take up jogging?*

She listened once again and heard thoughtful, precise steps behind her. Not in a rush, just a predatory movement. She was being played with, hunted. She started running again at full speed and tripped on an uneven cobblestone. She screamed as she went down hard on the ground. Her face bounced back from the pavement like a rubber ball. Once her face touched down again, she lay still for a second, trying to catch her breath. Then she heard glass shatter near her. *Well, that certainly brings back memories.* She touched her face and winced. *Ouch.*

She yelled again as if her life depended on it. Now the only thing she heard was her own heavy breathing. The quiet tentative footsteps faltered, waited, then started again.

Another set of louder and heavier footsteps echoed in the shadowy evening, but these were coming from the other direction. These footsteps were different, harder, bigger, more forceful. Her right ankle throbbed. She couldn't get up. She closed her eyes and waited. Then she tried again, but couldn't put any weight on her ankle. The gentle quiet footsteps disappeared into the shadows.

A stillness permeated the area, except for the sound of running at full speed coming straight at her. Her labored breathing and bells ringing in her head sounded like a cacophony to her ears.

Gingerly sitting up, she leaned against the wall and tried using the wall as leverage to get up once more, without putting any pressure on her now throbbing ankle, and couldn't. She had no energy left for a fight. She saw blood on her knees. Her elbows matched her knees, equally battered and bloody, and it felt as if the cobblestones were imbedded in her skin. Involuntary tears streamed down her face. She swiped them away in anger. She'd bitten her lip and saw smeared blood on her hand.

The few pieces of glass were a dagger in a previous life. Leaning down, she groaned as she tried to gather the pieces in a pile. Minola realized if she hadn't screamed and fallen she'd be dead. She momentarily closed her eyes to regroup.

Someone was almost upon her, but the steps now sounded familiar to her ears. She opened her eyes and stared up at Peter.

"What the bloody hell happened here?" Out of breath, Peter reached for Minola with trembling hands. He took stock of her injuries and slumped down beside her. His body shook. He didn't know whether from relief or rage. Most likely both.

"Peter...this time I was really scared. What are you doing here? Thank you being here." Minola's voice was shaky. She raised her hand to touch his face and put it down so he wouldn't notice the blood. He did.

"You were late, you told me where you were going, and I thought I'd meet you. I was worried. Yes, even with your phone call, I was worried, and it would seem I had every reason to be. What happened?" With his fingertip, he tenderly wiped the blood from her lips and cheek. He couldn't control the wobbly movement and shuddered when he saw her blood on his hand.

"I lost track of time, and then I heard footsteps—or I imagined them—but they turned out to be real. Strange, but I felt someone watching me. Close enough to see what I was doing, but I didn't see anyone. Then later I felt hunted. That is a truly frightening sensation." She couldn't control her wobbly voice.

Peter was the first to stand up. The street was empty and strangely quiet. He couldn't pursue the attacker with Minola here, besides he didn't know where to look. He knelt down and inspected Minola's injuries. She was bleeding, her lip was swollen, cheek bloody and bruised, and elbows and knees scraped. He swore under his breath.

"Peter, I want to go back to the hotel and shower." She tried to regain her equilibrium, but couldn't quite get up. The sharp pain in her ankle didn't relent. "Maybe I'll just stay here for a while. I may have twisted my ankle."

His trembling hands went over her body. "You need a doctor." He looked down at his hand again.

"Just give me a few minutes. With your help, I think I can make it to the hotel. Not far to walk..." She pleaded.

"You're not walking." Peter couldn't stop his hands from shaking. Rage like he'd never felt before overtook him. He took the pieces of glass, carefully wrapped them in his clean handkerchief, and put them in her bag. The mindless activity allowed him to calm down. He needed to hold her, and she was right. Their hotel was nearby. He picked her up and carried her back.

He deposited Minola on the bed, took care of her immediate needs, and called downstairs to arrange for a doctor. Then he called the local police and reported the attempt on her life. He turned and saw her smiling.

"What exactly do you find amusing about this situation?" He glowered at her and then turned away. He needed to regain some control over his emotions so that he could function.

"Remember Paris?" she asked quietly.

"Yes." He ground out the words. He couldn't quite manage a normal tone. Terror still lurked. "You're not to go anywhere without me. Do we understand one another?" His voice was icy cold and lashed out at her.

"Peter, are we back to that?"

"Do not…" He started pacing, something he always did when under extreme duress. "Just don't go there now." The knock on the door interrupted a further outburst. First to arrive was the doctor, who cleaned and dressed her wounds and bandaged the ankle. Based upon his examination, the doctor didn't think her ankle was broken, merely sprained. He issued the usual caution and noted that she would be sore, but was not in any danger.

The second to arrive were two police officers. They questioned Minola in broken English. She gave them all the information she had, but withheld details about the dagger. They demanded to know why she was there, who was chasing her, but treated it is as nothing more than a robbery attempt.

Minola patiently explained that she liked the scene and wanted to paint it. One officer asked to see the work. Peter took it out of her bag and showed them the sketches. The officer studied the drawings for quite a while, finally nodded his head, and smiled. The police left without promising anything, and Peter didn't really expect any results.

He stood by the window with his back to Minola and remembered Paris all too well. He didn't hear her hobble up to him and put her arms around his waist. "Peter, I'm bruised but still here, able to hold you. Let it go, I beg you."

Peter picked her up and carried her to bed, lay down with her, and wrapped her in his arms. His touch tender, he inhaled her scent. "I cannot."

He continued to hold her. His heart pounded, and he thought it would burst from his chest. Embracing her had a calming effect on him. "I'll start a shower for you. Then you need to rest." He took her face in his trembling hands and stared at her swollen lip and bruised cheek, took a deep breath, and in a whisper soft caress touched her cheek with his lips.

"Shower is an excellent plan." She clutched him fiercely, more to soothe his fears than anything else.

By the time she was done, Peter had coffee waiting for her. She drank a couple of cups and then went to sleep. Peter held on to her for the rest of the night.

Chapter 12

Watching her sleep peacefully this morning was even more significant. She was bruised, but safe and going to remain that way. There didn't seem to be a reason for the attack. Who knew about her? Certainly the Castigli family. The Deniccali's knew of her; she'd met Pia briefly, Dario not at all. That left Gio and Adriana, and he refused to believe either one was capable of that brutal attack.

Peter loved the early mornings, before she woke up and they made love, before she demanded her coffee. Those were the moments he counted his blessings for the joy she brought into his life. And today, through the terror, he counted his blessings that she was safe. He nestled her bruised body closer to him. When she snuggled, he tenderly put his hand on her waist, afraid to hurt her. He watched as she turned into him, opened her eyes, and smiled.

"I love you." He heard the muted whisper against his chest. "Coffee?"

"Good morning, my love. How do you feel? And yes, coffee has been ordered." He inspected her bruised face, the cheekbone swollen and turning a mustard green. Her lip appeared puffy and red. She really chomped on it this time.

"Hmm. I'm fine," she mumbled and ran her lips along his neck and shoulder. The knock on the door stopped her progress. Room service was prompt.

"Yes, I can see that. We'll stay here today." Peter handed her a cup, poured one for himself, and then watched her face as she gingerly savored her first taste. Her sheer delight always made him smile, today even more so.

"Staying in would be lovely, but I don't think that will be possible." Her cell beeped, and she answered it.

"That was Adriana confirming our meeting with Pia at the Deniccali Furnace. Apparently, Pia was gone for a while, and now she's back. No one knows where she went or why or, for that matter, when she left and returned."

"Did Dario go with her?" Peter sipped his coffee and continued to caress Minola. He couldn't stop touching her.

"Apparently so. Adriana said he returned with Pia. They were at the house, and then he disappeared again, nothing else about where they went or why. According to Adriana, Pia only tells you what she wants you to know. Their *palazzo* is big, so that may not be significant. They could have been hiding at home. Sally is coming, too. She has shopping plans. She wants a lamp for the baby's room. I think I'll get that for her as a shower gift. It will be something that will grow with the munchkin."

"It will be a treasured gift," Peter replied softly. The idea that they might have a child together brought him extreme joy.

"What are you going to do?" Minola asked

"Robert and I are going to meet with Gio. He wanted to have lunch. All this is hush-hush—he wouldn't discuss it over the phone. I'm going to take that dagger you didn't hand over to the police. Gio needs to see it and maybe, if we can, Jennifer, too. Be careful."

"I will. The ankle is better today, and I'll limp along. Maybe you'll find something out. The police should have at least confirmed the identity as a professional courtesy. Good thing Gio is working with us. We'll get information faster." She took another sip of her coffee. "I hope we make some headway; I want us to be married and not worry about murder. Your mother texted me. She'd like us to have lunch when they arrive. She wants to make sure we will marry."

"Yes, I know. She told me not do anything foolish to stop the wedding, or else...I have been warned." Peter set the cup down and gingerly took Minola in his arms. "Not a chance of that happening." He pushed some hair behind her ears and nibbled on her neck, enjoying her shiver. He loved how she always responded to him. "I think maybe we should dress for our respective meetings. Do you feel well enough to go out? The only reason I'm not going with you is that you won't be alone." He felt her lean into him and offer her mouth. His kiss was tender. Peter heard a groan and realized it came from him.

***

Peter and Robert waited for Gio at the same restaurant where they met with Matteo, far from peeping eyes and the ever present tourists with their incessant cameras. He forgot he was one of those tourists, except he was working. This morning, Peter had spent his time with Minola, concerned with her safety and comfort. He had nothing to eat other than coffee and a biscotti, so sandwiches were ordered while they waited for Gio. He requested the meeting rather urgently, and Peter was curious.

Gio arrived dressed as if he was about to model for a magazine cover—a white silk shirt, black gabardine trousers, and soft black leather loafers. Peter felt decidedly underdressed in his khakis and polo shirt. He smiled and remembered the first time he met Minola in Paris. His suit was wrinkled, his favorite shoes were worn with age, and he hadn't slept for at least twenty-four hours. He smiled as he remembered the glare he received when he was insufferably rude to her.

Gio's gloomy demeanor told Peter something was drastically wrong. Gone was the perfect smile, and he was distracted. He stared at everyone in the vicinity as if he suspected them of something.

Robert extended his hand and said, "I hope you won't think us rude, but we already ordered." Robert pointed to the sandwiches and coffee on the table.

"Not at all. Please. Good morning," Gio replied, his features grim. He sat down and placed his order as well. "I'm glad you started without me. I was detained...I had a visit from Carlo, a friend, also with the police. He paid a visit to the house under the pretext of a charitable event. He occasionally provides official security for our functions. One is coming up at our *palazzo*, and important people will attend."

"This is by way of an excuse. He wanted to keep a low profile. Why?" Robert asked.

"What happened?" Peter asked. He knew from Gio's visible frown lines that something serious had happened.

"You both pick up on things rather quickly," Gio commented. "Matteo has been murdered. The police are investigating…that is the common phraseology, I believe." He snapped.

"I'm sorry, Gio. I know he was a friend," Peter said softly. "How? What happened?"

"That is an excellent question. The police are in an uproar—one of their own has been killed. He was a good and honest man. I will miss him. He was also a good friend."

"My sympathies." Peter understood the loss all too well. Anytime a fellow officer was killed, a deep sense of loss was felt in the police community. Evan Welsey was his second sergeant. When Peter first started with Interpol, he was assigned a young green sergeant who wanted to prove himself and took unnecessary chances without telling Peter. He took one too many and paid with his life. When Sergeant Welsey came on board, Peter made sure they had a chat about following protocol at all times. Welsey understood well, and Peter never looked back, but always remembered and even now grieved for the loss. "How was he killed?"

"With a gold tipped dagger. He was assassinated, sometime last night. Matteo called me earlier that day and wanted to chat. This was supposed to be our second meeting. We set a time. He never made the meeting. I called and was told he died suddenly. Nothing else. I called Carlo, and he told me the rest."

"Where was he killed?" Robert was stunned at the news; he didn't understand the life Peter led, and he liked Matteo. Even though he'd been indirectly involved in both the Paris and Bath murders, Robert still had a hard time with this side of life and death.

"In the alley behind the Deniccali Furnace. They suspect he was killed with one of the Deniccali daggers, in the style of the old assassins." Gio spoke softly, obviously mourning his friend.

"Unlike Julio." Peter would mourn as well. He was a colleague.

"Unlike Julio," confirmed Gio. "He must have discovered something. They don't know why he was there."

"I don't for a minute believe that Pia or Dario would commit a murder that led directly to their door." Peter wasn't as convinced as he sounded.

"I don't, either. I'll see if Matteo left any information." Gio replied.

"Do you have any information on the murder scene? Any details at all?" Peter knew some things were being left out. He was sure of it, but not in any position to do anything. He would accept the meager offerings and bide his time. "Now would be a good time to fill us in, before anyone else is killed. Could we meet with Carlo?" Peter asked.

"I would prefer not to. I do not want to endanger his life. We may be watched. A classic dagger kill, nothing else. The tip was imbedded in his heart. A professional killing, one had to have had practice. Time of death was late last night. No defensive wounds. It would appear he knew and trusted his attacker." Gio gulped his espresso. "I don't know what Matteo learned, but watch yourselves. Adriana and Minola will have a security detail. They have become fast friends." When Gio saw Peter was about to object, he put his hand up, and continued, "Whether you agree or not, that will happen. Save yourself the trouble. I will introduce you, but the security will remain. I will also tell Evan. He needs to know. Adriana would have my head if anything happened to him." Gio turned toward Robert. "You and your wife are Minola's friends, and as such are not directly involved. However, you will also be included in the overall security. If someone checks at your history together, they might think otherwise. It is good there is the wedding. Guests are expected for the occasion and nothing more."

"I am not going to argue where Minola's safety is concerned, nor Sally's and Robert's. I am not a fool. I will, however, tell Minola what is happening, I will not keep that from her." Peter was adamant about his promise to share everything with her. "Sooner or later, she'd notice she was being followed." Peter took a deep breath. "I was not expecting this. Matteo seemed like a fine officer. I'm sorry, Gio." Peter offered his condolences.

"The police are now fully engaged in the investigation," Gio replied.

"I have some news, as well." Peter took out the dagger pieces and laid them on the table. "Minola was attacked yesterday, early evening. A serious attack, the aim was to kill." Peter heard a gasp from Robert.

"Is she hurt?"

"Yes, but not enough to take her to the hospital."

"Does she need anything? She hates hospitals. Do you remember Paris?"

"Indeed. She reminded me." Peter told them everything he knew. "This must end soon. Helping a friend is one thing. Putting Minola in harm's way is quite another."

"I'm happy to hear that Minola is safe. Matteo was honest, and that goes a long way. I will let you know if I learn anything else. In the meantime, let us be vigilant. If they killed a carabiniere, they will not hesitate to eliminate any of us, but I don't understand why someone tried to kill Minola." Gio's expression was tight with concern.

"I intend to find out. I agree more than one person is involved." Peter knew Gio was right, but he wanted to hear an explanation from him. "Once a cop, always a cop."

"Yes, of course, you want me to say it out loud. This is not the work of one individual. We have an assassin and the driving force behind the assassin, the one who paid the commission."

"Paid the commission—an interesting way to put it." Robert ran his hand through his hair. He was not used to the side of life that dealt with murder and other atrocities.

"It is a business," Gio stated simply. "Gentlemen, we'll meet again."

He stood up and was immediately followed by another man, who seemingly appeared out of nowhere. Peter watched as Gio turned back and waved. Peter wasn't sure if the wave included him and Robert or the man who followed him. He rather suspected Gio had his own security detail.

"This is rather frightening. I'm worried." Robert's concern was reflected in his voice. "I've never come across anything like this. Someone killed a carabiniere. I suspect they don't take kindly to that."

"No, they don't. I'm concerned, as well. If they killed a cop, they will not hesitate to go after any one of us. There must be a great deal at stake here. Look, Robert…" Peter didn't know quite how to tell him to keep out, but if anything happened to Robert or Sally, he wouldn't forgive himself. They had become his dear friends.

"I know what you're going to say. Sally and I will be careful, but we will be there for Minola and you. That is not open to debate, and Sally wouldn't hear about it. That being said, her extracurricular activities will be greatly curtailed. I will use the pregnancy as a reason. She'll listen, and besides, she has to finish the wedding preparations."

"Excellent. Minola and Sally are meeting with Adriana. Robert, this will be Sally's last meeting like this. Make sure she throws herself into the wedding. My family is arriving soon. Maybe they can plan a few tours, anything to keep them both out of harm's way." He understood the insidious side of greed and power and the loss of both. He learned that lesson all too well in Bath. What he didn't understand, in this case, was how it all related. He went over everything in his head and realized he had to prepare his chart and sort it all out. They walked back to the hotel in silence and parted company at their respective rooms.

Peter took out his pad of paper, sat down at the desk, and jotted down what he had so far. He had the glass sarcophagus, stolen gold daggers, two ostensibly unconnected murders—a police officer and the master glass blower with a past—a hidden design pattern, a wealthy family steeped in ancient rituals and history, another old family seemingly bred from the same cloth, many innuendos, possible adultery, a potential message hidden in the daggers, and who knew what else. Plus the attack on Minola. His head was beginning to pound.

He remembered Minola telling him about the exclusive shoe shop owner with ties to Pia Deniccali, and it continued *ad nauseam.*

The clues were piling up, but they lacked cohesiveness, the glue that would bind everything together. He didn't include Gio and Adriana. He trusted them. More to the point, he trusted Evan Welsey. Gio was Welsey's friend. Adriana far more than that. Peter was not so sure about papa Bruloni. Where did that leave Peter? *With a bloody headache, that's where.* He rubbed his head, pushed the pad away from him, closed his eyes, and promptly fell asleep.

Peter was not dreaming of his soon-to-be bride, but instead, he dreamt of a pool of blood, a sarcophagus made from glass, carved hearts with gold tipped daggers imbedded in them, and in the middle of the chaos, one lonely cop in a dark alley, water splashing all around him. He didn't know where to turn-he was surrounded by carnage, blood and water. He searched for Minola, and she seemed forever out of reach, separated from him by an endless canal of blood. Every time he grasped for her, the bridge moved out of his range. He saw glass daggers floating in crimson water.

He shuddered and tossed involuntarily while he slept. The cramp and following spasms in his arms finally woke him up with sweat pouring down his face and neck. *Bloody hell.* He ran his hands through his hair and felt dampness, as if he had just washed it. He closed his eyes, and a renewed sense of terror prevailed, as the nightmare continued.

Chapter 13

Minola found him in exactly that same position two hours later, slumped in the chair. She didn't want to disturb him, but saw that this was not a peaceful nor relaxing sleep. His brows were furrowed, his movements involuntary—arms flailing as if he was reaching for something.

She quietly walked up and tenderly caressed his cheek with her lips. A gentle kiss meant to wake him up out of a disturbing sleep. He was startled by her touch, and his arms thrashed in the air, trying to hold on to something.

"Peter, wake up," she whispered, her voice soothing and melodic. She wanted to wake him gently.

He shook himself out of the dreadful sleep and saw Minola bending over him. Her face clearly showed her concern, her touch tentative and sweet. She was safe. He took a deep breath. "I'm sorry. I must have fallen asleep."

"You had a nightmare...the murders?" She bent down and ran her hands up and down his thighs in a soothing massage.

"First and foremost, your safety," he replied casually. He didn't want Minola any more worried, but knew a moot point when he saw one. He promised to share and share he would. Besides, she'd witnessed his terrifying movements. Matteo's death rankled. He was a cop and, by all accounts, an honest one.

"What other things?" She called room service. He needed something to eat and drink. Then she went and sat on his lap, wrapped her hands around his neck, and held him. She felt him shudder, and with shaking hands, he pulled her closer against him.

"You always know what to do," he whispered.

"I love you. What other things?" She wasn't going to let go.

"Our wedding and…"

"We can reschedule or…" Minola refused to meet his gaze and closed her eyes. Her heart ached with pain.

"We certainly will not reschedule." He took her arms and pushed her away from him. "Look at me." The sadness he saw in her eyes almost moved him to tears. She bloody well was not cancelling their wedding—not at any cost. "Minola?" he whispered.

"If you have second thoughts, this would be the perfect time to cancel. Besides, I'm not at my best."

"You're always at your best. Cancel? No. Absolutely not. Never. Where would you get such a fantastic notion? I am deeply in love with you. I am committed to you for life." He took a deep breath. "I am, however, terrified that something will happen and I will not be able to protect you. I am marrying you. And you are certainly marrying me." He pulled her back into his arms and held her tightly against him.

"I just want you to be sure…" Minola answered the knock on the door and waited while coffee, biscotti, and other breads and sweets were set on the desk. She poured a cup and handed it to Peter. She then mixed her coffee and took a sip.

"Be sure. I don't often have nightmares. I am, however, concerned about you and the eminent danger to you." Peter took one shallow breath then another followed by a deep wrenching sigh. He would have to tell her. It might as well be now. "I have some news from Gio. I don't know how to say it gently. There is nothing gentle about this. Matteo was killed." When he heard Minola gasp in horror, he rubbed her back for comfort. "That someone killed a carabiniere tells me that he may have found something out, or witnessed something he shouldn't have, and they are frightened. As the saying goes, they are running scared. I don't want you in the middle, and yet you are."

"Where? How?" she asked, her voice a broken whisper.

Peter told her everything he knew and then repeated his concern for her safety. "You need protection."

"Peter, I won't do anything stupid. I promise. You will always know where I am. My cell phone is on. How are the police handling this additional murder? An all out search?"

"What about yesterday? You were supposed to be safe. I suspect there will be a thorough investigation of the movements of the Deniccali family, especially Pia's and her brother's absence. Probably the Castigli family, too. Most likely all persons involved."

"They must have something to lose, or maybe something to gain. This is such a strange and convoluted case." She looked down at her wristwatch. "I have to meet Adriana downstairs. Are you all right? Do you want me to cancel and stay?"

"I'll take a shower. I'm fine, my love. Be careful, I beg you." He felt her lips touch his cheek, and little by little, warmth crept over his body.

"Call me if you need me. I love you." Her lips touched his like a soft whisper. She stood up and hobbled over to the door.

Adriana gasped when she saw Minola. "What happened to you? Who did this?"

"I was attacked, but I'm fine." Even makeup couldn't hide the bruises. She wore long pants to hide the bandages on her knees and a long sleeve loose blouse to hide the bandages on her elbows. The ankle she couldn't do anything about. Minola explained everything and assured Adriana and Sally that it could have been worse. *Not much consolation, but I'll take what can.*

"Are you sure you want to continue with our plan?" Adriana asked, concern for her friend clearly marked on her face.

"Yes." Minola saw Sally had tears in her eyes and hugged her friend. "I didn't tell you because I didn't want you to worry. Peter found me in time. I'm fine."

"In that case, we will proceed as planned. But we must be careful in the future. After we visit the Deniccali Furnace, I arranged a lunch at my club. Pia would not miss such an opportunity." Adriana knew Pia well enough to know she'd do her best to mingle with the Bruloni family and other exceedingly rich and influential patrons. Pia's greed for more power and money never ceased to amaze Adriana.

"It actually sounds like a lovely morning. Loosen our concerns a little." Sally pointedly stared at Minola. "If you're okay, then lunch is good, too. I'm always hungry lately."

"I would suggest you show interest in a piece or two. That should not be difficult. Their work is fantastic," Adriana said.

"It will not be a problem. I actually want to buy a gift, specifically a lamp."

Minola heard a gasp from Sally. "You wouldn't be searching for baby's room lamp would you?"

"Oddly enough, I am. I want something the munchkin can grow with, and I want to make sure you would approve of my choice." Minola spoke softly.

"Now I can't wait. Let's go." Sally beamed.

Adriana laughed. "Excellent. You will find something, and if not, they will design it based on your specifications. They may be many things, but their artistry has never been questioned. Dario is obsessed with glass, the design and color selection. Everything that has to do with glass. My boat is waiting for us at the pier. We'll be in Murano in fifteen minutes. They are expecting us."

"Peter and I usually take the vaporetto, and it takes about thirty minutes, a fun ride both ways. I can see why Robert likes the water taxis. They sort of ride the waves, and heavy traffic creates many waves."

Once they arrived at their destination, Pia met them at the pier. She stared at Minola. "You were perhaps in an accident, Miss Grey?"

"Of sorts, but not hurt badly. I'm not a runner, but am seriously considering becoming one. It looks worse than it is." It seemed to Minola as if Pia almost willed her to lie. *What game is she playing?* She was surprised Pia remembered her. They'd met briefly, and Pia hardly spared Minola a glance.

Pia escorted them to the furnace and galleries. "Miss Grey, congratulations on your wedding. Peter is a handsome man, sensual as well," Pia Deniccali drawled in a seductive voice, and she never took her eyes off of Minola.

"I think so too." Minola felt uneasy under the scrutiny, and hearing Peter's name on Pia's lips sounded odd. Her comments were meant to cause discomfort, but Minola decided to enjoy the quality of the work displayed everywhere instead. She felt a slight twinge that she was contemplating buying here and not from the Castigli Furnace. The chandeliers were replicas of the Renaissance and Baroque styles, not many contemporary pieces, but the variety of tables and racks that could pass for bookcases were amazing, as were the colorful table lamps made from fused glass, mosaic tables, and even pieces of glass that appeared woven together to create a magnificent wall hanging.

"Miss Grey, I know you're an artist. Peter didn't mention your wedding at all, in fact he didn't mention you at all, as if…but I have heard about it from Adriana. How can I help?"

Once again, Minola was taken aback by Pia's use of Peter's name and the innuendo that the wedding was not worth discussing, as if Pia and Peter were friends or even more. Rather odd, and Minola was sure Pia did it on purpose. The woman watched Minola's face for any reaction. Minola was puzzled, but she did not give Pia the satisfaction of a response. Instead Minola decided to ignore the barbs directed at driving a wedge in her relationship with Peter. *This is insane.* "The vase on the stand is gorgeous, so many rich, vibrant colors. What is that something special to make them so alive? How are the colors enhanced like that?" She heard Pia roar.

"It is a secret, my brother would go to his grave before he would betray his secret."

"I read about the secrets of glass blowing and blending. My apologies for even asking. I love the design, the geometric pattern where one line flows after another. Beautiful." Minola gazed at the piece, and the more she looked, the more vibrant the colors became. *A magical piece.*

"Yes, it is one of my favorites as well. My brother Dario designed it, selected the colors. He does not blow glass often, but he did this piece. You have a good eye."

Minola didn't attempt to lift it, but Pia knew what to do. She didn't pick it up, but set it sideways on the table and showed Minola the signature on the bottom. Signed and dated by her brother, a one of a kind piece. She then set it down, took out a tiny lamp, and lit it from the inside. The piece came to life, and it dazzled. Minola couldn't stop staring. She saw it from all angles—first from the point of the artist, then the design, and finally the blowing process. This was perfection.

"I think you may have a sale, Pia. Minola is captivated." Adriana watched in fascination as Minola's gaze focused on the work of art.

Minola was jolted out of her stupor when she heard her name. "Simply beautiful. Peter will love it. I also would like to know if you have any lamps."

"This is Murano. Of course we have lamps. A chandelier perhaps?" Pia smiled, pleased with herself. She guided them to a showroom that was filled with chandeliers, and here Minola saw only stylized period pieces. None of the chandeliers were as stunning as that singular one she saw at the Castigli furnace.

Sally walked over to the table and saw the ideal lamp. It was larger than expected, with various hues of yellows, reds, blues, a rich burgundy that was reminiscent of the wine color, even an iridescent white designed in a way that looked as if the colors were dancing on top of each other. A sea ripple topped by sunlight. This was the one she wanted. She stared at it and walked around the piece, too afraid to pick it up. And once again, Pia came to the rescue. This one was also designed and blown by her brother, and one of a kind. Pia turned the lamp on, and the results were the same. A child would be mesmerized by the colors and the display of light. Minola saw Sally's face light up in joy.

Minola watched Sally's progress, and once she was satisfied that this was the one, she nodded to Pia to wrap it.

"Minola, you can't. These things cost a huge fortune," Sally exclaimed.

"I'll just paint more, and I'm buying the other piece for Peter. So that's it. I'm buying the lamp and the vase."

"For Peter, and not for you, how unusual," Pia hissed.

"I'll enjoy it, too. There's a perfect place on his desk in the office at home. It'll brighten the corner of the room. Peter loves sitting there. I never would have thought to illuminate what in essence is a vase." Minola's voice softened anytime she mentioned Peter's name.

"Min, he'll love it because you gave it to him. It is beautiful. Robert told me not to buy anything until after we move. We'll just have to come back to Venice." Sally anticipated another visit in the near future.

"Count me in. It is truly one of my favorite places. Paris and Bath hold a special place in my heart, but Venice is absolutely magical." Minola's voice rang with happiness.

"We have a date, right after the munchkin arrives." Sally radiated joy.

"Peter is a lucky man," Adriana answered wistfully. "And don't forget you have a commission to paint my father."

"I did forget." Minola watched as Pia's eyes widened—hard, emotionless—and then they narrowed down to slits, such a strange thing to see. Apparently, it was a big deal to paint a portrait of a Bruloni. Adriana knew exactly what to do.

"Please wrap both pieces." Minola gave her the address and was told the packages would be delivered tomorrow.

Sally threw her arms around Minola and tearfully thanked her. "This will become an heirloom…immediately. Wait until Robert sees it."

"I love it, too." Minola watched as Adriana bought a table and had it delivered to her home. She didn't even look at the price. They visited the rest of the galleries and the big drying room. They also watched someone blowing what would become a platter, and after that, they went to the office.

"Ladies, I think we can go to lunch." Adriana turned to Pia and said, "Thank you, Pia. Dario's work is really magnificent."

"Yes, of course, it is. He is truly mad about it, and nothing must get in his way," she replied sadly.

"What is the matter?" Adriana's voice was soothing.

"The family business, problems, that is all."

"You mean the glass blowing...Or something else?" Adriana prodded a little.

As if caught in a lie, Pia replied. "*Si*, of course...glass blowing."

"Maybe Dario could join us. We would love to hear about his techniques, at least those he's willing to share. I haven't seen Dario in a long time." Adriana spoke casually, as if it did not matter at all that he attend.

"No, that is *impossibile*. He is not well...*no, no impossibile.*" Pia's voice was jerky and uncertain.

"Of course, I am sorry to hear he is not well. Please extend my good wishes," Adriana replied graciously.

"*Si, grazie*. I will tell him," Pia replied.

"If we're ready, the boat is waiting to take us to Dominios. I have not been there in a long time. It is a lovely club."

Minola watched the exchange in silence, giving kudos to Adriana for playing her part so well. Pia was solemn and didn't say a word. Her smile didn't reach her eyes; they were cold, lifeless. Minola had an odd sensation of pure evil. She shook herself to get rid of the feeling and caught Pia staring at her. Minola returned the gaze and smiled. "It must be wonderful to be surrounded by such beauty every day."

"*Si*, probably just like you. You're a painter, are you not?" Pia's voice matched her eyes, icy cold.

"I never thought about it, but you see, I never keep any of my work, even though I own a gallery in Chicago. We promote the works of upcoming artists and some established ones, as well, but I still tend to work on a commission basis. Peter has a few pieces, but he paid for them—a charity auction in Bath." Minola smiled at the memory. She bought the gallery during her stay in Bath when she thought she'd be going home. It worked out really well, and Rebecca Standish helped to keep it going. Sort of a joint effort, and the concept was rather popular.

"You must be famous to receive such a commission from Adriana."

Minola laughed gently. "I don't know about famous, but friends are supportive. Peter and Gio are friends. Gio was once a police officer. Those roots go deep. Adriana and Gio are attending our wedding." Minola hoped this would establish Peter's and Gio's bond, and nothing would look suspicious.

"It must run in the family." Pia turned toward Adriana and continued, "Weren't you once involved with an Interpol man yourself?" Pia sneered.

"*Si.*" Adriana didn't offer any other insights.

Minola thought it rather interesting that Pia knew Peter was with Interpol. *Just how much checking has she done, and more to the point, why? She frightens me. Even when she handled the glass, I couldn't see any emotion. She took no joy, no delight in the beautiful artwork. No life. Avarice and envy, that is what I sense when I watch her.*

Their arrival at the club was greeted with fanfare, escorted not by one waiter but three. A Bruloni was welcomed with abundance, and this was no exception. The center table had a low rise floral arrangement, what Minola assumed was Adriana's favorite wine, already decanted, and a bowl of fresh fruit at one end.

Once everyone was seated, a bottle of Pellegrino appeared out of nowhere. Minola was fond of the sparkling mineral water or, as the Italians call it, *frizzante*. Minola wondered if Evan Welsey could get used to this high life. Adriana accepted it with graciousness and kindness, seemingly unaware of the attention, but then she was raised in that style. Minola sank down in the plush chairs and sighed in comfort. Her knees and elbows throbbed, and it felt good to sit. Once the food was ordered, Minola took stock of her surroundings. Gilded columns and Murano chandeliers and sconces were everywhere. The place was opulent and over the top.

She focused on Pia and saw the bitter resentment, malevolence, and hatred reflected in her eyes when she occasionally stared at Adriana.

The loss of Gio and the lifestyle she probably felt could have been hers? Perhaps she blamed Adriana for that loss. She needed to warn Peter. Suddenly she was afraid for Adriana.

"Why did you choose Venice for your wedding?" Pia asked.

"It is really rather simple. Peter and Gio are friends." Minola emphasized that point again. "I love glass, and a fellow artist from Chicago, Jennifer Castigli—you probably know her. The art world really is small. We're divided by an ocean, but still…at any rate, she and I are friends—thought it would be lovely to visit. And, of course, the Biennale Art Festival played a large part in the selection."

"Quite by chance…eh?" Pia asked. Suspicion was evident in every syllable.

"Actually, yes. As you can see, we have friends here, and others wanted to visit. It fit our needs perfectly." Minola knew Pia was fishing for information, for some kind of admission.

"I know Jennifer. I am friends with her husband…as you said, it is a small world."

"You're Antonio's friend but not Jennifer's?" Minola heard a distinct hiss from Pia.

"*Si*, Antonio."

"I own a piece that Jennifer did when she first started blowing glass. She's talented." Minola saw that Adriana was watching the conversation with interest.

"If you say so," Pia jeered.

"Nothing that compares to her recent work and, of course, that of the master blower they just lost. I believe his name was Julio—such a tragedy. I saw some of his work, not quite as masterful as your brother's, but close." Minola hoped for a reaction.

"Ha, Julio learned everything from my brother, and then he left. He betrayed the Deniccali name. His death is not such a great loss. He was never that good." Pia spat out the words.

Minola could taste the bitterness in Pia's voice. "You must take into account the brutal death. I read in the paper that he was stabbed. It is a loss. Every death is a loss." Adriana spoke quietly.

"*Si*, if you insist. How is Gio?" Pia turned toward Adriana.

"He is quite well. Eager to attend the wedding, as am I. We went shoe shopping, and of course, Katarina had the perfect selection." Adriana raised the wine glass to her lips and slowly sipped the local vintage. She did everything she could to provoke Pia. Maybe something would slip and help in the investigation. Help Evan.

"Yes, she does. All my shoes come from her shop. They are exquisite. She told me about your visit. You did not have shoes." Pia spoke in a calculating voice.

"Not for my wedding, no. Such a beautiful boutique." Minola couldn't understand the envy she continued to hear from Pia. Her family was reputed to be wealthy. Pia should be financially comfortable, certainly not to the degree that Adriana was, but few were. From all accounts, the Deniccali furnace was doing well. Who knew how much was inherited by the other suspected assassination business down the centuries? Why the need for more? *Is it just human nature or is there an underlying reason?*

"The food is delicious. My black pasta was superb. I don't think I'll ever get tired of it, and the cuttle fish was cooked to perfection." Minola nudged Sally.

"Sorry. I've been snoozing all along, my apologies. I think I ate all of my favorite pizza. My plate is empty so I must have been sleeping and eating," Sally patted her tummy. "I'm surprised my face didn't wind up in the pizza. It seems as if I need a nap after every meal lately."

"Any pizza is your favorite pizza, and yes, you dosed off a little, and we understand." Minola laughed.

"I'm glad you enjoyed your meals. Pia, what about you? Did you enjoy your lunch?" Adriana asked.

"*Si*, of course the eggplant was delicious. It is quite an elegant club."

"I'm afraid I must go back to the hotel. I have some work to do, and I would like to spend some time with Peter. Plus, Sally needs to rest." Minola heard Pia hiss when she mentioned Peter.

"You're a lucky woman." Pia lips twisted in a macabre smile.

"Yes, I am truly blessed," Minola replaced her napkin next to her plate. She needed something to do, Pia made her nervous. "Adriana, thank you for a delightful lunch. The food really was superb."

"It is. I brought Evan here once and even he liked it." She turned toward Pia. "Can we drop you off somewhere? Or you can stay if you'd like. I, too, must be off."

"No, *grazie*, I, also, have much work to do and must go to the furnace. *Grazie*, Adriana. *Ciao*." Pia left without another word.

"Well, we didn't get much, maybe a little nibble. She's a very unhappy person." Minola felt sorry for her.

"Ever since I have known her, she has been like that. Even before Gio. Nothing is ever enough. She is quite taken with Peter." Adriana looked directly at Minola, and her words sounded a warning.

"It was rather strange, and I understand. We'll be careful," Minola replied.

"I will schedule the ball, and we'll see what happens," Adriana replied.

"First things first, Evan is joining us for dinner and breakfast, and I would like to invite you. I'll leave Gio to Peter. We made arrangements to meet for breakfast at the hotel, and then Sally picks the dinner restaurant. Breakfast or dinner, your pleasure, or both." Minola considered Adriana a friend and wanted to help her with Evan.

"Are you sure Evan would come?"

"Of course he would. We're in the middle of a murder investigation. And Peter always worries about my safety, especially now, and Evan is always there to offer his help. He is an exceptional and honorable man. He doesn't need my vote of confidence. I just wanted you to know."

"I know exactly how honorable and how foolish he is. And stubborn. Dinner would be lovely, anytime you say." Adriana smiled.

"Today would suit." Minola nudged Sally.

"What? I'm awake, just resting my eyes."

"So I see. Where is dinner tonight?"

"At the hotel. I like their pizzas. The veggies are roasted nicely." Sally huffed when she heard Minola chuckle.

"You haven't met a pizza you didn't like." Minola smiled.

"Ha, little you know. I have a selective palette when it comes to pizzas. They just happen to be really good here."

"If it's a pizza, you like it, but I happen to agree with you. They are exceptional." Minola turned toward Adriana. "Dinner at our hotel. We eat early... five. The poor little munchkin's first word will be *pizza*." Minola heard Adriana laugh out loud.

"Thank you, Minola. I am grateful for your help. I find your relationship with your best friend to be amazing and am delighted to have met you."

"I agree. It is amazing, and we cherish it. And we're happy to have met you, too," Sally replied.

"I agree as well. And I'll make sure Evan shows up. Peter needs to chat with him anyway. This will be a good excuse."

"I will see you tonight." Adriana turned her head toward the waiter, and he appeared instantly to signal their boat was ready.

Chapter 13

Once they arrived at the hotel, Sally went to nap, and Minola went in search of Peter. The first place she tried was the hotel bar, and she found him with Evan. Both were drinking coffee and eating sandwiches. She heaved a sigh of relief when she saw that Peter was relaxed and enjoying his conversation with Evan. No pretense, no reservations on his part, he was happy to see her, and he showed it. He pulled out a chair for her and ordered another coffee.

"Evan, how wonderful to see you. I have a favor to ask." She saw Peter raise his eyebrows. She knew that look well.

"Please. How can I help? I am sorry you were hurt. From now on, one of us will be with you."

"Peter, this is your doing, isn't it?…Would you join us for dinner tonight, here at the hotel?" Minola felt Peter gently nudge her foot under the table.

"I would be imposing."

"You are our friend, and I need your advice." This time Peter was a little more forceful, and her foot was getting a workout. "Ouch."

"Is something wrong?" Evan's lips curved up a notch.

"No, just my foot. I'm a little sore, and so are my knees and elbows." She saw Evan smile and knew he figured it out. So much for subterfuge. "All right, Peter you can stop bumping my foot. I met with Adriana, and I asked her to dinner." Minola turned toward Evan. "She wants to talk to you, and I really like her, and I think she's admirable

164

and kind, beautiful, and…" She stopped when she heard Peter roar. "What? That is the truth."

"I agree with you. She's a remarkable woman. She's stubborn, opinionated, Italian, and stunning." Evan spoke quietly. "Thank you for the invitation, but I'm not sure that is a good idea."

"Evan, give her a chance. Stand by her. That is all she wants. She can't help that her last name is Bruloni. She's proud of it, as she should be. You can't hold that against her. Give her a chance and don't walk away. She is a worthwhile human being. I like her and admire her courage, and I just met her."

"I give up. I will be here for dinner. And thank you, Miss Grey…er…Minola."

"Much better. I know you have business to attend. Peter, I'll see you in the room. I bought you a present." Minola ran her hand gently against his back and walked out.

Peter excused himself for a moment and followed Minola to the elevator. Once in their room, his lips brushed against hers in a soft caress. "How are you feeling?"

"Peter, I'm fine. Please don't worry. More to the point, how are you?"

"I am much better, and I worry, so please be careful. What kind of present?"

"Glass."

"Glass? What kind of glass?"

"Murano glass."

"We're not getting anywhere here."

"On the contrary, I thought we were. You were about to kiss me again."

"I was?" His hand took her face and held it gently.

"Yes, you were." She lifted her head and ran her lips over his. His response was immediate as he deepened the kiss, careful not to hurt her.

He touched his forehead to hers and whispered, "I love you and missed you." He kissed her once again. "I need to love you, and you're bruised, and I have to go back downstairs." His gaze lingered on her face. He ran his fingertip against her swollen cheek. "I will be back shortly—just going through the security detail with Evan. Did I hurt your foot?" He brushed his lips against hers in a tender caress.

"No, of course not. You were gentle. Go back to your meeting." She pushed him toward the door.

On his way down, Peter once again wondered at the turn his life took. Every morning when he woke up, he was astounded at how much more he loved her. Such an evolving, delightful, and terrifying process. He really didn't know that the abiding love and passion he shared with Minola could ever exist. This encompassing emotion he felt for her terrified him, because no matter what he said and how much he shared with her, her safety continued to be an issue.

Peter joined Evan in the restaurant. "I'm sorry to have kept you waiting."

"No need, Sir. I understand. Other than the security detail, I have something to tell you. Gio phoned me this morning. He trusts you, but felt more comfortable talking to me. We met for coffee, as old friends you understand." Evan looked directly at Peter. "Matteo didn't keep any public notations or records of his investigation, but they had a way of communicating. Gio does not trust easily, but he trusts you. It seems as if Matteo and Gio communicated with each other by leaving notes in a bank box. To be safe, it is a bank that Gio and his family have a vested interest in. He also has a vault at the bank that houses an extensive gem collection. His visits appear quite normal and natural. Actually, the gems are Adriana's, but the box is used solely for some clandestine communication—Gio and Matteo worked some cases together, even recently. Gio has not quite given up the police force. He has been known to work undercover, it goes back to his days on the force."

"I suspected as much. What did you find out?" Peter asked.

"Matteo was to meet with Dario. Julio was blackmailing Pia, not for money, but to be released from some kind of guild. Julio wanted out, and the daggers he was working on were the key. Julio also had ancient pieces of paper with a code, and it listed some of the key members of this guild. The daggers were coded to tell the name of the head of the guild."

"I see. Let me fill you in on the assassins guild in Murano, everyone knows about them, but no one talks about them. Nothing has been written, nor is there any history about them, all whispers and hints of secrets, all innuendos. They go back centuries. A specific method was used to kill. Incidentally, it was glass daggers. The people in the know aren't talking, and the people who don't know are speculating—that would be us." Peter's voice was grim.

"It seems Julio wanted out, and someone wanted him to stay in. According to Gio, one never leaves the guild alive, and it is still going on and in the best of social circles."

"There must be more of a record somewhere, and someone must have known what Matteo was doing and eliminated him. Who, other than Gio, did Matteo share the information with?" Peter asked.

"That is exactly what Gio asked. Where do we go from here?"

"What else isn't Gio saying?" Peter asked candidly. He had the distinct impression more was to come.

"Gio went to the box. This was to be his second such meeting with Matteo, and there he found pictures of daggers and most likely the code to identify the family, along with a small gold triangle drawn on the top of the page, but no clue as to where it leads or what that means. It is not known if the pictures of the daggers are the ones stolen from Julio or if they are antiques and belong to the Deniccali family. Of course the Castiglis have similar daggers, but they're not bragging. Matteo suspected someone, but needed more information. Gio doesn't know if Matteo met with that someone else. All he knows is that Matteo was getting close."

"This is one of the strangest cases we have ever worked on. What else did Matteo discover? I think I need to meet with Gio. Can you arrange it? Or, since Adriana is coming to dinner, maybe Gio can join us. For those watching, it would appear as a social function."

"Excellent. I will call and invite him. I will also list everything that we have—that should be about two sentences—and everything that is missing—that should be a few blank pages. How is Miss Grey?"

"Minola is bruised and resilient. I, on the other hand, am terrified. I'll work on the sequence of events and will see you tonight. We'll sort it all out," Peter assured him, but he had his doubts on that score.

"I don't want Adriana involved in this. These are dangerous killers."

"They all are, Sergeant, but I agree with you. However, Minola won't stay out of it, and from what I've seen of Adriana, she won't either."

Evan and Peter went to their respective rooms to chart the next course of action, with limited access to the police force their options were severely limited. He also wanted time alone with Minola.

Chapter 14

Peter found Minola in the shower. Since she never showered in the afternoon, something must have upset her. He soon joined her. The hot water was soothing, and he watched as Minola let it wash over her. Eyes closed, her skin wet and glistening, her hair off her face, head bent back as the water cascaded over her body, she appeared positively sinful. He took a deep breath and groaned at the erotic picture she made.

Minola sensed rather than saw Peter enter the shower. She was lost in memories of their time together. Often in the past, when they had problems in their relationship, she would drift back to happier times, a sense of escape from reality for her. Peter was so important to her, to her life, that she tended to panic and question their connection, even now. She still couldn't believe the reality. Danger lurked once again, and all she wanted was to make love with Peter and forget everything else.

Peter took her in his arms and allowed the water to wash over them. "What is it, my love? Has something happened?" He tenderly took her face in his hands and forced her to look at him. "Tell me," he insisted.

"I spent some time with Pia, and she truly frightened me. I think she hates Adriana, is envious of her, and probably blames Adriana for her break-up with Gio. She's not crazy about me, either, and she used your first name. You're Peter to her, and I didn't like it. I got us into this mess, and all I want to do is make love with you, stay in your arms, and never leave. Peter, I think I'm losing my mind. The depth of my love for you is profound. That is the only way I can put it, and I feel as if I'm losing myself in the process."

"You're not alone. I feel the same way about you. What we have together is unique and incredibly special, and it will take time for us to sort it all out. We have been through a great deal together, and we are stronger. And yes, I want to make love with you all the time, too. I think about you all the time. I don't want to be separated from you. Ever. And I'm truly grateful you feel the same way. I'm grateful that you're always ready for me. That is what I've been trying to tell you. My obsessive fear for your safety is because I feel this amazing love for you." He took her in his arms and caressed her back, lovingly kissed her neck, and then reached for her mouth. He swallowed her sob in the kiss and proceeded to love her.

After they finished, he took a towel and dried her off, and she did the same for him. "I'm okay now. Thank you. You always know what to say and do. That is one of the reasons why I love you so much."

"I'm always here for you. Now tell me more about my present?" He wanted to take her mind off the murder and her fears.

"I'm surprised you remembered. I bought you a lit vase, almost like a lamp. I fell in love it, and I bought it for your office."

"I can't wait to see it." He pushed her toward the bed. "I need a little nap." He smiled and lowered her on the bed and made love to her once more. Careful not to hurt her, he took a deep breath as he stared at her bruises.

"I think we need to get dressed and head downstairs for dinner. It should prove interesting."

"That it should." He looked at her face for any sign of stress and found none.

"Peter, I'm all right. Just a panic attack. I haven't seriously painted in a while, and I miss it, a cumulative panic attack. Should I ask about our honeymoon or is Sally planning that, too?" Minola was blissfully happy, but even now, death was never far from her thoughts.

"I think she had something in mind. We'll have to ask her tonight," Peter replied.

"I would really like to stay in your home, and maybe go somewhere a couple of months later."

"Our home…that is most reasonable. We can decide later where we want to go for a honeymoon. Preferably somewhere where they don't have any murders," Peter replied.

The dinner provided some information. While Evan and Adriana settled their differences at least temporarily, Gio indicated that progress was made in the investigation. After a Deniccali family reunion, Dario contacted Gio directly and asked to speak with Peter. Dario didn't elaborate, but maybe he wanted outside help from Peter. Dario was afraid the carabinieri would destroy his family. Gio consented to arrange the meeting, but warned Peter it could be a trap.

Peter, eager to finish with this mess, readily agreed. The meeting was set for the next morning in the Deniccali gardens. Evan Welsey would accompany Peter. He didn't want Peter to go alone. Both Minola and Adriana insisted on being nearby.

***

After dinner, Peter excused himself and told Minola he wanted to visit the Deniccali estate to familiarize himself with the property just in case. He promised her he'd be careful, and since he wasn't expected until tomorrow and would not step foot inside, he felt safe.

From across the street, Peter spied two people in the garden. He couldn't identify them. The large, hooded dark jerseys and pants prevented him from even guessing at the identities. All he could tell was that one person was considerably larger. Big hands most likely indicated a man. Peter hid behind a large bush and watched with interest. One person seemed agitated. A vehement conversation took place. Peter could not hear what was being said, but watched a large envelope change hands, and then the larger, hooded man was shoved out the gate.

Peter followed him until they reached a cafe. The man sat down and waited. A few minutes later, Gio sat down at the same table and was handed the envelope. He opened it and glanced down. Peter could see the envelope contained old and yellowed papers. A furtive discussion followed, and the man left.

Peter felt comfortable in approaching Gio. He loomed over the table and waited for Gio to acknowledge him. "This is not what you think." Peter heard Gio's rich resonating voice.

"No? Perhaps you'd care to explain." Peter pulled out a chair and sat down.

"Dario wants to blow glass. That is all he cares about. He wants to be removed from the family business, whatever business that is. This was an undercover policeman who met with Dario and supposedly received a secret list or a secret history of the Deniccali affairs, other than glass, I can only guess what they are involved in. Dario wants protection for the family and survival of the glass business. He knew the information was coming to me. Matteo's death rattled him, and he is afraid."

"Are you working undercover? Is that why the police have not been asking us too many questions?"

"Yes."

"How does Dario hope to keep all this secret? And protect his family from what? How is Pia involved? And why did he want to meet with me if he's giving you the information?"

"As yet, I do not know, but maybe Pia is involved, and whatever Pia wants, she'll attempt to get. Frankly, it is beginning to look as if she has her eyes on you."

"Eyes on me, that is totally absurd. She managed to upset Minola. That I will not tolerate further. She cannot control this situation, and if Minola is at all threatened with greater harm than she already sustained, I'm done playing it safe. Please keep me informed."

"I will do so, but I cannot give myself away."

"I understand." Peter got up and left.

His intuition never failed him. He headed to the Deniccali furnace. He had no idea why. It just seemed a natural course of action. The doors were shut, but a single light shone through a small window. Peter took out his cell and called Welsey and waited for what seemed like an eternity. Other than the one bright lit spot, silence prevailed. He moved closer and peeked through the window and saw shadows moving. Then he saw nothing at all, except dirt.

Chapter 15

Peter raised himself up and saw Welsey peering down at him.
"What the hell happened?" His head pounded a steady rhythm. He
gingerly massaged his scalp and felt a sticky red warmth on his hand.
The skin was broken, but the knock wasn't severe enough to cause
major damage.

"Sir, move slowly please." Welsey extended his hand and helped
Peter sit up. "Someone wanted to let you know you were not welcome.
I interrupted, but the person was already running away. Sir, we need to
discuss your lack of proper police procedure," Welsey admonished.

"Yes, Sergeant. It would seem war has been declared on us." Peter
groaned and continued. "Just a tap to let me know I was seen. If they
wanted to kill me, they would have done so. Did you see anything?
Give me everything you have."

"I have nothing. The attacker heard me, but didn't seem concerned.
I agree this was a warning, not meant to inflict serious damage. You
were lucky, sir. It could have been serious. You had no way of
knowing. You cannot do this again. We are a team."

"Yes, we are. Thank you, Sergeant, it will not happen again. Were
you able to identify anyone?"

"I can't even say man or woman, not a large person, but whoever
hit you wore dark clothing. Someone was inside as well. I saw the light
switch off."

"Is Minola safe? Well, that means someone is running scared, but
why."

"She and Mrs. Jones are in the restaurant bar, enjoying the view. She will be...upset."

"Upset, Sergeant? That is an understatement." Peter took out his cell and called Minola to let her know he's been delayed. "Let's see if maybe they dropped something."

Welsey used his cell flashlight and inspected the area. Near the bushes that lined a narrow path, he found an old, folded piece of paper. He flashed the light on the paper that was yellowed with age and had tattered corners. He had no way of knowing how long it has been there, but at least they had something. He treated the area like any other crime scene. Some items were relevant to the scene unfolding in front of him, others may have been in the vicinity and were not relevant, but everything was collected and checked. He handed it to Peter. "Sir, you need to go to hospital. We can inspect the paper later."

"Sergeant, I'm fine, really, no need to fuss. We will not be reporting this latest incident to the police. We're inundated with old paper and glass daggers. And I have a beastly headache from this investigation. Let's go back."

Minola was pacing and stopped dead in her tracks when she heard the door open. One glance at Peter, and she ran into his arms. "What happened? How did you get hurt?" Panic and anger fought for supremacy. He was standing in front of her in one piece. "What happened? Why did it take you so long to call me? You cannot do this again. Ever. Just as you worry about me, I worry about you," she mumbled in his arms, and held on tight. "What happened, and why didn't you call?" She wanted to rail at him and hold him. Her eyes watered, and she willed herself not to cry, but the tears rolled down her cheeks.

"I'm sorry. I did call you." He felt her tremble against him.

"Not soon enough. Tell me what happened. Everything." She whispered against his chest. The now familiar panic welled in her throat, and the attacks on Peter in Bath flashed in front of her.

He reached down, kissed away the tears, and then explained what happened.

"What do we do now? You're in danger." Sheer black fright swept through her at the possibilities.

"No, I don't think so. This was only a warning, but you are. Your attack was meant to kill. Now, we have a little more information we didn't have before, and we have this." Peter took out the piece of paper and gave it to Minola. He watched as she carefully unfolded it with trembling hands. She listened as Peter shared the latest news, including Gio's apparent police status.

"I am all right," he spoke softly. "I am not the target. This was a warning," he repeated to soothe her fears.

"Yes, I can see that. I should have been there. Are we back to our issues in Bath?"

"No, absolutely not. Sergeant Welsey took great care, and besides, by the time you would have arrived, I would have been on my way back to you. I was not rejecting you. Never again. Never." His arms went around her waist, and he pulled her against him.

"Promise?"

"Yes."

"You need to rest, and I know what to do—wake you up every couple of hours." Her hands shook as she ran them over his body to make sure he wasn't hurt anywhere else. She ordered hot tea and sat on the bed. "Peter…" she whispered.

"I'm right here," he murmured, his gaze on her face tender and loving.

"I know. Maybe we should stay in tomorrow. I still need to finish a few things for our wedding, and…" She gulped hard while tears trembled on her eye lids.

"That is an excellent suggestion." His hand lightly traced a path over her cheek and neck. He desperately wanted to calm her fears.

They spent the time together and were no closer to solving the murder, but the attempt on her life and the odd attack on Peter meant someone was nervous. They just didn't know who or why. Minola drew a few scenes of Venice on small postcards along with their wedding date and location, and she finished Adriana's and Evan's drawing.

Peter focused on charting the information on paper. He always worked better with a plan in front him, listing the suspects. They worked and periodically reached out to each other for sheer comfort and joy at being together. Their day together was something both needed. It allowed them a sense of intimacy and contentment without rushing to an engagement.

***

While Peter and Minola relaxed, Adriana planned her engagement ball for her new found friends. Her invitation would include the Deniccali and Castigli families. They wouldn't refuse. An event at the Bruloni *palazzo* meant networking with many high powered and wealthy people. For that reason, she invited Katarina as well. She liked the woman, and she liked the idea of promoting exquisite products made in Italy and wanted to help her gain more customers. Along with the *suspects*, she invited her friends and business associates, anything to make it look like a real celebration, and in reality, the party was genuine.

Adriana set the date for the coming Saturday. Hand delivered invitations went out immediately, along with an apology for the short notice. She checked with Gio. Carlo would provide the security, again—something he'd done in the past. Everyone knew Gio had friends in the police force. She called Minola to make sure she didn't miss anyone and continued on her mission. The caterer and florist would never deny a Bruloni request, no matter how late and rushed.

Adriana always planned her own parties, preferring the personal touch, and this event was not any different. No time to go shopping for a dress. Her closet a veritable boutique, and she'd pick one that would send Evan Welsey to his knees, her perfect opportunity to win him back. She smiled and continued on her mission. By day's end, she was satisfied the trap was set. The rest would be up to the police, her brother, Evan, and newfound friends. She hoped no one would be hurt. Enough blood had been spilled already.

The opulent ballroom was almost ready. All that was needed were the flowers to transform the room into a magical and romantic dream. Huge wall to wall windows, brilliant Murano chandeliers and sconces, silk Turkish carpets, drapes, and many candles of all shapes and sizes added to the magnificent setting. Adriana sighed and smiled. She was pleased with the results.

Chapter 16

The morning of the ball, Minola scrambled for something to wear. Then she remembered the exquisite black dress she wore in Bath that travelled with her to Venice. She also remembered the effect it had on Peter, and she rather liked how he reacted to it. Thanks to Adriana she had gorgeous and sleek Italian black shoes to go with that long seductive black dress. She'd wear her engagement ring, watch, dangly colorful glass earrings, and Peter's opal necklace that he bought for her in Paris—she didn't need anything else.

Peter watched as she took the dress from the closet to inspect it, and his breath left his lungs. He was transported back to the hotel in Bath and the evening at the hotel restaurant when she barely acknowledged him. He walked over and took her in his arms and held her. "I remember this dress, and it is not a happy memory," he whispered in her hair.

"I know. I remember…but I love it, and if memory serves, you did, too. This occasion will be happy. I didn't want to buy something else when I already have…"

"You looked beautiful in it. You took my breath away, just as you will tonight. First dance will be mine," he whispered, his breath hot against her ear.

"Staking your claim early?"

"I've already staked my claim. You're all mine." He nuzzled her neck. "I need to meet with Gio and Evan. I'll see you this afternoon."

He kissed her once, picked up the bits of the broken dagger from the table, put them in his pocket, and walked out the door.

His last minute meeting with Gio came as a surprise. The bigger surprise yet was Dario, who requested it. Pieces were beginning to fall into place, but many things still did not make sense. Two murders. First, Julio's to silence him and his attempted blackmail. At this point, the only family to gain from that murder were the Deniccalis. Then Matteo's murder happened because he was close to a discovery. The pictures Matteo provided of the daggers had to come from the Deniccali family. Who was the leak? No matter which way he filled in his puzzle, the Deniccali family was front and center. *This is too easy.*

He went over everything in his head. Julio's stolen daggers-who took them? Why? Which member of the Deniccali family spoke with Matteo? Why the second meeting—a trap to kill him? All fingers would point to the Deniccali family. It couldn't be that simple. What were they hiding? Who was leading the pack? Peter hoped that the ball tonight would at least give up some secrets. His wedding day was quickly approaching, and he'd be damned if he'd share it with a murder investigation.

Before he knew it, he was at the café, and Gio and Evan were already seated.

"Gentlemen, good morning. What do you have?"

"Peter, good morning. Sit down and relax. We'll get to business soon enough. Coffee is on the way." Gio pointed to a chair.

"Has something happened? Is Dario coming or did he just request the meeting?"

"He is coming. After this, we will change our meeting place, should another one become necessary, for obvious reasons."

"In that case, here." Peter took out the chunks of the broken dagger. "I brought them because I knew Dario would be here. Maybe he can identify them."

"Someone meant business." Gio stared at the shards.

"Indeed, if Minola hadn't tripped..." Peter let the rest of the sentence trail. He had no wish to relive his worst nightmare. "Why attack her?"

"I think maybe Dario will have an answer. Ah, here he is." Gio pulled out a chair. Dario sat down, ordered an espresso, and glared at the contents on the table.

"Where did you find this?" Dario demanded.

"That dagger was used in a murderous attempt."

"I see. Let's get the pleasantries out of the way. It is a pleasure to see you. We will, of course, see each other tonight, but I wanted—let us just say that my sister is out of control and needs to be stopped." Dario stared at the glass and did not blink once, as if mesmerized.

"Are you saying she's the killer?" Evan asked quietly.

"I do not think so, but her erratic behavior is progressing, and she will eventually destroy this family, and that I cannot allow." Dario glowered at Peter as if blaming him. "She is captivated with you. She has this romantic image of you and her together. She is obsessed with you. She has fixated on other men before, but not to the extent that she has you."

"That is absurd. I hardly know the woman." Sheer fright swept through him, and Peter gritted his teeth. "We met twice, enough for me to identify her as your sister. That is all."

"That may be, but you're her hero. She feels you belong together."

"That is frightening. Is she unstable enough to want to kill my fiancée?"

"She hates Minola Grey with a vengeance. She couldn't stop talking about her. '*She has everything.*' The usual Pia envy. I grew up with it and didn't think anything of it, but lately, it has become a problem. I took her to Rome to see a doctor, and he gave her some medication, but it has not helped."

"Is she capable of murder?" Peter insisted. His stomach twisted in knots at the thought of Minola in danger.

"We are the Deniccali family." Dario smirked. "Surely you have heard rumors."

"Are you admitting that fact?" Peter asked.

"I am admitting nothing."

"You are going to sit here calmly and tell us that your sister is capable or may be a murderer, has made an attempt on Minola's life, and we are supposed to listen, do nothing, and pretend it is business as usual. I want proof, and I want her stopped." Peter voice was ice cold.

"I have no proof, but that dagger or what is left of that dagger is ours—one of our priceless antiques. There are only a few left. I'd recognize it anywhere."

"I thought you might. That is why I brought it with me. Who has access to them?"

"Only our family, they are kept locked in a safe. As I have said, they are irreplaceable and valuable."

"Well, that certainly points to your family, does it not? I checked. No fingerprints. Whoever attacked Minola wore gloves." Peter watched as Dario made an attempt to touch the broken pieces. Peter stopped him by calmly folding the handkerchief over the glass and putting the contents in his pocket. "Why would she destroy a priceless antique?"

"A ritual or tradition. Why don't the police have this? Evidence, is it not?" Dario asked.

"We kept that to ourselves for a while. Eventually, the police will have everything." Gio wanted to make sure Dario understood and did not share anything with the police. A warning from a Bruloni went a long way, even for a Deniccali. "Dario, what is it that you want from us? You have no evidence that you admit to and, so far, you have wasted our time."

Dario reached into his pocket, pulled out a small ledger, and handed it to Gio.

"What is this?" Peter peered at the notebook and shrugged his shoulders. "Wonderful, more paper, because we need more paper."

"My sister's accounts, those she keeps in her personal safe. I have not been able to decipher them, or maybe I simply do not wish to do so. Take your pictures. I have to bring it back."

Evan, who so far had not said a word but took copious notes, started snapping pictures of every page.

"What, precisely, are we looking at here?" Evan asked.

"Initials, dates, and amounts—two columns for the amounts, and they are split evenly. A high price to pay for whatever service was provided. All seems rather straight forward. If we can identify the initials, maybe that will tell us who or what we're dealing with. Did you notice anything unusual?" Peter pointed to a page.

"Yes, in the corners… the tiny triangle on each page." After he finished, Evan handed the notebook back to Dario. "Gio, maybe you can identify some of the initials."

Gio took out his cell and took his own photos. "I will see what I can do. Is there anything else, Dario?"

"No, *grazie,* Gio. I will see you tonight." Dario stood up, pocketed the ledger, and walked away.

"Triangles? A logo of sorts? Wasn't there a triangle formed with daggers on Julio's body? Gentlemen, the plot thickens," Gio commented.

"Yes, indeed, like a thick pea soup. Why would he give up his sister? The ledger proves nothing, unless we find out that people with those same initials happened to die suddenly. Even then, it'll be hard, if not impossible, to prove anything," Peter replied.

"I know the woman. She probably has an alibi for everything. To think, I almost married her." Gio shuddered."

"I don't know what tonight will accomplish, but Adriana will be watched by me, and Gio make sure your security is good," Evan warned.

"They'll be safe. I'll have a full security detail on the premises. We'll see you tonight."

It felt as if a trap was set. Peter just hoped they weren't the bait. He had no expectations. All he wanted was to gain some information and for someone to make a mistake. Then again, murderers who have been in business a long time, and in this case, centuries, were formidably trained by others before them, and they didn't make many mistakes. Terrified for Minola's safety, he headed back to the hotel.

Dressed in a tuxedo, Peter was ready for the formal ball. He waited while Minola finished. When she walked out of the bathroom, a shudder passed through him. He wasn't sure he could keep his hands off her body, so he did the only thing he could and took her in his arms. "I certainly do remember you in this dress. You are beautiful." He kissed the tip of her nose, and his hands slipped up her arms to bring her closer. "How is the ankle? You moved the bandage so you could wear the shoes, didn't you?"

"Hmmm, just a wee bit. You are rather stunning yourself." She put her arms around his neck and touched her lips to his. The gentle massage sent currents through her body, and she snuggled into him. "Are we ready for tonight?"

"Stay off your feet as much as you can, please. And yes, as ready as we'll ever be. You'll be close to me at all times." He reluctantly let go of her.

The knock on the door announced Sally and Robert. She wore an elegant peach maternity dress, and Robert wore the obligatory tuxedo.

"We're all ready for this adventure. I can't wait to see Adriana's home. I have no idea what to expect, except it will be grand." Sally delighted in this newest adventure.

The private water taxi was already waiting for them at the hotel pier. After gingerly getting in the wobbly cab, the driver took off in the choppy waters. Traffic on the canal was heavy. "Hmm, all those taxis, what an amazing sight! Hope they're not all going to the ball." Sally giggled and settled in the comfy leather seat.

The ride was short, and Sally gasped as they approached the Bruloni *palazzo*. Someone was waiting for them to help them disembark.

Adriana was at the pier and rushed to greet them. She wore a bold black and burgundy dress that accentuated every curve she possessed, black open toe suede stilettos, along with a diamond pin that held her hair up. Minola had never seen anyone more beautiful, and what made it special was that Adriana seemed unaware of her many charms. Minola saw Evan Welsey staring at Adriana. He couldn't tear his eyes away from her.

"Adriana, thank you for the taxi, and even from here, your home is beautiful," Sally said.

"A pleasure! Please come inside and let me introduce you to my father." Adriana graciously took them past a gigantic foyer and what could pass as a huge receiving room. Papa Bruloni was smoking a cigar and chatting with Gio and another guest. He waved when he saw Adriana, and she walked over and introduced her newfound friends. Papa Bruloni shook hands and welcomed everyone with an offer of a drink. Even here, antipasti plates were everywhere, along with fresh bread, crackers, an assortment of Italian cheeses, fruit, and an espresso stand. Minola couldn't resist and headed straight to the machine to make herself a cup. Before she had a chance to pick a cup, someone appeared to make it for her. She graciously accepted. *"Grazie."* She took a sip and licked her lips. *Best espresso I've ever tasted.* She walked over to Peter and saw he was smiling at her. "What a magnificent machine," Minola said.

"We're in this home with unbelievable art work just in this room alone, and all you could see was the coffee." His gaze on her face felt as soft as a caress.

"On the contrary, I recognized a few pieces hanging on the walls. I noticed the lights. The tapestries are magnificent, as is the carpeting and the sheer size of this room. It is like a museum, but seems lived in. And, yes, I noticed the coffee, and it is sinfully delicious. So there." Minola saw Adriana approach them. She glanced at Minola's hand and laughed. "Adriana, this coffee is amazing. I'm staying close to this machine for the evening."

"Have no fear. We have another such machine in the ballroom— along with various biscotti and cookies. We all love coffee here. I also have a gelato bar, for those of us who appreciate Italian gelato. Please have some antipasti. We will serve dinner a little later. It is buffet style. I had this prepared, because Sally would probably be hungry."

"I believe she is." Minola pointed to a large table filled with an assortment of Venetian style pizzas, and Sally appeared to be in heaven. "That was a lovely thing for you to do."

"I want this to end as well. Gio has not been himself since Matteo's death. The buffet will allow us to watch the guests and who they talk to, their expressions. We will be vigilant. I learned a few things from Evan."

"It is an excellent plan," Minola replied. They walked over to the pizzas and watched as Sally loaded her plate.

"What? I'm hungry, and the little one is starving."

"Yes, I can see that." Minola laughed and took a slice of the vegetarian pizza loaded with grilled eggplant. "This is truly delicious."

"I told you so." Sally bit into a slice.

Minola took a closer peek at papa Bruloni. He appeared to be jovial, smoking his cigar, but Minola was sure he knew exactly what everyone was doing, a careful man who didn't miss a thing. Why was he watching everyone? Minola wondered how many security people were here already.

She glanced at the various tables laden with food and assortment of salads and anything else anyone could imagine, and this wasn't even considered dinner. Adriana outdid herself—not a pretentious effort, judging by the pizza spread for Sally, but rather to please her guests. Minola observed Welsey staying close to Adriana, who acted oblivious, but she was totally aware of his presence, and unobtrusively watched him.

The rest of the guests began to arrive. First to enter the room was Pia Deniccali, followed by her brother. She left little to the imagination. Her bold crimson dress had no back and not enough of a front to conceal her ample cleavage. Minola watched as she made a beeline to Peter, completely ignoring Minola, as if she wasn't even there.

"Peter, how are you? You simply look magnificent." She caressed his arm and leaned up to kiss him. Anticipating her move, he instantly moved out of her reach, grasping for Minola, and was grateful that she was close to him.

Minola watched as Pia's eyes narrowed almost to slits, and then she walked away, as if nothing happened. "Peter, what was that all about?"

"You're asking the wrong man." The exchange shook him, and he put his arm around Minola's waist and moved her against him. He needed her softness and gentleness.

"If this is just the beginning, it should prove to be an interesting evening." Minola leaned into Peter as she saw Adriana and Katarina approach them. She glanced at Katarina's shoes and wasn't disappointed. She wore a pale blue, baby soft leather pump, open heel and toe that fit as if molded to her foot, matching her rather simple blue dress. Elegant and not overstated, the shoes were the center piece. Minola was sure they were handmade and quite an advertisement for her exclusive shop. Katarina was a shrewd businesswoman.

"Adriana, you have done a marvelous job. Everything is perfection." Minola sighed.

"I'm happy you like it. Let's mingle." Adriana's took Minola's arm and moved forward to greet a guest. Peter followed behind. The ballroom was filling up. The massive doors were open to the veranda and gardens below. Miniature lights were hanging in the veranda and the steps that led to the gardens. The effect was at once romantic and necessary, lighting the stairs. The potted plants near the veranda were also dimly lit, but the bushes that were tucked farther into the garden had no lights. The area was dark and shadowy in direct contrast to the brilliant and festive atmosphere above stairs.

Minola needed a breath of fresh air and stood near one of the open doors, watching as the staff brought out the food. Three large tables alongside the walls were filled with Venetian specialties, and the pizza table was refilled with fresh pies. One table had various wines, and Minola was sure they'd represent Venice well. *I'm drooling, and if I keep eating the way I have been, my dress won't fit. All I'll have to wear are my shoes and most likely a bandage. It should make quite the picture.*

Peter and Robert were introducing themselves at every opportunity, and soon Gio joined them. Dario stayed close to Pia, who appeared to be sulking, and Katarina was mingling with a few society types of the male persuasion. Sally was sitting down near the pizza table and was observing all the action or lack thereof.

A quartet started playing, and Minola closed her eyes and swayed to the music. Peter watched her for a little while and then walked up to her, took her in his arms, and started dancing. He moved slowly, careful of her ankle. Soon others joined in.

The massive room held tables and chairs for those who wanted to sit and eat. Guests were walking with plates in their hands, and waiters with white gloves served additional appetizers. The dancing continued. It appeared to be a relaxing affair, and all the while Gio and Carlo and a few plainclothes officers kept watch. The quartet stopped, and normal activities resumed, guests catching up with the latest gossip.

Peter escorted Minola to the balcony for a breath of fresh air. "Let's sit down and rest your foot. Please stay close to me. I have a bad feeling about this."

"I've been watching everyone, too. Adriana and Evan are inseparable. I think he's worried as well. Peter, people are having a good time. I can't imagine something going wrong." They relaxed for a little while and then wandered back to the ballroom.

"Observe our key suspects. All is not well. They aren't having a good time." Just at that instant, Jennifer and Antonio Castigli walked in. Jennifer was in front of Antonio, and he was scowling, his fists tight. Peter suspected an argument between the two, or Antonio was forced to come and wasn't happy about it. Pia acknowledged the arrival with a smirk and walked over to her brother.

Minola greeted Jennifer and Antonio and received a lukewarm welcome.

"As always Adriana outdid herself. This ball is to honor your wedding, Minola? I didn't know you knew each other that well," Jennifer commented, while Antonio just nodded his head.

"It is a small world. Gio, Evan, and Peter are connected. I'm to paint a portrait of Giuseppe Bruloni, a wonderful gesture on Adrianna's part," Minola replied.

"I see Pia is up to her old tricks," Jennifer commented, her voice bitter.

"Antonio, you seem upset? Is something worrying you?" Minola asked.

"I have work to do. This is a waste of my time."

"I'm so sorry. Adriana invited our friends, and I thought…." Minola said regretfully.

"I'm sure I can find my way back. You don't have to stay." Jennifer's voice was as cold as the arctic.

"I'm sure you can," was the swift and brutal reply from her husband.

Jennifer watched as Antonio turned away from his wife and left. She hiccupped and spoke in a whisper soft voice, "I think that pretty much ends it."

"We'll take you home. Please talk to each other," Minola pleaded, and Jennifer nodded. Whether in agreement or just to acquiesce, Minola wasn't sure.

Peter focused on Pia and Dario. They were observed in a heated argument, after which Peter watched her go out to the balcony and then disappear. A few minutes later, she walked back in and once again argued with Dario. He walked away in a huff, and Pia stood there as if mesmerized. She seemed to gather her wits about her and again headed for the balcony.

Peter and Minola casually walked toward Gio, and they were finally introduced to Carlo, who had little to say, but his shrewd assessment of the activities said plenty. He didn't miss a thing and knew where all the suspects were. Sally and Robert were sitting down and chatting with another couple. It seemed like a normal party, yet a great deal of explosive tension existed in the massive room.

Peter observed that Pia returned to the ballroom and occasionally glared at him, and her glances at Minola were venomous. He was worried, but Minola was never out of his sight. Peter decided on a bite to eat, and by the time he walked back to Minola, Pia had disappeared. He felt uneasy and asked Minola to stay with Sally and Robert.

"Peter, we're staying together. She has you on her mind, too. Together, Peter." Minola's fear for Peter's safety hammered at her.

"Fine." His voice was sharp. One attempt on Minola's life was more than enough. He couldn't risk another. Minola was at his side as he asked Dario where Pia was, and he seemed unconcerned. "She's probably chatting with someone. She decided to behave. We had a little talk."

"That is all well and good, but she doesn't appear to be chatting with anyone. In fact, she is gone again." Peter, accompanied by Minola, walked toward Gio, who was still chatting with Carlo. Gio was not one to mingle. They walked out to the balcony in hopes that she would turn up as she had done previously. Other than a few guests sitting down in the plush garden chairs, the balcony seemed deserted in comparison to the ballroom. Gio and Carlo went back to the ballroom. Peter called Evan. He was not about to expose Minola to greater danger.

Peter waited for Evan and then, together, they walked down the steps, Minola beside him. Nothing but darkness greeted her. The garden had a few dim lights along the stairs, and a few shadows seem to lurk directly below, but beyond, only gloom. He used the flashlight on his cell and continued walking. The scent of fresh flowers and various shrubs made him wish this was just a leisurely stroll in a beautiful garden with the love of his life. Instead, he was hunting a potential murderer with Minola by his side.

He saw a few flowers had been smashed along the edge and knew that was not part of the maintenance process. He'd only known Adriana a short time, but long enough to know she would never allow such sloppy gardening.

Peter walked a little farther, saw a broken branch from a shrub, and then heard a sharp breath from Minola. Evan bent over a lifeless form on the ground, his fingers touching a pulse point. However, Peter knew the effort would be pointless. The victim had been stabbed once through the heart. Someone had known what they were doing.

Pia Deniccali had been murdered.

Peter stood up, took Minola in his arms, and rubbed her back for comfort. "We can't do anything else, we'll muddle the crime scene." Without moving a step, Peter crouched down for a closer look and then called Gio. He saw Minola nod and continued his inspection. He didn't expect to find a weapon or anything that would give the killer away. At least they didn't leave any additional footprints. This was a professional job. Why Pia, if she was the killer in the business? Did she have a partner? Was it Dario? He seemed unconcerned about her absence. Peter thought he saw him in the ballroom at all times, but he wasn't sure.

Once Gio and Carlo arrived, Peter and Minola returned to the ballroom. He wanted to observe the guests. Peter glanced at the assembly and saw nothing unusual, other than Gio and Evan returning without Carlo.

Standing on the balcony, Carlo took the lead and quietly called his men. Two officers remained with the body, and the other four stayed in the ballroom to make sure everyone was accounted for and no one slipped out.

Gio found Dario, put his hand on his shoulder and told him what happened, he lowered his head and said nothing. Gio then made an announcement about an unfortunate accident and that no one was to leave. Oddly enough, everyone took the information in stride and continued business as usual. "This is a seasoned group. Nothing interferes with networking, but then we didn't announce a murder…yet. Let's stay together, please. It will be easier for you." Gio told his friends who had gathered to be with Sally and Robert. Adriana soon joined Evan and her brother. Minola waved to Jennifer. She was chatting amicably with Dario and acknowledged Minola with a slight wave of her hand, but remained by Dario's side.

The coroner arrived alone.

The police were lagging behind. Carlo had taken charge, and he was one of their own. Carlo met him, and together, they went to the scene of the crime. Procedures were followed, and the body was removed the same way it was found—discreetly. Carlo could now question the guests. Where were they? What were they doing? Did they go out to the balcony or garden? Did anyone hear anything unusual? The usual questions came with the usual answers. No one saw anything. They were sorry, but busy having a good time.

Minola looked at everyone and hesitated, shook her head, and continued to focus at the wall near one of the doors to the balcony. As she lowered her eyes, she was observed as well.

"What did you see?" Peter asked. A few people were milling about, but he was sure Minola noticed something.

"I'm not sure, Peter. I…so odd, and it should be familiar to me. I can't point a finger to it."

"Others are watching you. I don't like it. Think, what stood out? Was someone missing, in the wrong place? What did you see?" Peter insisted.

"Just now, I really didn't pay attention to people coming or going for that matter. I was thinking about the…It'll come to me," she whispered, still shaken from seeing Pia's body.

"In the meantime, you're not to leave my side." His voice was harsh, and when he saw she was about to argue with him, he added. "Do not, my heart. I need to focus, I beg you, and you agreed earlier." He brushed a stray hair behind her ear to take the sting out of his voice.

"I won't leave your side. Is the party over?"

"Not according to the police. It shouldn't be long." Peter watched as each guest was questioned, and names and addresses were being written down in a notebook.

Minola turned to Adriana and said, "I'm so sorry. Who could have done such a thing with so many people about?"

"Frightening, isn't it? I didn't notice anything, other than people having a good time. We didn't find out anything at all," Adriana observed wistfully. She'd hoped that the murders would magically be solved.

"We didn't, but someone did." Minola stared at Adrianna's beautiful shoes and gasped loud enough for Peter to hear.

"What is it?" he demanded.

"Shoes," she gulped, and felt shiver of panic.

At that moment, the lights went out, and other than the candles, the ballroom was in darkness. Either this was a power outage, not unknown in Venice, or someone needed to escape. Slowly, various flashlights from the cell phones cast flickering shadows on the walls and created eerie moving apparitions. Gio was the first to move and head for the main circuit breaker located near the kitchen, but they were all in place, most likely a temporary power outage. Seconds later the power was back on, he then spoke with two of his own security people. On his way to the ballroom, Gio saw a couple of them head up the stairs. Two were searching rooms on the same level as the ballroom. One agent went to the first floor to see if anyone was hiding there. Gio walked quickly back to the ballroom to assess any damage.

The activities in the ballroom were lively. Guests discussed the outage and accident, glasses clanked as wine was poured, and people ate. Gio overheard a discussion on the accident that most likely was not an accident. Security agents were everywhere, above and in the garden below. Gio listened attentively, but heard nothing other than mere speculation. He reached Carlo and the circle of his new friends in quick strides.

"It would appear we have a missing guest, Katarina Ivanov," Carlo spoke quietly.

"So it would." Gio took stock of those still present. "She couldn't have gone far. The gate is electric, but not turned on, and the power did go out for a second. I checked, no one was seen outside. I had security posted everywhere. Maybe a climb over the gate, but that is doubtful."

"Did you see anyone leave the ballroom?" Peter asked.

"No, and that is odd, because someone would have to have known where the breakers were, and they weren't touched," Gio announced.

"A few know there is a bathroom near the kitchen. I love to cook and often entertain friends in the kitchen. Dario, Katarina, and even Pia have been in the kitchen, and they knew where the breakers were. They were here for lunch at another time when the power went out." Adriana shivered with chill and fatigue.

"Who is involved? Dario is still here. Did anyone notice him disappear for a split second, turn them on, and then quickly off? For what reason?" Minola was concerned about her friend. Jennifer looked dejected and frightened. It would seem that the murderer was not afraid to destroy anyone who stood in the way. Three people had died.

Gio asked for attention and received it. He wanted to alert his guests before the full force of the police arrived. He told them what happened, didn't elaborate further, and refused to answer questions. He finished just in time for the police to be announced.

The investigation proceeded with no additional discoveries. Fingerprinting and all the usual procedures were followed. Since Carlo already had much of the information, the process moved along quickly.

Peter turned toward Minola and asked, "What did you see earlier?"

"Katarina's shoes."

"Her shoes?"

"Well, you asked. Yes, shoes."

"What about them?"

"I don't think they were the same."

"The same as what? Work with me." Peter smiled in-spite of the situation.

"When Katarina first arrived, she wore blue shoes that fit as if molded to her feet—they were handmade and fit to perfection. All the shoes in her shop are handmade. They were gorgeous. I saw her shoes after the murder. She was standing near the doors that led to the garden. She seemed so relaxed, but the shoes were a little big. I think the color was the same, hard to tell from that far, but I know the shoe was too big for her foot. The open toe was too big; you couldn't see it. I know it is a strange thing to notice, but there it is. And, Peter, she saw me looking at her and her feet. I didn't think anything of it at the time."

"Does that mean she killed Pia, stepped in the blood, and needed to change? Were there footprints around the body? Where did she find another pair of shoes?" Sally yawned, her bed time long gone.

"Excellent point, Sally. No footprints that I could see, but we didn't have much light. It'll all be speculation at this point," Peter replied.

"Peter, it could also all be innocent. She noticed I looked at her shoes and panicked. She has shoes in her boat. I remember she told us about her excellent customer service. She sometimes personally delivered shoes to her clients. Or she could have gone to her boat after the shoes became stained, put on another pair, and threw the stained ones in the canal. She was frightened." Minola ran her hand through her hair. "I'm pretty sure her shop is successful, if the customers and prices are anything to go by."

"She is successful, and it is true, she has delivered shoes for me a few times in the office and at home. She also has a few pairs for her special clients in case of a *fashion emergency*, as she mentioned once. At the time, I thought that was just silly, but then I know several of her clients," Adriana said.

"Jennifer was talking to Dario. Katarina was close by." Minola ran her hand through her hair.

"But why?" Robert has been silent up to now, keeping a close watch on Sally. Her head drooped down, and she was exhausted.

"That is the big question," Gio answered. "Our guests can leave. It has been a long night. I would recommend you stay in the *palazzo* to remain on the safe side. Arrangements can be made for your immediate needs."

"I have a closet full of things I have never worn. The sales tags are still on them, and we always keep toiletries on hand for any occasion. The rooms will be made up immediately." Adriana called with instructions for her staff.

"That is also my case," Gio confirmed. "And, Evan, we still have a few of your things in *your* room."

"My room?" Evan looked at Adriana, saw her blush, and sighed deeply.

"*Si*," was Adriana's short reply.

"I, for one, appreciate the gesture. Sally is beyond exhausted," Robert said.

"I have kept the full security detail, just in case. You understand," Gio spoke quietly.

"*Bueno*, it has been decided. Breakfast will start a little later at nine and continue until everyone has eaten." Adriana stifled a yawn.

"It'll be just a few minutes. In the meantime, we need to say good bye to our guests and make sure they leave the property." Gio nodded to Carlo. He would be spending the night as well.

Jennifer left with Dario, and some guests had their own watery transportation. For others, water taxis were summoned, and the palazzo was once again at peace. Some of the catering staff remained to clean up, and Adriana saw to their departure as well.

Once in the room, Peter took Minola in his arms and held her. He had every reason to believe she was in danger, and he felt safer in the *palazzo*. The room they occupied was fit for king and queen. The massive bed was fitted with silk sheets. He was pretty sure he was standing on a silk rug. The colors changed subtly as they glistened in the light.

"Peter, I'm worried about Jennifer. Can we call Antonio just to make sure she's all right?"

"She wanted to go home with Dario, thought she could help him, but call Antonio for your own peace of mind." Minola's call went straight to voice mail, and she left a message. She hoped he'd call her back. "Is Katarina hiding somewhere on the property?"

"The police and private security went through the estate," Peter reassured her.

"But...if she killed three people, she's good at her job. Could she have done so?" she insisted.

"Yes, I think so. That is why Gio kept the security here. It'll be easier in the morning. We'll start early," Peter touched his forehead to hers. "Now, we're going to shower, and we're going to sleep, my love."

"That is an excellent plan." She watched as Peter checked the windows to make sure they were locked securely.

Chapter 17

The following morning, Peter and Minola were up early. Another call was unsuccessfully placed to Antonio, and then they found their way to the kitchen and coffee. Adriana was already sitting at the table with Evan.

"I hope you slept well. I'm an early riser, no matter how late the night." Adriana gulped down her coffee, went to the machine, and asked Minola how she liked her morning cup. Minola indicated a latte or capuccino would do. Peter took a cup and watched as the staff worked on breakfast preparations.

"This is a well-run household," Peter observed.

"Yes, I often come here for my morning coffee and haven't been asked to leave yet." Adriana smiled. "I am spoiled."

"You certainly are," Evan replied and clasped her hand in his.

"I see progress has been made, and I'm happy for you both," Minola exclaimed.

"Has anything happened?" Peter thought Gio would be up already.

"No, Gio and Carlo, along with the others, are inspecting the property, but so far nothing. I was asked to stay here, as Gio put it, to keep Adriana safe in the kitchen. She wanted to go with them." Evan raised her hand to his lips. Her warmth was reassuring. She allowed the gesture and didn't pull back. He heaved a sigh of relief.

"The police are investigating. They have a prominent body in the morgue and a potential escaped suspect for murder from a prominent event. I'd say they have their hands full, but I think we may have a little more to go on." Peter scratched his head and tried to remember if they indeed had anything at all.

Peter didn't for a minute think Jennifer was connected to this mess. He wasn't so sure about Dario. After their earlier meeting, Peter felt Dario was capable of anything to protect the family business, but whether just glass or the assassination business, that as yet was not clear. Did he want out like Julio did and Pia wouldn't let him? What was the meaning of the ledgers with the initials and split amounts?

"I have more questions than answers. This needs to end before more people die. The first thing we should do is look at the report Dario provided. Evan, you have your cell. Let's get to work. Maybe Adriana could identify a few of the initials," Peter suggested.

Was Antonio Castigli somehow connected? Why did Pia hold such sway over him? What about the daggers? The bloody glass sarcophagus, what was its significance? The triangle on the body and Pia's notebook, how was that connected?

Evan found the photographs and handed his phone to Adriana. When he heard her quickened breath, he knew they had something.

"What is it, *carissima*?" Evan's voice was husky.

Peter's astonished expression at Evan's use of *my dearest* and in Italian, no less, had Evan blushing. Peter saw Minola smile. She was right once again. Evan was deeply in love with Adriana Bruloni.

"I recognize two initials, but it is a guess on my part. Recently, two brothers who refused to sell their company to a big conglomerate died in a mysterious boating accident while on vacation somewhere in the Caribbean. One brother was married, and the wife inherited the company and promptly sold it. I visited their headquarters in Rome last year. My father wanted to do business with them. Does that mean something else...a murder, not an accident?" Adriana glanced at the sum listed next to the initials and pursed her lips. "That shows eight hundred thousand Euros split in half. Is that how much two lives are worth?"

"In reality, if the conglomerate is worth billions, that was a small investment. I wonder...Let's take a closer look at that company and verify the names of the stockholders. Nothing big, but substantial. If this was indeed an assassination, it certainly is worth more than what was paid." Peter's Interpol instincts were working just fine.

"You're checking to see who perhaps has recently acquired a few shares." Evan voice held a tinge of excitement.

"Indeed, I would say a million Euro's, a little less or more."

"Peter, what do you suspect?" Minola asked.

"An additional payment, perhaps a gift or investment, anything really."

"I have an office here, as does Gio. We can start after breakfast." Adriana took a bite of biscotti that had been discreetly placed on the table earlier. "*Grazie*, Maria." She thanked her chef for the cookies.

Breakfast was served in the small dining room, right off the kitchen. The room was for the family and friends who spent the night. The spread included juices, eggs, various meats, potatoes, and polenta— because Adriana loved polenta with her poached eggs—along with cheeses, assorted seasonal fruit, various fresh breads, croissants and breakfast pastries, and the magnificent coffee machine. After seeing how much Minola enjoyed the coffee, Adriana decided to buy one as a wedding gift.

"I would like to thank you for coming into my life. True friends are few and rare, and even though we have just met, I...to good friends." She raised her cup of coffee in the air, and everyone did the same.

"What did I miss?" Sally walked through the door, Robert behind her, and saw the raised cups. She noticed the buffet on the sideboard and grinned.

"We were just toasting to good friends. I didn't want to wake you. You were so tired last night." Minola took a sip of her coffee.

"The food looks wonderful. I think I woke up because I was hungry."

"If you have a taste for something else that is not on the table, please let me know." Adriana smiled and watched as Sally first went to the plate filled with assorted small pizza tarts, and then she sampled a little of everything.

"Adriana, this is a feast. Did something happen? Anything new?" Sally asked.

Minola proceeded to fill Sally and Robert in on the latest events. "What now? Katarina is still missing. Maybe I should call Antonio again?"

"There is no need. I have already done so." Gio walked through the door and headed straight for the food, Carlo and others behind him.

"Well…is Jennifer home?" Minola demanded.

"No, but Antonio indicated she called him last night. He was extremely worried about his wife, and she told him she was fine and staying with Dario. He sounded relieved."

"Does that mean Dario is home?"

"If he is, he is not responding to the police. They were there last night and again this morning."

"And what, they just left?"

"*Si*. The bigger issue is where is Katarina?" Gio asked.

"I thought you said no one could leave unnoticed."

"The fence was not electrified. I did not want an accident. She must have left just before or as the lights went out. The lights went off everywhere in the area—a short power break, a legitimate interruption. I can't blame her, but her timing was excellent. I do not know how she left."

After breakfast, Evan, Peter, and Robert followed Gio to his office and did a little research. Robert's financial acumen came in handy, and working undercover gave Gio access to confidential information. They were able to find out that Pia became a shareholder in the company to the tune of over a million Euros. With Adriana's help in the kitchen, they checked a couple of other names, and the data was similar— accidental death and Pia an instant shareholder.

Katarina was not part of these financial transactions. It appeared as if the ledger was indeed a list of assassinations and payments made for the service—the assumption being that Pia and Katarina worked together. Except this partnership was not equal. Did Katarina know of the added sums paid to Pia's account? Was Katarina even involved or was she frightened of something?

The rest would be left for the police to research, and Gio had already been in contact with them and was told that a water taxi picked up a single female in the vicinity of the estate at about the time the lights flickered. Based on the description given, she had been identified as Katarina Ivanov. She disembarked at the Piazza San Marco and blended in with the tourists. Her boat still docked near the Bruloni estate was searched, and they found shoes on board, but none that matched Minola's description.

After several hours of churning numbers, the men returned to the dining room only to find the ladies discussing the wedding. Gio shared the information they discovered.

"I didn't expect a murder at the ball, just a little meaningful gossip. Let's go back to the hotel. Katarina has to surface. She owns an exclusive shop. She's smart and likes money. She'll figure something out." Minola wanted a few minutes alone with Peter. She missed him.

"That is reasonable. I don't think anything will happen at the estate. Carlo is keeping a couple of uniformed officers in the open. Please be careful. You do realize this is not over?" Gio replied.

"Of course we do." Evan turned to Adriana. "Please do not go anywhere until this is over. I want your promise you will stay home. Your promise, Adriana." The determined glare on his face spoke volumes, and she nodded in agreement.

Their transportation was ready within minutes, and they agreed to keep in touch. Once back at the hotel, a stop for coffee and an early dinner at the restaurant was just what was needed. The view of the Grand Canal and the dim candlelight at the table restored the soul.

"Peter, I've been thinking. At least Antonio called and said that Jennifer is with Dario. Maybe Katarina is with them. Maybe they are together."

"That would be rather strange. What do they all have in common?"

"They know one another and most likely are friends. Jennifer was certainly chummy with Dario at the ball, and Katarina is an ambitious and shrewd woman. She knows how to network. I've watched her. Maybe Katarina was frightened. Maybe she found the body, and somehow her shoes became dirty, and she panicked." Minola hoped that Katarina was safe and innocent. She'd liked the woman.

"That is a distinct possibility. For that matter, I'm sure the police are searching all possible locations. Where would be the best spot for them to hide?" Peter asked.

"How about the impossible place? For instance, somewhere near where Julio's body was found. Someone knew about it. At least two people had to be involved in order to move the body and all that glass. It is dark, seemingly deserted. Who would look there?"

"Who indeed? I love you, Miss Grey." He kissed the tip of her nose. "I'm calling Welsey, and we'll take a walk."

"Not without me. Where you go, I go. Together, Captain Riley."

"Together, Miss Grey. In that case, I'll notify Gio as well."

Minola called Robert to keep him in the loop. Peter thought it best to go while dark. Any light spotted would be a giveaway. When they discovered Julio's body, only the moonlight and the glow from the lantern on the Gondola lit the area. Otherwise, it was rather ghostly. At the time, the ambiance seemed perfect for a romantic ride. Discovering the body, however, had dimmed that mood quickly.

They took a water taxi and were let out at another pier, and they walked along a narrow path to their destination. No need for the taxi to wait since Gio was coming with his entourage, namely Carlo and a few uniformed officers. Peter hoped it would be a quiet arrival, so as not to scare off anyone hiding.

It was dark and eerily quiet. The water lapped against the stone, a drain somewhere steadily dripped, and water sloshed against a brick wall. Tonight, darkness surrounded them rather than moonlight. No light anywhere helped brighten the way. Peter did not want to advertise their arrival, just in case someone was in the vicinity. They walked along the path in single file. Peter saw a tiny glimmer, and through a broken window, a candle was snuffed out and then darkness again.

Peter motioned to the entrance of the building. As in many others, the first floor was the disembarkation point for boats and during floods or heavy rains would be under water. Their movements were slow and precise, rhythmic in its intensity.

Minola was sure anyone could hear her heart beat double time, and she wondered how Peter could do this job, and yet she had become a part of this world with him, and she wouldn't have it any other way.

Peter opened the large metal and wood door, heard it creak, and stopped his progress. Nothing moved, yet he was sure someone was there. The darkness was now total, and Peter had no option but to use his cell for light. They were going in blind, and the terrain could prove treacherous. *As if a killer wouldn't be*. Peter smirked.

They continued walking single file. Minola was in the middle and Evan behind her. Peter motioned to go up, because that is where he saw the flash of light. The stairs squeaked, and Peter was sure their arrival has been announced earlier. Not much else to do but keep going up. The first door they reached was open, and the room was vacant, not even a sliver of furniture could be seen. The second door was closed, and that is where Peter had seen the light. He motioned Minola to stay behind the wall. Evan was on one side, and Peter on the other. He kicked the door with his foot and immediately pulled back, taking cover next to Minola just in case someone had a gun and wanted to use it. The door was old and worn and gave way easily.

Peter shone the light and saw a table and a few chairs. Dario was in one chair, and Jennifer in another. Both were tied securely to their chairs, and both had gags over their mouths. Katarina was not with them.

Evan and Minola used their cells and now more light was available. Peter walked over to the table and saw the spent wax was still warm and soft in the candle. He untied them, removed the gags, and he heard Jennifer whimper.

"What the hell is going on here?" Peter demanded.

"We need to get out. Katarina is hiding somewhere in this building. She heard you." Jennifer coughed, and her voice sounded hoarse to her own ears.

"I suspected as much. Where is she?"

"We don't know. She blew out the candle and left. She'll be back. We're loose ends that she intends to tie up. She owns this building and knows her way around. She used it as her warehouse, for more than just shoes. Somehow I don't think you'll trace the ownership back to her easily." Jennifer was on the verge of tears. Her eyes sparkled in the flashing light.

"How did she find you after the ball?" Peter asked.

"I went back with Dario to his furnace. He wanted something to do. He was devastated about Pia, and I wanted to help him. She had her problems, but she was his family. I thought I could be there for him and forget my own issues for a little longer. I didn't want to go home. Katarina was waiting for us. I think she thought we knew more than we did. I really don't know anything about what has been going on." Jennifer rubbed her neck in agitation.

"Katarina boasted about her successes in her businesses. Pia didn't share everything, and when Katarina found out, she was furious. During the ball, she spoke with someone and found out that Pia owned a few shares in companies they did business with. You can surmise what that business was. They had an argument outside, and Katarina killed her. Katarina was always prepared for any emergency. Pia was my sister, I suspected but refused to believe she was capable of killing. But I knew...my father...I knew," Dario said softly. He sounded beaten.

"Yes, we figured a few things for ourselves, but we weren't sure who did what."

"Sir, I think we need to leave this building." Evan spoke quietly, but firmly.

"An excellent suggestion, Evan," Minola replied.

With the flashlights on, any pitfalls could be spotted as they walked out the door, making it much easier to see a shiny gun pointed at them from the hallway.

"Which one of you killed Matteo?" Peter asked no one in particular, just waited for a reaction. Katarina's back was to the staircase, and she was inching forward. Peter backed up a little and made sure Minola was behind him, but she casually stepped up and moved alongside him. *Bloody hell.* He saw Evan standing near Minola, watching for any opportunity to protect Minola and disarm Katarina. Jennifer and Dario were standing near the doorway in the back.

"Pia did. And together we killed Julio," boasted Katarina. "She designed the glass shroud. She started with the blue-grey palette…Julio stole the formula from her. Little by little, he was stealing everything before he left her. Then she just used any glass she had to complete it. He betrayed her." Her eyes were cold, no emotion showed in her stark glare.

"I see." Peter tried to stall for time and hoped Gio was on the way.

"This way, if you please." Katarina moved slightly and pointed the gun in the direction of the stairs.

"I know this is trite, but you will not go far. The police are on the way." Peter voice was calm and even.

"In that case, I'll need a hostage, a valuable one." She spat out the words, and moved the gun toward Minola, but Peter stepped in front of Minola.

"Miss Grey, step forward. I will not tolerate any games. Step forward now, or I will shoot your lover. It will cost me nothing to do so, but I will be careful not to damage your shoes." She snickered as she shoved Peter aside with her gun, pointed it at Minola's head, and told her to move ahead.

Peter's whole body shook in fury, but he could not risk Minola being hurt or worse. He nodded at Minola to warn her. To distract Katarina, he turned off his flashlight, and for a second, she was caught by surprise and stumbled. Peter took the opportunity to push her away from Minola, and she tumbled down the stairs. First, he checked to make sure Minola was not harmed and then quickly ran downstairs to see Katarina. She was on her back lying in an unnatural position. Her right leg was twisted like a pretzel. She was dying, but her parting words to Peter shook him. "There were three, and only one is left." She gasped and was gone. A twisted grimace lined her face.

Peter went back up, took Minola in his arms, and with trembling hands, he inspected her face in the dim light. He took a deep breath and exhaled with profound gratitude. Then he heard a commotion and saw bright lights and Gio enter the premises. "You're a little late."

"Yes, my apologies. This time I had to clear it with the department before I could get additional official help. My security detail should have been here already." He saw Katarina was beyond help. "We'll let the police handle this. We can talk in the boat. I brought my own."

"We do need to talk, but not now," Peter whispered and escorted Dario and Jennifer to one of the police boats. He watched as Gio spoke with the officers, after which, Gio headed to his boat.

Minola and Evan were already on board. Peter sat down next to her, took her hand in his, and held on.

Once Gio settled himself comfortably next to Evan, he looked at Peter, nodded, and demanded answers. "Tell me."

"You're rather good at giving orders. This isn't the end. Katarina's dying breath was a confession of three partners, and only one is now left. A threesome running the business. A triad. Who is the third party? Most likely the senior, invisible, and shrewd cohort. As you indicated earlier, this is far from over."

Minola nestled against Peter and closed her eyes as she relived the most recent terror. Peter didn't hesitate to step in front of her, and she knew Katarina would not have hesitated in shooting Peter. *How does killing become a business?* She opened her eyes and felt a wetness on her cheeks. With a trembling hand, she angrily swiped away at her face.

"We are fine, my love," Peter whispered and pulled her closer against him, his face buried in her hair. He took a deep breath and then another one before he could finally relax enough to keep his body from shaking.

"We're going back to my home. We need to talk and make a few inquiries, and I have the capability. As a precaution, for the time being, Jennifer and Dario are being held at the police station." Gio slammed one fist against another. Matteo's death was nearly avenged.

"I thought you might arrange for their safety. I would even hazard a guess that you know who the third person is," Peter replied.

"As do you, but we have to confirm it."

"Mine is only a guess and based solely on a possible little lie."

"Peter? It can't be." Minola's voice trembled.

Minola watched as Adriana met them at the dock and ran to meet Evan. She threw herself in his arms and sobbed. Evan took her face between his hands, bent his head, and kissed her.

"Enough. We have work to do." Gio smiled, happy that his sister and his trusted friend were finally together.

"I'm going to call Robert," Minola spoke.

"Let us go to the kitchen. We can find something to nibble on. It is late, and I can only surmise that it has been a difficult endeavor," Gio said.

"Yes, it has." Minola recounted their adventure as she followed Adriana.

Evan and Peter followed Gio to his office. After a few phone calls, additional information gathered from Interpol, and using Gio's connections, they had enough evidence for an arrest, rather than just suspicion and innuendos. Once they knew who to look at, it became easier to gather pertinent information. Gio notified the police with instructions on how the arrest would be handled. Even at the late hour, Gio personally took Minola and Peter back to the hotel, while Evan stayed with Adriana.

Chapter 18

The following morning, Minola and Peter went to visit Antonio Castigli at his furnace. He was in his office. Shocked at seeing them, he closed the file he'd been working on with a loud thud. With a heavy voice, he asked if Jennifer was dead. When told she was quite alive and in police custody for her safety, a rage Peter had never seen replaced the astonished pretense. A deep purple vein quivered in his forehead, his eyes narrowed, and Peter swore they turned an arctic cold. His glare was piercing. Then suddenly, he slouched in his chair and his face crumpled. He said, "You know." He slowly reached into the drawer of his desk.

"Yes. Before you do anything more stupid, the police are in the front and back, and right behind the door. You will not get away." Peter's voice was fueled by contempt and rage. He saw Antonio give up the attempt and rest his hands on his desk.

"We came as a courtesy to Jennifer. Why, Antonio?" Minola asked in a choked voice.

Antonio waved his hands in the air and chillingly replied. "Simply, Pia and Katarina—we were quite a threesome. I became bored with Jennifer, but she kept trying to work at it. She would not give up. She should have just walked away. I no longer wanted her. Dario became a threat once he realized what Pia was doing. And of course, the money, though not as much. Julio, because I didn't trust him. He didn't know about my involvement, but one can never be sure. Especially after he stole the formulas from Pia and tried to blackmail her. It is about trust.

Matteo, poor Matteo trusted Pia, and he knew too much. And Minola, Pia desperately wanted Peter. By eliminating you, Minola, she thought Peter wouldn't be able to resist her considerable charms. She was becoming a liability, somewhat delusional."

Peter shuddered at the cold and precise description of the murders and attempted murder of Minola. "The money, yes a great asset, except in your case, not quite so straightforward. You were put on several boards that helped your business. Certainly not direct compensation, but rather worthwhile nevertheless to have a voice with politicians and business leaders. There is considerable power there."

"If you say so. Mine is an old family. That is important." Antonio's voice was proud and dismissive at the same time.

"It won't get any older. You have no siblings, and you and Jennifer had no children. It dies with you. All those precious centuries, end with you." Peter's brutal summation gave Antonio pause. His face almost turned scarlet in his fury. Then he seemed to shrivel. His face had blue and red splotches. Wrinkles suddenly were visible around his eyes and mouth. The transformation was amazing. He went from a middle aged man to an old one virtually in seconds. The arrest of Antonio Castigli went without fanfare.

Gio met Peter and Minola at the police station, and once they were done, they agreed to meet back at the hotel. Later, Evan and Adriana would join them in the restaurant.

Minola needed to talk to Jennifer, make sure her friend had all the support she needed, but as it turned out, her friend was not all that welcoming.

"You shouldn't have come to Venice. Dario will help me with whatever I need. Maybe if you hadn't become involved, none of this would have happened." Jennifer's voice was bitter, and she laid the blame squarely on Minola.

"You asked me, and I tried to help you. Antonio was in the killing business before I arrived on the scene. How can you accept it so casually?"

"He didn't kill anyone. Pia and Katarina did. We could have worked it out. No one has a perfect life, except maybe you," was the stinging and bitter reply.

"I see. If you need anything, call me." Minola ended the conversation, and she couldn't stop shaking until she felt Peter's arms around her.

"She'll have to come to terms with her life, and with Antonio. Her relationship with her husband was based on a lie. It is difficult to suddenly realize you've been married to a killer." Peter's voice was soothing as he continued to hold her. "It will be up to her to decide if she wants your friendship. Her life was saved because of your involvement. She'll realize that quickly enough."

"It doesn't matter. She has changed. She was so gentle and kind…Now look at her. She's resentful and disappointed. Some of Antonio's ruthlessness must have touched her. Let's take a vaporetto back to the hotel and walk from the stop. I think I can use a little of the local humanity."

"Excellent plan."

Exhaustion settled in as soon as Minola sat down in the vaporetto. So much had happened in such a short time. Jennifer was alive, and Minola took comfort in that fact. As the saying went, life continued. Maybe not as before but always as a learning experience, sometimes dark, but thankfully most times not. She reminded herself she was to be married to a man she respected and admired and loved above all. A man who brought light and passion to her life. Who eliminated darkness whenever he could. A man who cared about others. She did, in fact, have it all in her life with Peter and silently gave thanks.

Gio was already waiting for them in the restaurant, as was Sally, Robert, Evan, and Adriana. Minola smiled when she saw Sally run up, or what passed for a run by an extremely pregnant woman, more like a balanced waddle. They hugged in silence.

"I ordered. Your coffee is on the way, and we can have a peaceful lunch." Sally took Minola's hand in hers. "I'm so sorry. Gio told us what happened in great detail. Jennifer will come around."

"It is up to her. Her life could not have been easy. There is nothing more I can do. What are we eating?" Minola reached for Peter's hand and laughed out loud when she saw a large pizza delivered to Sally. Normal life felt good.

"Don't laugh. The munchkin really likes pizza. He kicks every time."

"He? Maybe he's trying to tell you to order something else for a change. Did you ever think about that?" Sally brought so much joy everywhere she went, Minola once again counted her blessings. The munchkin would have magnificent and loving parents.

"No, he likes pizza," Sally said with confidence.

"I could use coffee, and we didn't stop for breakfast this morning. I'm famished, too." Suddenly, Minola was in a mood for a pizza, also.

"Peter, why did Antonio lie about that phone call from Jennifer? Such a silly thing to do," Robert asked.

"Overconfidence, arrogance, he certainly had plenty of that. I'm assuming he wanted to keep the police and us from looking for her. I think, ultimately, he would have killed Katarina after she eliminated the people that potentially threatened him," Gio replied.

"I hope Jennifer will come through this. Maybe Dario can help. He's now free to keep the glass business going. I don't think the police will do anything to him." The haunting and deepening evil Minola felt since they discovered the body had lifted. Could three people cause such feelings? *Yes, it's pervasive. There is peace now. How did Jennifer not feel it? Why didn't she simply walk away?*

"There really is no evidence linking him to the murders. The police have plenty linking Antonio, and his confession to Minola and Peter helped as well. Those old papers Peter found when he was attacked included Antonio's crooked deals, dates, and theft of several new formulas for new glass processes from other furnaces. He knew all was lost and confessed to everything. Even to the triangle on Pia's ledger and the three daggers placed on Julio's chest that formed a triangle. Goes back to the three of them—a triad. That being said, he hired an excellent attorney. However, the corporate espionage will not go unnoticed. He is finished in the glass business, and I suspect elsewhere as well." Gio was sure he would not survive much longer.

"Let us concentrate on the wedding. It is time for a little happiness." Adriana looked at Evan, and her breath stilled at the sensuous flame in his eyes as he gazed at her.

"That is an excellent suggestion. My parents are arriving in two days," Peter confirmed.

"Becky and Kirk, as well, and I think David and Ashby, too," Minola reminded Peter.

"I think you need some time before the wedding just for yourselves. It has been difficult. Robert and I, along with Adriana and Evan, can finish up the wedding arrangements. You and Peter spend some time alone. How is that?" Sally suggested.

"Sally, I think that is a splendid suggestion," Peter replied, grateful for the respite.

"Thank you, I'll take you up on it." Minola noted that Adriana and Evan were all smiles, most likely looking forward to a test run for their own special day.

They stayed a little longer, enjoyed the lunch, made plans, took pleasure in the unruly traffic on the Grand Canal, and even ordered dessert with coffee. Peter asked if she wanted another Gondola ride since they never really finished the first one, and Minola vehemently nixed the idea, stating too many things lurked in the shadows of the small canals.

Minola and Peter spent the rest of the afternoon and early evening strolling along the many narrow alleys, small streets, and many bridges. Somewhere along the way, they stopped for coffee and gelato, and Minola spoke with a few artists whose stalls lined a street along the Grand Canal.

A quiet and romantic dinner in the hotel restaurant finished what started as a horrific day and ended peacefully. A hot shower helped relax them, and Peter tried not to relive the horror of seeing a gun pointed at Minola's head. He trembled as the hot water washed over him. He couldn't stop until he felt her hands wrap around his neck and she pressed herself against him, her touch at once soothing and erotic.

She sensed his mood and reached for him, his touch an ecstasy she would never take for granted. They loved and slept and loved some more.

Tomorrow, they would have dinner with Sally and Robert. Otherwise, the day was theirs.

Chapter 19

Minola, nestled in Peter's arms, woke up to a blaring cell. She answered and heard Jennifer's voice. "I want to apologize for my behavior yesterday. I know you wanted to help."

"Yes, I did." Her voice was shakier than she would have liked.

"I'll need some time. I will not come to the wedding. It would be too uncomfortable for me. Your vases are all wrapped and will arrive tomorrow at the hotel. And, also, I saw that Peter bought Julio's beautiful chandelier. Please tell him that it is being packaged and shipped to his home in England. Antonio…was supposed to do it. Obviously he had other things on his mind."

"What chandelier?" Minola heard a rousing *bloody hell* and knew immediately what chandelier. "Thank you for taking care of the shipment." Minola waited for Jennifer to say something else, and when the silence continued, Minola said, "Call me if you need anything or want to talk. Goodbye, Jennifer." Minola heard a muffled goodbye, and the line went dead. She knew a permanent *goodbye* when she heard one. Minola would always remind Jennifer of what her husband had done.

Minola turned toward Peter and kissed him. She felt blissfully happy and fully alive. Peter's enormous generosity countered that of Jennifer's meager offerings as a friend. "I can't believe you bought that magnificent chandelier. I don't know how to thank you."

"I can think of a few ways." He chuckled and nibbled her neck, and then his lips came coaxingly down on her hers.

She drank in the sweetness of his kiss, a perfect caress for her tired and battered soul. "Thank you, Peter. I don't know what else to say. Thank you for loving me the way you do, and thank you for your incredible thoughtfulness and generosity." She kissed him, a slow drugging kiss that left them both breathless.

"I know this had been difficult for you, but your involvement in this mess saved Jennifer's life. You have to remember that is all that matters." Peter nibbled on her neck.

"I understand, and I love you for trying to make it easier. I'm marrying the most wonderful man. A man who picked an amazing and thoughtful wedding gift. I can't get over that fact."

"It was simple. I knew how much you loved it."

"Peter, you know you're enough? You do know that? That was an incredible thing for you to do." Minola stared with longing at him then buried her face against his throat. She was overwhelmed with love and simple gratitude. "I love you, Captain Peter Riley."

"I know you do, and I bought it for the same reason I bought you the opal in Paris. Except this one, you can't wear around your lovely neck." The tips of his fingers brushed her neck seductively.

She stifled a moan at his sensual caress. "That is a magnificent chandelier," she mumbled.

"Hmmm." He pulled her against him and made love to her. They needed an intimate release from the accumulated tension of the past few days, and they hadn't really had much time alone. This was perfect.

"I would like to spend more time loving you, but need to wait a little." Peter wrapped his arms around her and held her. Then a little later made slow languid love with her.

Sated, she snuggled closer against his body and murmured. "I think we need to dress and go have breakfast downstairs. And coffee."

He wrapped his arms around her waist. His lips brushed against hers as he spoke. "I'd rather stay here." He reached for her mouth again and massaged her lips with his. She opened for him, and he deepened the kiss. They spent the better part of the day in bed. Room service provided any additional sustenance they needed. They slept, talked about their future, and made love and napped.

The ringing phone forced them to move apart. Minola answered sleepily and heard Sally's happy voice. "You have twenty minutes to get downstairs. Time to have dinner, and I'm hungry."

Minola smiled. "We'll be down shortly." She turned back toward Peter. "That was our wake up call. Let's go or we'll be late for supper. She's hungry."

"Well, she is eating for two, and frankly, I'm hungry, too." Peter got up and pulled Minola out of bed.

Sally and Robert were waiting for them. "I'm happy to see you look rested. I'm sorry about Jennifer and Antonio." Sally spoke in a hushed tone.

"So am I, but... not much any of us can do. He was responsible for his actions. Never would I have guessed where this case would end. Let's talk about the wedding," Minola suggested, trying to set aside the tragedy.

"I'm glad you two weren't hurt. I heard from Gio that this could have ended differently." Robert leaned back in his chair and relaxed.

"Yes, much too close for my comfort," Peter admitted with quiet emphasis.

"I spoke with Adriana. We looked at a few tours for the guests. She offered one of her bigger boats for the duration. What an amazing woman. Anyway, I have a few restaurants selected for lunches and dinners. I think everyone will have a memorable time. I almost forgot, Adriana will send over hand embroidered lace masks for everyone from Burano, and yes, that includes the men. According to Adriana, as long as Murano was represented, she wanted everyone to see the work from Burano, too."

"That is incredible. If anyone wants, they can be framed. Min, I think we're ready for your big day."

"Yes, I can see that. It sounds incredible, a dream wedding, and the best part, we made new and lasting friendships."

"Gio is helping as well. He's sending three cases of his favorite local wine. Let me see—Amarone della Valpolicella. I think he ordered it the first time we met him." Robert delighted in being included in the preparations.

The rest of the evening was spent discussing the final plans and, afterward, a short stroll for gelato. As the moon shone brightly on the shimmering water and across the way, a gondolier sang a soulful romantic song. This was the Venice Minola would always remember.

Chapter 20

Peter's parents were due to arrive today, and that meant the rest of the Riley contingent was not far behind. His mother adored Minola, and Peter knew that she'd be a welcome addition to the family. He had so many things to be grateful for. Minola was finally going to be his wife. Wife. He tasted the words on his lips, and they were immeasurably sweet. She was sleeping, nestled against him, and he closed his eyes and remembered the first time he met her. He knew then she'd be his. He heard a muttered *I love you* against his chest, and he pulled her closer against him.

"After coffee and teeth, I'd like to do a quick sketch of Evan and Adriana then turn it into a portrait for their wedding."

"Wedding…whose wedding?"

"Theirs, of course. Coffee, Peter," she mumbled as her lips massaged his neck.

"On the way. I placed an order last night." His voice shook, and he buried his hand in her hair to keep from making love to her. He didn't want to be interrupted by room service.

She kissed him and raced to the bathroom, and he followed.

They gloried in the time they were able to spend alone, and Minola even had an opportunity to work on the drawing. They talked about Julio and the events that led to the final discovery. Most of all, they talked about Matteo, a fellow policeman. The loss touched Peter deeply. It felt good to be able to talk about all that had happened without the threat of further danger.

Time disappeared until Minola heard the phone ring. She put her hand over the mouthpiece and whispered that his parents had checked in early. "We'll be right down." She set the phone on the dresser and said, "Let's go meet your parents. They're in the lobby. They had their luggage delivered to the room and are ready for a cocktail. I love your mother's zest for life and her kindness. She helped me so much in Bath…" Minola's voice trailed off as she remembered the horrendous three days in the hospital. She blinked back the tears that threatened to fall and felt Peter reach for her.

"Don't go there, my love." He spoke softly, as always totally and completely aware of the woman he loved above all. A woman he almost let go. He had behaved like an idiot, and it cost Minola a great deal of pain, and he almost lost her. Never again.

"I'm sorry. Your mother is an amazing woman, and she raised a remarkable family. An incredible son. Let's go." She took Peter's hand, and together, they went to meet his parents.

All the while, just from a few furtive glances, Minola knew that Peter still felt a nagging sense of loss. Matteo was an officer, like Peter. It cut close to home. She understood and wanted Peter to relax and not think about it for a while. She wound her arms around his back to offer comfort.

Once the elevator door opened, Minola was enveloped in a huge bear hug. George Riley was the tall, silent type with salt and pepper curly hair, tall and lean, not unlike his son. "It is good to see you looking so relaxed, Minola. I trust my son has been making you happy." He peered at Minola's face then glared at his son.

Minola laughed and kissed his cheek in welcome and replied, "Yes, he has." She felt a tug on her arm and saw Clara Riley reach out to her as well. She turned and hugged the woman who would soon become her mother-in-law, but in fact, Minola considered her more of a mother.

"Welcome to Venice. Yes, I know the cocktails await." Minola turned toward Peter, smiling with pure joy. "Peter, you should say hello to your parents."

"It would seem I do not matter. You're all they care about." He grinned happily.

"Now, son, behave. We are happy to see you-together," replied Clara Riley.

"See, all they care about is you." Peter took her hand and tucked it in his arm. "As it should be." He bent down and kissed his mother's cheek.

They entered the bar next to the restaurant. The view of the Grand Canal was just as spectacular, and if Minola reached over the railing, she could actually touch the gondolier who was picking up a guest at the hotel. The location never ceased to amaze her, and she never tired of the view. Maybe a five minute walk to the biggest attraction of Venice, the Piazza San Marco, yet secluded enough to avoid the huge tourist throngs that populated the area from morning until dusk. A quiet, serene place, one side faced the Grand Canal, and the other a small and local canal. She leaned into Peter. Her contentment at that instant overwhelming, she whispered in his ear, "Can you hear the water lapping against the gondola, the whispered echoes of romance floating over the water?"

"Yes, you taught me to appreciate these instances." He smiled down at her. That was all he could do at the moment.

"Peter…" She didn't take anything for granted, but recently more often than not, she appreciated the quiet, tranquil time she spent with him. As long as he was by her side, she felt at peace, a rather unique awakening for someone so afraid and timid of relationships, whose trust had to be demonstrated over and over. This proved to be life changing. *Thanks to Peter, I grew up and took a chance on life and him. I'm eternally grateful that I did so. My life is fulfilled with him in it.* She felt Peter squeeze her hand in affirmation. *He didn't give up on me.* "Thank you, Peter," she whispered in his ear.

"Mother, please order for all of us. I need a moment with Minola." He took her hand and walked to a secluded and private spot near the business office. "What is it, my love? What is worrying you?" He ran his finger against her neck and felt her shiver. When something troubled her, his response was always if at all possible to handle it immediately, rather than let it fester.

"Not a thing." She touched his cheek with her lips, a gentle caress like a fleeting breeze. "I'm just exceedingly happy. I often tell you how much I love you, and yet it doesn't seem to be enough. I show you when we make love, and I tell you as often as I can, yet it never seems to be enough. I had this epiphany when I saw your parents, the perfect moment of utter peace and contentment. This is right. You and your parents are my family, but it also frightens me." She ran her lips over his neck and behind his ear.

Peter felt that potent touch all the way down to his groin. "It is right. That is precisely how I feel all the time when I'm with you and when I think about you. Which, by the way, is all the time. You have brought joy and wonder and trust into my life. I don't remember what it was like before I met you." He bent down and kissed her as if his actual survival depended on it, because he firmly believed it did. "Also, at moments like these, I feel a profound terror that something will separate us. That your safety will once again be in jeopardy. I understand how you feel."

"I think we'll be fine as long as we're together. Peter, I'm sorry about Matteo, sorry about all of this, but it is behind us. I know he was a colleague, a different force but a colleague none-the-less. I wanted to let you know I understand, and I feel your loss. I just needed to be with you for a moment. Let's go back to your parents." She put her arms around his neck and pressed her lips against his. She felt his immediate response as he deepened the kiss. Her lips parted to his assault as if parched. "I think we need…" she mumbled.

"I know. Let's go back," he whispered in her hair and gave her one softer kiss. "I need more time alone with you and soon." He took her hand, and together, they walked back to the bar.

"Is everything all right?" Clara Riley looked at Minola's red cheeks and swollen lips and smiled in satisfaction. "Tell us what has been going on, the plans, tell me everything."

"I'm not sure you want everything, Mother," Peter replied grimly.

"When I say everything, I mean everything, son," was the quick reply.

"Well, in that case, here we go. Minola found a body, and there…"

"What?" George Riley couldn't stop himself.

"Well, mother said everything." Peter proceeded to tell them what had happened since their arrival in Venice.

His mother sat there stupefied and oddly comforted that even with this latest adversity, her son was content. No strain lines or dark circles were visible under his eyes. He was happy, and being a typical mother, she couldn't have asked for more. She loved her future daughter in-law like a daughter. She was creative, independent, and demanded equality in her relationship with her son. And most importantly she loved him deeply. Clara Riley heaved a sigh of relief and listened to her son regale them with their latest adventure. "Minola, you have a remarkable talent, and I do not mean your astounding artistry. Tell me about all your wedding plans," Clara Riley demanded.

"It is rather funny that you should ask. I would like to know a few things myself."

"There is another story here, isn't there?" Clara watched Minola's lips curve up in a smile.

"There is, indeed. You will have to talk to Sally. She planned everything. I can show you my dress, and yours as well. Everything was delivered to our room."

"What do you mean 'my dress'? I brought one with me. I love my dress. I went shopping especially for my dress," Clara replied and heard Minola burst out laughing.

"Sally will explain, but she's napping at the moment." Minola saw Peter grinning, and once again felt an inordinate overflowing happiness.

"I'm wearing the dress I bought," Clara Riley replied.

"It is a *Carnevale* wedding. We all have costumes. Sally planned it, and I had no idea until we arrived in Venice."

"And you're going through with it?" Clara Riley asked.

"Yes, somehow it seemed appropriate, considering this is Venice, and the dresses are simple enough. At least ours are. I'm not sure about Sally's. She's my maid of honor."

"By the way, Peter, I stopped at the house before we left just to make sure everything was well. Your addition to the stable is quite impressive." Clara Riley watched as Minola shook her head vehemently.

"What addition?" Peter demanded.

"I…I must be mistaken," Clara Riley replied.

"Mother, what addition to the stable?"

"Err…I need to use the powder room." Clara Riley set her napkin aside and stood up.

"Mother, either you tell me or I'll call Dobbs."

"Peter, I bought you a wedding present," Minola whispered, wringing her hands together.

"You bought me a horse? You bought me that horse?" Peter was stunned and intense astonishment touched his face. He never would have guessed she would do something that magnificent.

"Yes," she mumbled and felt a tingling in the pit of her stomach at the sound of his husky voice.

"My apologies for saying anything, but it never occurred to me that you would…" Clara's eyes were moist.

"Did I make a mistake? You wanted it so badly. I don't know anything about horses. Peter, talk to me?"

"I'm speechless. You most certainly did not make a mistake. I'm just at a loss for words." He grasped her hand and squeezed. The woman literally took his breath away.

"That is a beautiful horse. Dobbs is taking good care of the household," Clara Riley said.

"When I found out it had been sold, I was so disappointed. How did you manage it?"

"That was the easy part. I called the owner. Then I called Mr. Dobbs."

"The devil you did? He never mentioned a word about it."

"He knew it meant to be a wedding surprise. Do you realize that we found out about our respective presents in a similar manner. Peter bought an incredible Murano chandelier. I couldn't take my eyes off it, and he just went in and bought it without telling me—an incredible surprise." Minola spoke in a soft voice. She still couldn't believe that beautiful piece was theirs.

"Your life together will be wonderful to watch." Clara Riley's tears glistened in the light.

The joyful reunion continued. Then Minola took Clara to their room to show off her dress as well as Clara's. The costume Sally selected for Clara Riley was that of a milk maid, George Riley was a court jester, and of course Peter was a nobleman, simple and elegant.

Peter and Minola had a few precious minutes alone. They used the time to make love and awaited the arrival of Rebecca Standish and Kirk Adams. Minola only met Kirk briefly before she left for Paris, but he made Rebecca happy, and that is all Minola cared about. She knew she'd have to go over the murder in detail for Becky and Kirk, and by now, she had it down pat, except for the latest tragedy and ending no one foresaw.

Chapter 21

The arrival of Becky and Kirk caused a mild uproar. Rebecca Standish was a force to be reckoned with. She had an astounding zest for life and a temper to match. She arrived at the hotel with four suitcases and several carry-on bags, and those were just her things. Minola's wedding was a small one, so Becky decided to bring a gift for everyone—a print of one of her favorite new artists that she took under her wing. Lovely drawings of the city Minola loved, her hometown of Chicago.

Becky couldn't wait to meet the man who finally captured Minola's heart. "Kirk, let's surprise them. Minola told me what room they're in."

"I don't think we have to bother." Kirk saw Minola run up to greet them. Hugs were exchanged, and Minola saw a ring on Becky's left hand and let out a shriek of excitement. "We have to celebrate. When is the wedding?"

"Not soon enough," replied a gruff voice.

"Kirk, how are you? Strange, Peter said something similar. Such a beautiful ring. I'm so happy for you both," Minola turned and hugged Kirk Adams. "A pleasure to see you again. I have been kept informed about your own adventures, except for that little addition." Minola gazed pointedly at Becky's left hand.

"It just happened last night, rather fantastic timing. Kirk wanted to propose before out trip, sort of a romantic escape for us. I'm celebrating my engagement and your wedding in Venice. And besides, I thought I'd surprise you." Rebecca extended her hand to see the ring.

"I still can't believe he did it. More to the point I can't believe you're marrying your Peter. Hey, when am I going to meet this exemplary man? So far I love Venice. The water taxi ride was a hoot. Kirk wants to retire here and pilot the water taxis." Becky took a deep breath and reached for Kirk, her happiness obvious to all.

"They are fun, aren't they? I love that you're here. Let's go to your room and make sure everything is all right. Your luggage should already be there. All of it." Minola remembered Rebecca did not pack light. "You'll meet Peter in a minute, and we have dinner reservation. Sally picked an incredible restaurant, right in the back of the piazza."

"That would be the Piazza San Marco. I did my homework. The location of this hotel is incredible." Rebecca felt herself being pulled by Kirk straight into his arms.

"Let's first take a quick peek at the restaurant and bar." Rebecca dragged Kirk to the restaurant for the astonishing view of the canal.

"The view is spectacular." Kirk's hand went around Rebecca's waist, and he nuzzled her neck and whispered softly in her ear so that only she could hear. "I'm so deeply in love with you, Becky. I'm never letting go. Never." He closed his eyes for a second to savor the euphoria he felt. Then he turned toward Minola. "Would you object if we had some time alone?"

"Of course not. The is the place for romance and love. You need to celebrate privately, and Venice is perfect for that. One of the most romantic cities in the world. You can go on your own anytime—well, except for the wedding and dinner tonight. I think Sally planned a couple of tours. Just let her know what you want to do. I'm so happy for you both." Minola grinned and hugged them. They returned to the lobby raving about the hotel, and Kirk was enchanted with his first trip to Europe. "I want our honeymoon here," he exclaimed.

"That could be arranged." Rebecca reached up and kissed him. "Speaking of honeymoons, where are you going for yours?" Rebecca asked.

Minola thought Peter's home first to relax and then decide. She'd be happy anywhere, as long as Peter was with her. "I have no idea.

Maybe Sally knows." Both burst out laughing and headed toward the elevator.

After seeing their room, Minola took them to meet Peter. Minola knew he was on the phone with Gio and gave him the few extra minutes needed.

Matteo's death rankled and probably always would, and Peter understood the choices a cop made, but one never forgot a colleague's death. The murders had been solved, and Minola was no longer threatened. He could live with anything else. Now, he could move forward with his life. He exhaled deeply. The knock on the door jarred him out of his stupor.

Minola reached Peter, kissed him, and then introduced her friends.

Rebecca hugged Peter. "So you're the man who finally captured Minola's heart? And more to the point made her happy." She extended her hand to Peter.

Peter laughed and replied, "I am indeed." He looked down at Rebecca's hand. "I would hazard a guess that congratulations are in order. My best wishes to you both." Peter turned and shook Kirk's hand. "It is a pleasure to meet you."

"Maybe we can stop and have a drink in the restaurant, if you'd like. We have early dinner reservations so it'll have to be quick. I think Sally mentioned something about five. You must be tired." Minola didn't want to intrude on their time together.

"Not really, I'm excited and happy…and frankly, I want to spend some time with Kirk. I hope you don't mind." Rebecca reached for Kirk. She needed to acknowledge the depth of her feelings for him and felt his arm go around her waist.

"I know the feeling, and not at all." Minola smiled. "So what is happening in your life? I only hear tidbits." Minola watched as Rebecca extended her left hand and wiggled her finger. "The engagement is still new for me. I don't want to take away from you, but…"

"Becky, stop it. We'll celebrate at dinner tonight. Good news is to be shared at all times. We certainly know enough of the other kind." She momentarily closed her eyes. "I'm so excited for you." She hugged

Becky and then turned toward Kirk. "You're a lucky man, Kirk Adams."

"Don't I know it?" Kirk's hand slipped up her arm, bringing her closer to him.

"When is the wedding?" Minola hugged Rebecca again.

"We'll be expecting you two to attend, so we'll wait until after your honeymoon," Kirk replied. "Give us the rest of the news. Sally shared a little. Another murder? Something odd about creative women and their adventures." Kirk smirked and felt Becky pat him on the back.

"Excuse me? You do know the person you're engaged to owns an art gallery?" Minola was happy for her friends, and Kirk could be grumpy, but she knew he loved Becky deeply.

"Yup, sure do." Kirk's lips caressed Becky's hair. He always needed to touch her. "I'm her handy man, because we firefighters always have second jobs." He chuckled and pulled Becky closer against him.

"I have heard that somewhere. I wanted to make sure you included your fiancée in the *odd adventure and creative women* bit." Minola grinned, her eyes bright and cheerful. "Sally was taking a nap, and I don't want to wake her. You'll meet Peter's parents at dinner. They are joining us."

"Sounds wonderful. I still can't believe how our lives have changed. I remember when you left for Paris. By the way, the jerk asked about you. He recently stopped at the gallery. He heard about your adventures and that you're now a celebrated artist. You and Peter made the papers back home, too."

"The jerk?" Minola asked puzzled.

"Yup, the reason you left for Paris, remember?"

"Oh, that jerk…yes, I remember."

"He apologized to you via me and asks your forgiveness. I am to extend his apologies, and he wants to know if he still stands a chance, and if not he hopes the man in your life has the patience of a saint…like I said *the jerk*." Rebecca laughed.

"Amazing…" Minola laughed out loud. "I don't know what to say."

"I do. Please extend our sympathies, but Miss Grey is engaged and shortly-to-be married. Quite soon in fact." Peter quietly moved closer to Minola and took her hand in his.

"Yes, to a really patient man." Minola couldn't stop laughing. She had a lucky escape. She remembered the reason for her adventure in Paris. Little did she know just how much her life would change, all because of the man standing next to her. "Becky, I'll call you thirty minutes before dinner. Enjoy your time together."

"Thanks, Min…I haven't called you that in ages. As odd as that sounds, I want to take another quick peek at the view from the restaurant. Would you mind coming with us? Then we'll go to our room."

"Of course not, even now I do the same thing. I call it Venetian magic. Believe me, I understand," Minola replied.

They went downstairs, and Rebecca stared at the Grand Canal and listened to the sound of the water swishing about, the waves rocking the gondolas, and the creaky oars as the gondoliers moved into position to pick up their guests, and she exclaimed, "I love this hotel. It is exquisite. I agree with Kirk about our honeymoon spot, right here in this hotel."

"Works for me. The sooner the better. I wish I'd known what I've been missing." He pulled Becky against him and nuzzled her neck. She was the love of his life, and he wasn't letting her go. He turned toward Minola. "We'll see you in the lobby at the appointed hour. I want some time with my fiancée. Hey, I like the way that sounds." He took Rebecca's hand in his and tightened his hold.

"So do I." Joy could be heard in Rebecca's voice. She loved him deeply.

"Dinner is at five. We'll call you if anything changes. Otherwise, see you in the lobby. We know where you're staying…have a good time you two." Minola once again hugged her friends.

"See you," Becky and Kirk replied in unison.

Minola headed back to the room. She locked the door and reached for Peter.

"Your friends are delightful, except for the *jerk,* of course."

"The *jerk* doesn't count. He's not a friend, never was. Peter, how are we going to handle the wedding with everything that has happened? It seems odd to celebrate when four people are dead, and one in prison. And we can't ignore our family and friends. They flew a long distance to be here for us."

"We won't. Life is to be celebrated. The only death that mattered was Matteo. Katarina and Pia were going to kill you. They were assassins. I cannot waste any sympathy on their loss. And Antonio…well, he certainly qualifies as evil. When I was on the phone with Gio, he told me they found other evidence tying him to the killing business. In fact, he was the mastermind. His was the first contact with the business associates, then Pia, and ultimately Katarina. He was the salesman for the company. Cold bastard. No, we shall celebrate our lives, our family, and Sally's new life that she's bringing into this world. We have Adriana and Evan, your Becky and Kirk. We have much to celebrate."

They dressed and went to meet their friends. Everyone was waiting except for Peter's parents. Peter called them and was told by his father that his mother couldn't decide what to wear and they would be down shortly. Peter chuckled and relayed the message. By the time he was done, his parents were exiting the elevator. Introductions were made, and everyone followed Sally to the restaurant.

"I know exactly where it is—so that no one would be disappointed, Robert and I had dinner there just to check it out. It was delicious," she relayed with great satisfaction.

"I know how diligent you are in your research. It is much appreciated." Minola took her arm, and together, they led the way.

The narrow side street off the piazza was filled with restaurants and souvenir shops, along with gelaterias. Tourists flittered from one place to another. The dim lights added to the romantic ambiance. The restaurant was the perfect spot for comfortable conversation, and everyone knew exactly where they were. They could see the Piazza San

Marco just around the corner. Seated immediately, they settled on the drinks and wine selection.

"So that everyone knows, I arranged a few tours for us. I thought, if anyone wanted to, we could go together. I'm good at arranging things." Sally felt Robert's arm around her now impressively large waist.

"I assume we all know about the murders. Our resident sleuths were at it again." Clara Riley radiated happiness.

"We heard a little. Please tell all, but before the tale begins, I'd like to make a suggestion. We have a couple of days before the wedding. I would like for us to at least have breakfast and dinner together. I know Sally planned a couple of tours, and that is wonderful, too. This is just such an unusual and happy gathering, and I want to partake." Rebecca brushed her hand against Kirk's arm.

"That is a splendid suggestion. We are all in agreement," Clara Riley replied.

Peter laughed. "Breakfast and dinner, it is, and a couple of tours. Sally, please pick the restaurants. Your research so far has been excellent."

"Breakfast has to be at the hotel. It is scrumptious, and Minola needs her coffee first thing. And maybe a dinner as well. The place is beautiful in the evening. So romantic." Sally rubbed her tummy in contentment.

"Now the murder story please," Rebecca requested.

The food was ordered, and everyone picked a Venetian specialty, from black pasta to sardines with onions to Sally's favorite pizza to calamari with pasta. Along with the wine, the conversation flowed smoothly, a perfect setting to get to know new and old friends. Once they finished, Minola recommended one of her favorite gelaterias down the street from the restaurant. On the way back to the hotel, they stopped in a café for an espresso served with a tray of biscotti. A delightful ending to the day, time that was much needed to regroup and to continue. The tragedy certainly had not been forgotten, but rather set aside so that life could resume with all its uncertainties.

Since becoming involved with Peter, Minola valued each moment. She'd learned that life was fleeting and should be cherished.

Chapter 22

The tours had been arranged, chief among them was the Doge's or Ducal Palace. The sites were nearly impossible to see without a prearranged tour. The lines were extremely long, and the wait could take hours. Piazza San Marco held many of the Venetian treasures, and the square itself was a place Minola returned to on a regular basis. She wanted to share all the sites she loved with family and friends.

Minola didn't mind revisiting the Doge's Palace. As any tourist would agree, certain places could not be missed. The palace had been home to many leaders of Venice for almost a thousand years. Filled with art, sumptuous rooms, and the famous Bridge of Sighs so named by Lord Byron, the beautiful view of a canal, a lonely stop for some who were going from the palace to prison, indeed a poignant scene, a last breath of Venice, a walk from elegance and sumptuousness to a hard, cold and damp stone dungeon.

Minola wanted to share a little of the vast history and age of the place, and over breakfast she talked about the history. "This building is amazing. The first palace was a fortress finished in 814. Fires in 976, in 1106, 1574, and 1577 destroyed many masterpieces, and restoration continued slowly until the 1880's. Today, it reflects the massive and majestic power that was once Venice. For me, every step in Venice history, beauty, and art beckons. I really hope you love it as much as I do. Maybe I should become a tour guide." She grinned mischievously.

"Now I really want to see it." Rebecca took a sip of her coffee.

"Good, that was the idea."

Minola knew they would enjoy the visit and couldn't wait for their reactions. She had been delighted when all agreed to go together. The morning and early afternoon was spent touring Venice. Peter and Minola opted out of a gondola ride and settled instead on a cafe to wait for everyone. She still couldn't bring herself to step foot in a gondola, and Peter didn't pressure her, either, firmly convinced she'd find something to investigate. He wanted to be married.

***

After the tours, they agreed to meet at the hotel for dinner. Peter noted that Minola was becoming restless and wanted to make sure there would be no regrets. He knew she loved him deeply, but he also understood her reticence in what she considered a public affair, even though the wedding only included family and close friends. He knew she preferred a more intimate setting for taking her vows, and he felt the choice was as close to perfect as possible. He needed to reassure her. Once in their room, he took her hand and led her to the window. The drapes were open, and she was able to see the amazing traffic on the Grand Canal, the teeming life that so majestically sustained Venice.

She stood in front of him. His arms were around her waist, and he felt her lean into him. "It will be a perfect wedding. Our family and friends are here to celebrate with us. We have new friends as well."

"I know, and I cannot wait to marry you, but I can't stop thinking about Jennifer. She is virtually alone now, and she changed so much. How does that happen? Is it because Antonio no longer cared, if he ever did? Peter, she was living with a murderer, and he tried to kill her. How does a person survive that?"

"Even professionally, I cannot explain it. You can reach out to her a little later, after she comes to terms with what has happened and faces the truth about her husband, but now she needs time."

"I promise never to look anywhere that I shouldn't."

"I may hold you to that, and our home should be safe enough. Before I forget, Fitzhugh and his wife are arriving this evening. And the rest of the Riley contingent, too. Edward had to finish something at work."

"Good. I had a message from David Abingdon. He and Ashby will be here as well. He rang off with a *ciao*. I hope they worked out the problems they had in Bath. He sounded happy." She turned toward Peter and kissed him.

"Do you realize even at this date, essentially a day before our wedding, my mother is admonishing me? She wants to make sure I'm taking good care of you." Peter smiled, his happiness showed in his eyes, his relaxed stance, and light steps when he walked. The proverbial walking on air applied rather well. Even with everything that had happened, his primary focus was his bride-to-be.

"I'm a lucky woman, welcomed by a loving family with no reservations, nothing but true unconditional love."

"I can attest to that. According to my mother, their plan is to make sure I become married to you, and that nothing goes wrong. My mother was explicit. I'm to keep you from any and all mysterious discoveries."

"I'm ready, and I'm not letting you go, and I'm most certainly not looking under any rocks or glass." Minola felt a sense of peace for the first time since her gruesome discovery. Peter offered her everything—passion, peaceful contemplation, joy, and laughter, all that was good. She promised herself she'd never take it for granted.

Minola's bruises from the attack had healed. Some discoloration could still be seen on her elbows and knees, and a little on her face as well. Her badge of survival, and she was sure she would not be the first bride with a couple of healing bruises. Her wedding included only friends and family anyway, and as long as Peter was beside her, she didn't care.

The vases from the Castigli Furnace arrived as scheduled with an additional, bigger and wider vase. The colors were muted, an alabaster mixed with earthy tones, a nutmeg, deep shining bronze, and splashes of maroon. To add texture, the lip of the vase was in the shape of a rope that matched the bronze swirls in the vase. An amazing piece that was at once subdued and striking. Jennifer signed her work, and she included a note thanking Minola for her help, and she promised to keep in touch.

Minola, grateful to acknowledge the generous peace offering, sent one of her drawings of Venice she did as gifts for her guests, also promising to stay in touch. She knew they would never reach the stage of great friendship, for those were few, but she'd be happy to correspond, and help if she could.

Sally took charge of the vases and confirmed the delivery of the flowers for tomorrow, the day of the wedding. Minola's drawings would serve as an added souvenir of the special day. Adriana personally dropped off the lace masks, each one beautifully boxed and wrapped, along with the masks, Adriana delivered her wedding gift— the highly coveted coffee machine.

The simple decorations in the small ballroom were almost done. The soft ivory linens the hotel provided were perfect. The tablecloths gleamed in the light and provided another touch of romance. Sally had selected various *Carnevale* masks to hang on the walls to keep the theme going. She also picked Minola's favorite gelato flavors for the sweet table along with biscotti, Tiramisu and other Italian favorites.

Candles on every table, low flower arrangements for cozier conversations, and the chandeliers hanging above would set the intimate mood. The decor was simple and elegant and perfect for Minola. Robert even had a hand in the process. The music was forgotten, but Gio came to the rescue and recommended a quartet he had used previously. With Gio's help, after all no one said *no* to a Bruloni, Robert was able to book them at the last minute. Since Minola did not like loud music, the quartet was perfect. He also took charge of the wine that Gio had delivered, along with the choices at the bar.

On the last evening before Minola's big day, Sally along with Adriana set up the small room next to the restaurant. The tables were in close proximity to each other. A long table graced one wall with a coffee stand and the usual accoutrements, along with hot and cold milk, various coffee flavors from vanilla to hazelnut and an assortment of biscotti.

On another table, the gelato bar was set up. Minola's favorite mocha with dark chocolate and dark chocolate chip was in the center, and what passed for a sweet table occupied the wall on the other side of the room. It included Tiramisu, the *Carnevale* favorites *galani*, fried cookies that look like ribbons, and *frittele*, round small donuts with powdered sugar on top, sometime stuffed with candied fruit, but Minola loved hers stuffed with Nutella. Sally did not spare anyone's waistline with the sweet delicacies.

The bar was outside the dining room and faced the Grand Canal. The Bellini, was the main draw, a traditional Venetian drink made with Prosecco, a white sparkling wine, and pureed white peaches, a cool and refreshing drink. Gio's wines, sparkling water, and anything else one desired, it was a fully stocked bar. Peter had a hand in the drink selection along with Robert.

The final preparations did not take long, and by the time Sally locked the door, she was satisfied with the results and ready for dinner with her friends.

Chapter 23

The wedding morning dawned bright and sunny. Minola spent the previous night in a room alone. She stuck to some traditions. Now she wished she hadn't, she missed Peter. Nor was Peter happy with her decision, and he seemed somewhat disgruntled at the prospect of spending a night without her.

She rang him at six in the morning and was told in no uncertain terms that he hadn't slept at all, he missed her in their bed, and he needed coffee. She ordered coffee to be delivered to both rooms, and she told him she'd see him at the restaurant for breakfast.

Theirs was going to be an intimate ceremony with a vicar, Peter's friend who'd tended the family for many years. He came from Slough especially for the occasion. Minola was delighted with that arrangement, and she had her future mother-in-law to thank. It made Peter especially happy. They were long-standing friends. The ceremony was to be held in the same room where dinner was to be served.

Minola was nervous. The wedding was finally going to happen, her friends were with her, and she was going to be married to the love of her life. She counted her many true blessings. Everything was finished. All she had to do was be ready at the appointed hour. A knock interrupted her musing. Sally, still in her pajamas, was at the door.

"This is such a magnificent hotel, and I'm in my pajamas, but I can get away with it because I'm pregnant." She stuck her tummy out to prove her point.

"I have coffee, milk, and a few sweet rolls. I ordered enough." She poured some hot milk for Sally. "Okay, what do we do first?" Minola asked.

"We have the milk and coffee, sit, and relax. A sweet roll would be lovely! Then we dress and go have breakfast. That's what. I just came to say hi and tell you I love you."

"I love you, too. Thank you for arranging all of this and making it perfect. It has been a glorious last couple of days. You're going to make me cry." Minola hugged her best friend.

"I loved every minute of it. You know that."

"This has been an unbelievable journey. I still cannot believe I'm to be married this afternoon. Such a traditional wedding."

"Ha. Nothing traditional about your wedding. First, your best friend planned your wedding. The vicar will perform the ceremony in the dining room. The only thing he'll have is a small table with flowers, and he's staying for the festivities. You're wearing a costume. Do you want me to keep going?"

Minola laughed out loud. "You arranged everything—well, except for the vicar, and he's a family friend. Of course he's staying."

A knock on the door interrupted. Peter wanted to see his bride-to-be. "I missed you." He took Minola in his arms, saw Sally, greeted her as well, and watched as she took the sweet roll in one hand and the milk in the other.

"We need to dress, almost breakfast time. See you downstairs. Don't be late." Sally waved with the hand holding the sweet roll and waddled out the door.

"It has been a long night and an even longer engagement. I can't believe the day is finally here." He stared with longing at her, and every time his gaze met hers, his heart turned over.

"I can't, either, and I cannot believe our incredible friends." She reached up and tenderly touched his lips with hers.

"I don't want to let you go, but am afraid Sally will come looking for us if we're not downstairs." His lips curved up in a grin. He kissed the tip of her nose and left.

Minola was ready in minutes and joined everyone already at the table. Even Adriana and Evan were there.

Kirk was the first to speak. "I booked this hotel. We're coming back for our honeymoon."

"Have you set a wedding date yet?" Minola asked.

"No, we haven't, but the honeymoon is booked." Rebecca shared a smile with Kirk.

"That is an excellent plan." Adriana gazed lovingly at Evan and then flashed her ring finger in the air.

"I believe congratulations are in order. Well done, Evan," Minola exclaimed in delight before poking Peter in the arm.

"Speaking of honeymoons, have you and Peter decided where yet?" Adriana asked.

"Sally hasn't mentioned anything about a honeymoon, but we thought to maybe go home for a couple of weeks and then decide." Minola laughed.

"You should be able to handle that on your own. Geesh," Sally replied.

"The reason I ask is, if you would like to go to Barcelona, my father recently bought a hotel, and I could arrange your stay. I do not mean to interfere, but the location is perfect, and…I hope I'm not imposing," Adriana spoke softly. She loved the new acquisition and wanted to share with her friends. She knew Minola loved art and architecture, and Barcelona certainly had enough to spare.

"That might be quite wonderful. Thank you, Adriana." Minola was touched at the offer. So many people to be grateful for. Today of all days, she truly gave thanks.

"I've never been to Barcelona." Sally heard laughter surround her.

"In that case, maybe Barcelona is the right choice." Minola smiled when she saw Peter nod in agreement. She had no problem with Robert and Sally joining them, and apparently, neither did Peter.

The breakfast took over two hours. Between the delicious and varied selection of things to eat at the buffet, the wonderful coffee, conversations between friends and family, and the many future plans, time disappeared.

The Riley's quickly grasped the deep abiding love and friendships shared at the table and found it rare indeed. David and Ashby seemed to have come to an understanding, and Fitzhugh's wife delighted in all things Venice.

After breakfast, everyone went their own way, either to tour or relax in the nearby garden or walk amongst the tourists at the piazza. Ashby and David opted for a vaporetto ride. Adriana and Evan went to his room to discuss wedding plans, as Adriana put it. Sally and Robert went back to the room, as well. Sally needed to rest. No plans were made for a lunch get together, giving people more time on their own.

Peter and Minola lingered over coffee, enjoying the view and each other. Peaceful and serene. "I never thought about Barcelona. Gaudi's work alone is worth the trip."

"As long as you promise to avoid finding anyone not breathing due to foul play, I'll agree to anything," he quipped jokingly.

"I promise."

"I happen to have a friend who lives outside of Barcelona, a retired Interpol man."

"Retired?"

"He was wounded and could not return to work." He heard an indrawn breath from Minola and reached for her hand. "A hazard of the profession, I'm afraid, which brings me to this…I would like to leave and run the estate and…"

"No, Peter, this is what you do and do well. I do not want to be responsible for your decision. You will regret it, and that I could not bear."

"I have thought about it since our time in Bath. It is the right time. I need to protect you. I need to keep you safe. My primary focus is always on you, not my job. That is not a good thing if I continue working."

"You'd be giving up your profession."

"I thought about that, too, just wasn't sure when to bring it up. I could join the local force, somewhere in the vicinity, to keep my hands in the police business. I'm not making the decision because you want me to. It is my choice, my focus, but you must agree."

"All I ask is that you seriously think about it. Thank you for talking to me and letting me know how you feel."

"I promised you I would do that. I already think of you as my wife. It is rather odd."

"I know. I almost called you my husband yesterday." She stayed quiet a moment. "I suspect Evan is probably thinking of leaving as well."

"He is. We talked about it in one of our meetings. Gio recommended he become a private investigator with offices here and in London," Peter spoke casually.

"He mentioned your involvement, didn't he?"

"You know me a little too well. Yes, Gio did mention a partnership, and that included my friend in Barcelona. He cannot walk a long distance and uses a cane for the short time he can, but he is a computer genius and an amazing researcher."

"This truly is an eventful trip. Just remember, where you go, I go."

"Understood, and I wouldn't have it any other way. The cases would be what are known as white collar crimes—forgeries, art thefts, things along those lines…"

"Just a thought, what happened in Venice…was that considered white collar crime? Paris? Bath?" She was determined to be by his side. With Interpol, she could not, but in a private capacity, he wouldn't be able to keep her away.

Minola understood he tried to make it sound less dangerous than his profession and the exploits they shared together. Truth be told, she looked forward to new adventures. As Sally once pointed out, anyone could get run over crossing the street. During their time together, they met some incredible people—helpful, determined to do the right thing. This allowed her to keep her faith when she met the other kind—the kind that killed and maimed.

"Dammit, your point is well-taken," he replied with emphasis.

"All I can say is that we're on an amazing adventure, and life will not be boring."

"I can vouch for that, and we'll make any decisions together after our exceptionally long honeymoon," Peter agreed.

"I can live with that." She caressed his cheek with her fingertips.

***

In a few hours, Minola would become a wife. Recently, she thought a great deal about her life, the chances she took, and the man she loved. She would not change a thing. Maybe she would have accepted Peter sooner in Paris, but that was in the past.

Minola continued to brush her hair. She had it cut just above her shoulders, a few layers scattered around her face. She always styled her own hair, and today was no exception. With no veil, Minola opted for a few flowers pinned in her hair. She did her own make-up, preferring a light touch.

The dress lay on the bed, and Sally was already dressed and on her way to help. In two hours, Minola would take her vows. Once again, she found nothing wrong with the traditional vows that many took before. She and Peter already worked out their difference; the rest was up to destiny. She was prepared to take the biggest step in her life.

"I love this dress. That is so you." Sally twirled the dress then opened the door to accept the coffee she ordered to calm her friend.

"That is perfect, thank you. And you look beautiful." Minola took a sip.

"Robert is helping Peter. He seems a little…excited. Apparently, he cannot wait."

"Neither can I. Okay, here it goes." Minola put her dress on. It fit beautifully, a simple maiden's dress, yet much more. The color was a rich ivory with touches of gold that shimmered in the light. The long sleeves puffed near the shoulder, slenderizing the arms. The lace in the front softened the dress further, and with the Empire waist, it flowed smoothly as she walked. Minola picked up the shoes and thought about

Katarina. She shuddered and stopped mid stride. *Why couldn't she be happy with the beautiful store? What drove her to such extremes?*

"Minola, the shoes are beautiful. She's gone. She would have killed you and Peter. Let it go and put the shoes on." Sally hugged her friend.

"I know. You should have seen her eyes. They were so cold, so empty, as if killing someone was a fact of life. She was so nice and lovely at the shop. Antonio, too. I thought he was worried and loved his wife, was jealous of her perceived affair. And he didn't care at all about her. He wanted her dead because he was tired of her, and she didn't leave. I don't understand. Poor Jennifer."

"I know, but we found new incredible friends in Adriana and Gio. Jennifer is safe. Think about that. Think about Peter."

"What would I do without you?"

"You wouldn't be having a *Carnevale* wedding, for starters." Sally laughed.

She watched as Minola put on her shoes, and the effect was startling. The color was perfect, almost a vanilla. The gold bows on the shoes picked up the golden threads in the dress.

"Any jewelry?"

"Yes, Peter's opal and my engagement ring. That is I all need."

"Perfect, you look stunning. Put some lipstick on."

"Not a fan."

Sally reached into a bag she brought with, took out a light pink gloss, and applied it to Minola's lips. "There, that is perfect."

"Peter won't like it."

"He'll have to handle it for a little while. Time for you to marry." Sally handed Minola her simple bouquet of wild flowers then took Minola's hand. Together, they went downstairs.

The guests were already seated at the tables. Peter, Robert, and Edward stood near the vicar as Minola walked in. George Riley stood up, took his place by Minola's side, and walked her to his son.

Peter's breath caught in his lungs as he gazed at Minola. He literally could not breathe. Robert's hand grabbed his shoulder. Then he took a deep breath. He felt Minola reach out to him, and he grasped her hand in his and turned toward John Windham, a lifelong friend who would perform the ceremony uniting him forever to Minola.

He listened to the solemn vows and answered where he was prompted, surprised that he could do that much. All he could think about was Minola. In a few minutes, she would become his wife. To love and cherish...he watched Minola as she took her vows. Her answers were quiet but firm, no hesitation. She never glanced away from him while the vicar spoke, and even when he pronounced them man and wife, her gaze remained steady and reassuring and, above all, loving.

Peter was married. He had a wife. The love of his life. When he heard John Windham repeat, *Peter, you can now kiss your bride,* he smiled and finally indeed kissed his bride. And rather well at that.

"Peter?" He heard the intimate, soft whisper.

"I'm deeply and passionately in love with you. And I cannot yet believe you're mine. My wife. You are stunning, beautiful," he murmured in her ear.

"So are you, and I firmly believe I have been yours since the day we met. I love you, too-deeply and passionately," she whispered back, moving a little closer to him.

Their intimate moments in front of the vicar were necessary to them, a shared joy of unity and commitment. John Windham blessed them and then took his seat. Peter and Minola turned to face their friends and thanked them all for coming and for sharing the joyous occasion.

After the congratulations from everyone, and while appetizers were being served, some guests headed to the bar to sample the famous Bellini or Gio's local Veneto selection. Peter asked to be excused to have a few minutes with his bride. He escorted Minola past the bar to an intimate spot, a corner that faced the Grand Canal and was currently unoccupied.

"You have survived, Mrs. Riley, and you're mine. My wife," he whispered.

"I am that, Captain Riley. I like my new name on your lips."

"So do I. I cannot begin to tell you how much you mean to me, how much I love you, but I aim to show you for the rest of my life."

"As do I." That was Minola's solemn vow.

Peter kissed her, his demanding lips caressed hers. "I love you." His mouth recaptured hers, more insistent this time. There was a dreamy intimacy to his touch. Burying her face in his neck, she planted a soft kiss there that sent him reeling. He heard distant chords of an Italian love song, a gondolier serenading his guests. "Dance with me, Mrs. Riley. I need to move." He swirled Minola in his arms and started a slow, languid waltz.

"Always, Captain Riley." She put her arms around his neck and pressed herself closer to him.

Soon, others joined in the celebration, while still others swayed in place. The musicians settled near the bar and continued what the gondolier began.

Dinner was announced, and Peter reluctantly let go of his bride and followed her to the dining room. There were speeches made, memories recounted, and toasts given to the bride and groom, family, and friends.

Amidst subdued lightning and candles, the various colorful masks—many with feathers, gold trim and glitter—shimmered in the dining room. Truly a magical evening in mystical Venice that no one would forget.

Minola could not have imagined a better wedding day. Everyone she cared about was here to celebrate their special day. She gazed at Peter, and the love she saw in his eyes left her breathless. She wanted to be alone with him, and she wanted to savor and prolong this evening, a strange moment filled with contradictions. *I am a married woman. And I don't think it is possible to be any happier.*

She saw Adriana and Evan, and they were inseparable. Rebecca and Kirk, too. He had eyes only for her. Sally and Robert were as close as possible. Her new mother-in-law and father-in-law were chatting happily, as was her sister-in-law and brother-in-law, Mary and Edward, and her niece and twin nephews. There was a new sleeping baby, too.

So much love in the room. The ugliness had been set aside.

Minola walked over to her new parents and hugged them both and was welcomed to the family with open arms. The guests were given the souvenirs and were delighted with their presents. Minola thanked Adriana for the masks and credited Gio with the excellent wine. Everyone recognized Minola's work, and the prints were treasured.

The dinner included local specialties, and the gelato bar was a huge success. No one wanted to go home, and people lingered long after Peter and Minola left.

"This has been a truly amazing day. I am now a married man, and as such, I want to spend some time with my bride. We'll come down a little later and see if anyone is still standing. Please enjoy! Everyone is staying at the hotel, and we have the room and bar until we're done." He took Minola's hand and started to walk off. Minola put her hand on his arm to stop him.

"I don't think we mentioned it, but Sally arranged a breakfast for everyone— sometime around ten. If we don't see you a little later, then at breakfast. Enjoy while I spend a little time with my husband. See you soon." She felt Peter tugging at her.

Peter opened the door to their room and, per tradition, picked Minola up and carried her over the threshold. He set Minola down and saw the room had been decorated. The scent of flowers infused the room. Then a bigger surprise awaited them. Battery lit candles were everywhere. More masks—a few leaning against the desk and cabinet, others hanging on the walls—and huge bouquets of flowers filled the room. On one side, hanging on the wall, was a base of milky white ribbon of glass, blended with the same colors used in the small vases, etched and filled with gold leaf, and it read, *Congratulations, Captain and Mrs. Riley* with the date of their wedding. She read the note attached on the desk and started crying, and she couldn't stop the waterworks.

"What is it, my heart?" Peter took her in his arms and held her. She handed him the note from Jennifer, a last minute gift.

"She apologized and came to the realization that she's alive because of us and that we do have something unique. And, and…she wanted to let us know that." Minola hiccupped, while Peter tenderly dried her tears with his fingertips.

"Our wedding has been exceptional in all aspects, and she's right. We have something unique, something I'll never take for granted. That is my way of letting you know I will never take you for granted...And now, I want to make love to my wife."

He savored the words on his lips, his gaze on her face as soft as a caress. His hands cupped her face and held it gently. Then he lowered his head, and his mouth covered hers hungrily. He felt her arms go around his neck, and she pressed herself closer to him. His lips then seared a path down her neck. "I love you in this dress, but it has to go."

Peter proceeded to remove her dress and waited while she took off his clothing. He then gently eased her on the bed and loved her. He kissed her again and whispered his love for each part of her body. His hand reached her abdomen and moved seductively down to her thigh. She was his to love and cherish, and that was what he did when she welcomed him into her body. Their passion grew and the pleasure became explosive. Breathless, together, they soared to shuddering ecstasy.

Minola's emotions whirled and skidded with every touch, and blood pounded in her brain and heart. She trembled with each intimate stroke, nestling closer to him as their legs intertwined. She was his as much as he was hers. His murmured words of passion while he loved her shattered her. Together, they found the tempo that exploded in fiery sensations. She gasped as she climaxed and heard his groans as he followed her.

"Peter, I have no words, but I can't let go of you." She clung to him as if her life depended on it and felt him respond, his touch at once possessive and tender.

"Neither can I. You're my world. My everything. I want you again, but I'm exhausted." His heart thumped erratically. He buried his face in her neck, waiting for his trembling to subside.

Peter knew his life was bound in the woman he was holding. His wife. No matter what the future held, what decisions they made about their future, Peter knew it would be done together. Whether he stayed with Interpol, went into the private sector with two other remarkable men, or remained closer to home on the police force, it would be done together.

In the meantime, even before they left for Venice, Peter ordered that a room be converted to a studio for Minola, with a view of her favorite garden and the perfect light. He knew she would love it.

"Peter, since we're both exhausted, I vote we join our family and friends and savor our time with them. I know that is not the norm, but…"

"I couldn't agree more, Mrs. Riley."

They decided to join their friends, because many came a long way for the occasion, and Peter and Minola had the rest of their lives together. This day was to be celebrated with family and friends. The dress was simple, no train and easy to wear. Minola decided to wear it again. Besides, Peter loved seeing her in it.

Downstairs, it seemed as if no one wanted to leave, and the party was still going strong. Sounds of joy and merriment could be heard as Peter and Minola, holding hands, entered the bar area. Tables were moved so that more could sit together.

"Welcome back! Join us. You look rested." Sally snickered and raised her glass of orange juice in the air.

Laugher followed Sally's comments while Peter replied, "Indeed. I have never felt better."

"Neither have I. And I didn't want to miss all the wonderful things we have to celebrate today with our friends. A baby, old friends, new friends, and two upcoming weddings. We are, indeed, all blessed," Minola felt a bottomless peace and happiness, married to a man she loved and respected. For the first in her life, she had a loving family. She glanced down at her wedding ring and momentarily closed her eyes. Immediately, Peter's hand encircled hers. A simple ceremony with powerful words to live by, her vows enveloped her totally. Peter was her husband to love and cherish. That was so easy to do with Peter.

Peter glanced down at their intertwined hands and took a deep breath. He walked to the quartet and asked a song be played. He watched Minola as she heard the first notes of their song *You're My World* being played. Peter walked over and cradled his bride in his arms. He stood without moving, her soft curves molded to his body, and he could barely breathe. He whispered, his breath hot against her ear, "I love you, Mrs. Riley. More than life, I love you." He pulled her closer to him and swayed to the sound of the music.

Minola closed her eyes and then put her arms his neck, nestling her body closer to his. She whispered the same words he just uttered. "I love you, Captain Riley, more than life I love you." She felt his hot breath in her hair, and together, they danced into the next adventure of their lives.

The End

Author's Note

Dear Reader,

Venice is one of the most romantic, extravagant and stunning cities in the world, and it has captured my heart.

Every step taken is filled with art, history and romance. I couldn't think of a better place for Peter and Minola to marry. This is their adventure of love and passion, along with a mystery, but it is a romance first and foremost.

I used the carabinieri as the main police investigating body, and I did so because I found their history fascinating. I was able to include that history in the story. It also made it much simpler to have just one police organization in the investigating process.

Law enforcement in Italy is rather complex. There are two factions of police, the military and civil guards, and all police units fall under the jurisdiction of Ministero dell'Interno, and through the Department of Public Safety all laws are enforced.

Below I outlined the three national police forces:

Carabinieri along with police duties, serve as the military police for the Italian Military.

Polizia di Stato is the civil national police of Italy.

Guardia di Finanza- a military force that falls under the jurisdiction of the Minister of Economy and Finance, but is also a police force.

The *Carabinieri, Polizia di Stato and Guardia di Finanza* are all public safety agents, and as such are always on duty, even during vacation and leave.

Locally, as in Venice, the *Polizia di Stato* falls under the authority of the Prefetto, who works with the Questore, the local chief of police. The local police are under the authority of the mayor.

The above is just a quick and rather simple glimpse of Italian law enforcement.

Venice is portrayed from the point of view of a tourist, the impressions of romance and sheer magic of the Grand Canal, Piazza San Marco, and many other wondrous sites, as seen through the eyes of Minola and Peter. It is their Venice.

Like any major city in the world, there are issues of survival and crime, and all the things that make our world a rather sad one at the moment.

I left those issues where they belong-in the news, and our daily life. I write romance stories with happy endings, a short escape from our everyday reality.

—*Margot Justes*

About the Author

Born in Poland, Margot Justes has lived in some of the world's most wonderful places, including Israel, France and South Africa. Currently living in the East Coast, she has taken her love of art and travel and cultivated it into unique settings and stories for her writing, 2007 brought her a contract for her first novel *A Hotel in Paris* .

A Hotel in Bath was released February 2013, *A Hotel in Venice* was released July, 2015. Margot is currently working on her fourth book in the hotel series, set in Barcelona, Spain. She is also hard at work on a sequel to *Blood Art* .

A Fire Within, set in Chicago was released February, 2014. The story first appeared in the *Hearts and Daggers* anthology. Her other projects include a novella also set in Chicago, *Dazzling Diamonds,* scheduled for release January 2016. She also writes travel articles and blogs.

Margot Justes is a Member of Romance Writers of America, the Chicago North RWA Chapter, as well as the Georgia Romance Writers. She is a past president of the Chicago North RWA Chapter, and the Chicago Chapter of Sisters in Crime.

She loves to hear from readers.

www.mjustes.com

margot@mjustes.com

Made in United States
North Haven, CT
10 July 2024

54578774R10143